Dragons in the Water
By JH Wear

Plus JH Wear's bonus novella:
At The Edge Of Darkness

Published by
Melange Books, LLC
White Bear Lake, MN 55110
www.melange-books.com

ISBN 978-1-61235-062-2
Dragons in the Water, © 2010, 2011, JH Wear

At the Edge of Darkness, © 2006-2011 JH Wear,
Originally appeared in Night Moves Digest - 2006

Credits

Editor: Nancy Schumacher
Copy Editor: Taylor Evans
Format Editor: Mae Powers
Cover Artist: A. Bratt

Dragons in the Water
By JH Wear

When Harry accepted an invitation to join a dragon boat racing team by the eccentric Sheldon, he was plunged into the world of paddling, festivals and romance. But with Sheldon there is always a mystery and unknown forces involved as well.

* * * *

At The Edge Of Darkness
By JH Wear

Can Rodney, a claustrophobic suffering vampire find romance? Rodney wants Irene. Her friend Shelly feels uneasy about him. And meet Sheldon, a whole other mystery.

* * * *

Also by JH Wear at www.melange-books.com:

Shadows and Sensations

Castle 1 - The Fall to Domum

Castle 2 - The Return To Domum

Dragons in the Water
By JH Wear

Chapter One

I peered between the trees, straining my back as I stood on a clump of weeds that scratched at my bare legs. There couldn't be any mistaking that booming voice of Sheldon. I had been enjoying a peaceful stroll along the walking path by the river when I heard that hardy voice. The truth was I wasn't certain I wanted to see what he was up to, but morbid curiosity drove me forward.

Sheldon is a loud mouth, a know it all, and generally aggravating to be around. Annoying, actually. To say Sheldon is eccentric might be too mild a term to describe him. Lots of white hair. His face, like his personality, is large, with sky blue eyes, and a big hooked nose that stands over a mouth full of white teeth. He's clean-shaven to show off his strong jaw and, for some odd reason, women find Sheldon handsome. What belies his elderly facial features is a body of an athletic thirty year old. Like I say, he's annoying.

My name is Harry Webster. I'm thirty plus years old and I'm on the tall side of six feet. I guess I'm a bit on the heavy side as well, but I keep pretty active so the pounds are reasonably distributed. So far I've kept most of my black hair, though I have a couple of grey hairs sneaking in.

I write a column in the local paper about community events and keeping readers abreast of the social calendar. That may sound a bit boring work for a journalist but I also write under the name of Edwin Drood. My alter ego writes about the supernatural, ghosts, vampires, aliens and other assorted mysteries. Some are hard to believe but I always try to make sure there is a grain of truth in the story. No one but my editor knows who Edwin Drood truly is; it makes my column more interesting having that mystery. Well, almost no one else but my editor. During the course of following up on a vampire story, Sheldon casually mentioned to me that he knew Edwin's identity was me. How he found out I haven't a clue, but Sheldon is a mysterious man. More about him later but suffice to say that his nephew claims Sheldon is a warlock and it's as good an explanation as any.

Thus curiosity, and a lead to a possible story, compelled me to seek an opening among the white bark birch trees, the thistles and sprawling elms to find out what he may be up to. By the way, thistles and bare legs are a bad combination.

"Nice job pulling water. Timing was a bit off but that's what practice is for." The speaker was a woman with her blonde hair tied in a ponytail. She was sitting backwards at the front of an oversized canoe, a canoe that held two rows of ten paddlers. In addition to the blonde speaker, there was a steersman at the back who held an oversized paddle to guide the boat.

"Can we do another race piece?" This was from Sheldon who was sitting in the middle of the boat and was holding a black paddle. His voice carried across the river easily, causing several ducks to take flight. The other paddlers quickly agreed to his request, though a few dropped their heads forward, looking exhausted.

I was fascinated. I had never seen such a huge canoe before and never heard Sheldon mention his interest in paddling. I watched as the boat was manoeuvred towards the middle of the river, and then the paddlers stopped, allowing the boat to slowly drift backwards from the flow of the river.

The blonde woman yelled, "Attention, please!"

The paddlers in unison held their paddles vertically just above the water.

"Go!"

The paddles plunged deep into water and then pulled backward. Water was ploughed upward as each paddler frantically repeated another stroke. To my surprise, the huge boat appeared to lift partially out of the water, as if it was trying to leap upward.

"Lengthen now!"

The paddlers, almost in harmony, reached forward with their paddles and slowed down their stroke.

"Timing, timing."

Some of the paddlers adjusted their stroke, trying to pace with the lead paddlers better.

I watched Sheldon twisting in seat with each stroke, his big arms pulling his paddle with force.

"Power on three. Three, two, one. Power now!" the blonde woman shouted.

The boat, even though it was travelling at a good clip already, surged forward. It raced through the water as each paddler looked like they were trying to dig a hole in the river.

The steersperson, a tall, olive skinned man, stood easily on the rocking boat and moved his body with the strokes of the paddlers. He shouted out instructions to the paddlers close to him and they responded to his encouragement.

"Finish now!"

The paddlers somehow managed to increase their efforts. The boat raced down the river, creating a wake behind it.

"Let it ride."

The paddlers suddenly stopped, allowing the boat to glide. Some of the paddlers slumped forward, others reached for their bottled water. Sheldon's chest was heaving but he remained sitting up straight and then patted the back of the paddler in front of him. "Good job, Steven. You really pulled water that time."

His pat on the back caused the smaller paddler to almost fall forward.

"Damn show off." I turned away from my vantage point and promptly tripped and fell. I coughed out a mouthful of a green weed and stood up slowly, brushing some of the dirt and plants off me. My interest in the trees and bushes soon became lost as I thought what Sheldon could be up to. I followed the river path to where I knew a dock was used to launch small boats and I wasn't surprised to hear Sheldon's voice carry through the trees.

"Atta boy, Denny! You did a fine job of paddling there. I heard Denny's reply, a deep voice but not near the volume of Sheldon's. Now Sheldon claims to have had training as an opera singer, he really does claim many things, and he talks like a drill sergeant in front of a company of soldiers.

A group of the paddlers emerged from the small path that disappeared to the dock. A mixture of men and women, most wore waterproof sandals and clothing. All of them looked to be good shape as they carried their paddles to a grassy area to discuss whatever paddlers discuss when not in a boat. I'm guessing beer and pizza. Sheldon emerged, talking to two young women who were smiling away as they eagerly looked up at him. One would think he was telling them how to make a million dollars overnight the way they were hanging on to his every word.

"Harry!" He boomed out my name.

I cringed. There was Sheldon wearing bright red shorts, yellow sandals, and a blue T-shirt under a black life vest. "Hello, Sheldon. I see you're doing some canoeing."

"Canoeing?" He laughed aloud, bringing out grins from his companions. "No, no, no, Harry. We most certainly do not call it canoeing. Dragon boating is an entirely different technique and is a very difficult sport to master."

One of the ladies objected. "Oh Sheldon, you make it look so easy. You're just a natural dragon boater."

He gave one of his broad smiles, teeth sparkling. "I just have some very good instructors." Both of the women next to him blushed.

Lord, give me strength. "I see. Well, it does look you're enjoying dragon boating." Especially with those two women by your side.

"Why don't you hang around here for a few minutes Harry? We can go for a drink afterwards."

"Sure." I wasn't sure at all to be sure. First, he can dominate any conversation, and afterwards you feel like you had just completed a university lecture. Second, somehow I always manage to end up paying.

I listened to a lady with red hair address the group surrounding her.

"Now remember to focus in the boat. Practice is twice a week but that doesn't mean you shouldn't be doing workouts during the other days. Now let's get together."

The entire group huddled together and extended their hands toward the centre.

"Okay, on three. Who are we?"

"River Rodents!"

They repeated the chant three times, each time louder. Sheldon's calling was the loudest, causing a noticeable air draft.

"So, Harry, do you have your car nearby? I jogged here for today's practice."

I nodded as I looked at his damp shirt and shorts. "Do you need to change first?"

"Naw, I feel fine the way I am. Come on, I need a cold drink." He immediately stomped towards the parking lot, not giving me an opportunity to argue.

I put down my window as I drove. The combination of Sheldon's sweat, and the river water, filled the car with an aroma that I hoped air freshener and Lysol could cure afterwards.

We went into the lounge side of Devon Pizza and there were several members of the dragon boat team already enjoying a drink. They shouted Sheldon's name and waved us over.

I was introduced as Sheldon's "old" friend and soon was sharing a pitcher of beer with them. I have to admit they were a friendly group and certainly all of them seemed to be in good shape.

Allison, a lady of around thirty, asked if I'd ever been on a dragon boat and I shook my head. "I have paddled in a rowboat a few times." I smiled but they didn't look too impressed. It seemed rowboats were not held in high esteem and not worthy of a comment.

Danielle, a red head with freckles, leaned towards me. "We could use one or two more men as extras. We're going to Kelowna for a festival and could use some extras just in case some can't make the trip."

I thought about it for a few seconds. I'm in pretty good shape. I run and bicycle a fair bit and I'm no stranger to rowboats either, thanks to being invited to Sheldon's cottage to go fishing a few times. How difficult could it be to paddle in a dragon boat? I was to learn that lesson a few days later. "Sure, I can give it a try."

Sheldon beamed. "To our newest member, Harry." He raised his glass and took a drink that emptied its contents and immediately refilled it. He then called the waitress over.

"Jill, could you bring us another round of shooters? Harry has agreed to join out club and we should celebrate. Put it on my tab."

"Sure, Sheldon." She gave him a warm smile as she traced her fingertips across his shoulders.

The shooter wasn't bad, a brownish sour tasting concoction. The beer and food was great. Service was good and my new team mates friendly. It was too good to be true and I would soon learn I was right.

Sheldon clapped me on my back and announced he had to start back home.

"I have a social engagement I have to get ready for, so I shall bid farewell for now."

One of the young ladies, a short hair brunette named Stephanie, piped up, "Social engagement, Sheldon? Would that be a date?"

He smiled broadly. "Only if I get kiss from her at the end of the night."

Stephanie grinned. "Well, don't stay out too late. Save your energy for paddling."

"No worries there." Sheldon had a glint in his eye. "She has a photo shoot to do in the morning."

Trust Sheldon to get a date with a model. There is no justice. I started to rise, figuring I had to drive him home, wherever that was. He stalled me by placing his hand on my shoulder and pressed me back down.

"No need to drive me, Harry. I need to run off these calories."

He walked off to the waves of his teammates.

I was thinking that at least my car would have a chance to air out when Jill placed a bill in front of me. "Sheldon said you would take care of this." She giggled. "He said he left his wallet at home." She smiled happily. "He's such a nice man."

I looked at the bill. Two pitchers of beer. One order of nachos. And eight shooters. I closed my eyes. Death for Sheldon, "such a nice man", would be too kind.

Chapter Two

I wore old shorts and a T-shirt to my practice, leaving a change of clothes in the car. I wanted to be able to change after seeing what the practice did to Sheldon's clothes.

Sheldon arrived just after I did, riding a mountain bike with what looked like about twenty gears. It looked more expensive than my car.

"How are you doing, Harry?" He was energetic and boisterous as usual.

"Just fine." I hesitated as we approached the dock. "And you?"

"Feeling fantastic. What a wonderful day for paddling on the river."

Of course, he was feeling great. As always. Have I mentioned how annoying he was?

"About the other night after practice when you ordered that round of shooters and food…"

"Think nothing of it, Harry." He clapped me on the back, temporally removing all air from my lungs. "You can buy a round next time." With that he strode forward, getting hugs from many of the female paddlers. I gripped my paddle shaft tightly, pretending it was Sheldon's neck.

They put me near the back of the boat and on the right side. My bench partner was a pretty lady named Chelsea, with medium length wavy dark hair interspersed with blonde streaks. She looked to be average height and even with her life vest on I could tell she had a curvy body. I smiled brightly at her. No doubt young and thus impressionable, I casually mentioned my name and occupation.

"Harry Webster, you may have seen my name in the paper. I write the column Views and News."

I was surprised she didn't do much more than smile and comment how interesting that must be.

"And what do you do?" I hoped she was old enough to have finished high school.

"I'm just finishing my masters at university."

I gulped. "In what field? Art?"

"Math. I found calculus fascinating so I majored in it."

Math? Calculus? Masters? Maybe I underestimated her just a tad.

* * * *

Dragon boating is simple. One only has to learn the trick of twisting into a pretzel while dragging a paddle through water fast enough to launch a space shuttle. This has to be in time with the other nineteen pretzels in the boat of course.

Chelsea tried to help me, telling me I needed to use my legs to lock myself on the seat and against the side. Then, keeping both arms straight, I twist my body and reach forward as far as I can with the paddle. From there it would be simple to plunge the paddle into the water and pull it straight back to my hip, rotate and repeat the procedure. All this had to be done while looking forward to the lead paddlers to keep time.

I was dying as we paddled down the river, passing several small towns until we reached the ocean or it might have been the Hudson Bay. Mercifully, a break was called and I gulped down water from my water bottle.

"Are you all right?"

"Fine," I lied. My body was hurting from this simple warm up. I pretended this was a simple task for me. "Is this all we do, Chelsea? Paddle up and down the river?"

"Oh no. This was just to get into position. We're going to do a race piece pretty soon."

"Race piece? How long is that?" I now remembered watching the dragon boat race down the river. I began to get worried.

"About three minutes long. Most dragon boat races are five hundred metres long."

Now I was truly worried.

"Attention please!"

"Go!"

I worked the paddle as hard as I could as we tried to lift the boat out of the water. My arms began to burn at the shoulders. We continued the furious pace for a few strokes before the call was made to lengthen the stroke. The burning sensation reached my elbows. I could feel my heart pound in my chest and I tried to gulp precious air into my lungs.

Commands were shouted out and in my blurred vision; I tried to watch the lead paddlers. My ribs hurt. My back ached. How much longer could this go on?

"Power now!"

No! This can't be. She wanted us to put even more effort into the stroke. I ordered my weakened body to reach into the reserves it had and continue.

It was torture. I would confess to any crime at this point. Then, finally, after what seemed an hour of racing, the cry of "Finish it now!" rang out.

I poured myself into the race, borrowing energy from the next two days.

"Let it ride!"

I collapsed. I vaguely heard Chelsea's voice call out, "Sheldon, I think your friend is dead."

I wondered if they were going to just dump my body into the river, letting the sharks devour it.

Gradually I recovered. Chelsea opened up my water bottle and helped me swallow the precious fluid. I was going to live after all!

Sheldon called out, "Can we do another race piece?"

If I had had the strength to lift my paddle, I would have clubbed him with it.

Chelsea saved my life. "I think some of us need a bit of a recovery period first. Maybe we can have a coaching session on our weak areas."

Weak areas. For me that would be my lungs. I listened to the coach tell us how we needed to change our stroke from the start to when we lengthened our stroke.

"It's basically the same stroke people. All we're doing is just reaching a little further. But the critical part is the timing, as always. Follow the lead paddles because after the start there is a tendency to hurry too much. We have our cruising speed after the start and now all we need to do is maintain it. This also gives us time to recover for the next part of the race, such as the power and the finish."

What she was saying all made sense to me. It's one thing to know what you're supposed to do, though, and another to do it. I learned that to be an effective paddler takes lots of practice and a good set of lungs.

* * * *

We returned our paddles and life jackets to the storage shed and then had a group meeting. I listened to the words of encouragement and the plans for the upcoming festival in Kelowna. The speaker was a long-haired brunette, one of the more experienced paddlers. Tanya was tall, lean and full of energy. One of her roles on the team was to lead the warm-up before practice and she helped with some of the coaching.

"Our last few practices have gone really well. The last item is the Kelowna Festival. So far we have just enough paddlers but we do need extras." She looked right at me. "I hope Harry decides to come with us because we can really use another strong male paddler."

Several of the women paddlers cheered as they looked at me. I gave an embarrassed smile.

"Trina is looking after the accommodation, so make sure you let her know your plans. So far, we are putting two couples per room, three women per room and two men per room. We have fewer men so it just worked out that way. Now Mila is going to drive down there and has room for two more passengers. She's leaving two days ahead of the festival. Contact her for more information. If that's everything, let's bring it together."

We moved in closer and reached in with our hands or paddles, trying to make sure we were in contact with each other. After the shouts of "River Rodents!" we broke apart. I began to stagger towards my car.

"How did you like your first practice?" This was from the redhead named Danielle.

It was torture of the worse kind I wanted to say. "Fine. It was fun."

Chelsea came up from behind me. "He did really well for a newbie. I think he was a little tired after the race pieces."

She was a master of the understatement. "I need a bit more time to get in shape I guess."

Chelsea smiled. "You'll get there. Are you going to Kelowna with us?"

"I don't know. I doubt I'll be ready in time."

Allison shook her head. "We all feel that way at times. Sign up. If you don't feel you're ready, you can be a back up but still be a part of the team. As long as you can drink beer you'll be fine."

Chelsea rested her hand on my shoulder. "Come on, we all have a good time when we're down there. It's part dragon boat race and part party."

I nodded. "Alright. I guess I can go as a back-up." I knew I was setting myself up for more torture during practice, but having a pretty woman placing her hand on my shoulder won me out. As any man can tell you, pretty women can cause more problems than a tornado.

Sheldon called out to us, "Hey, you guys coming for some drinks? Harry, you better. It's your turn to buy a few rounds, you cheapskate." He laughed as he walked away with three women going with him.

I pictured myself holding his head under water by the dock, letting him take a gulp of air and then plunging it down under again. I repeated the procedure in my mind and felt better. "Sure."

The after practice drinks were entertaining again. Chelsea sat next to me and I was glad I had a chance to change to different clothes before we came here. That wasn't easy trying to slide my shorts off and replace them with jeans under a steering wheel. The horn going off in my car was a minor setback in getting unneeded attention, but it was better than wearing wet clothes to the bar.

Sheldon, of course, was leading the conversation when I arrived.

"Of course, there was considerable danger as I made my way down the Himalayas, and not just from the storm that was brewing. Earlier that week we came across the footprint of a yeti not far from our campsite. I didn't have a choice with one of companions injured. So I ventured out of the tent into the blistering wind and headed to a higher peak so I could radio for help."

I saw the others were listening to another of his tall tales. I find it incredible that they believed him but he makes it sound oh so convincing. The simple truth is he has pulled me into his story telling. He told me a story of a vampire that, I must admit, had me lying awake at nights.

"Then, out of white haze of flying snow, I saw a white shadowy shape approach me. The creature roared at me with that strange yell the yeti is known for. But I stood on that peak and screamed back at him as I waved my arms at him. I admit I was scared; however I needed to get help for those at the campsite."

Chelsea whispered to me, "He certainly has had some interesting adventures in his life."

"Yes, well, if you believe all that he has to say."

"You mean they're not all true?"

I frowned. "Well, I can't prove they aren't true. His stories just seem to stretch the boundaries a bit."

"So, you aren't sure?" Chelsea gave me a small smile.

"No, I guess not." That was it in a nutshell. I just wasn't sure about anything about Sheldon.

"The Yeti decided not challenge me after that and ambled away. I set up the transmitter and was able to get help for my companions."

Hans, a big blond hair man took a drink of his beer and then asked Sheldon, "So you saw a Yeti? Is it anything like a Sasquatch?"

"No, not really. A Yeti is related to the gorilla family, not too smart and rather unsocial. The Sasquatch is along the lines of humans but an evolutionary dead end. They are, however, quite intelligent and stick together in groups."

I whispered to Chelsea, "He has a logical explanation for everything. The danger is if you listen to him you'll find him so convincing you'll expect to see a yeti yourself."

Hans wasn't giving up. "How come we don't see any Sasquatch remains?"

"It is believed they bury their dead, being social creatures. Of course, if you go deep into the woods and look carefully, you won't find the remains of bears, either. We know bears exist but they are just more common than the Sasquatch. Perhaps we should believe those of us who have seen these magnificent creatures."

"You have seen a Sasquatch?"

Sheldon waved his hand towards the table. "Of course I have. I wouldn't tell you something I didn't know was true. But that is a story for another time." He stood up. "I must go and help a friend paint his car. He has not done it before and wants it done perfect."

With a grin, he left with several goodbyes to those at the table. The women in particular seemed sad that he left, calling out his name as he left.

Jill placed the bill in front of me shortly after. Sheldon managed to escape without paying again. I think you could buy a wallet from that man in brand new condition.

Hans was frowning. "Do you really believe he saw a Yeti and a Sasquatch?"

I reached for my wallet. "I not only believe he saw both those creatures but managed to get them to buy him a round of drinks."

Chapter Three

I would like to say the next practice was easier, but it wasn't. No matter how much effort you put in they want you to try a bit harder. I was getting better but the bar was also being raised. I was told to twist more, reach further, pull back harder and make sure my paddle went deep. Each part of my stroke was reviewed and the coach offered suggestions on how to improve. I was told I was doing great for a beginner but I was wondering if I'd ever master how to paddle effectively. However, Chelsea was encouraging me and I didn't want to give in to my collapsed lungs. What was even more annoying was how Sheldon could paddle without showing any signs of exhaustion. True, he was sweating and you could hear him gulp air as he paddled, but he recovered within seconds and was ready to go again before anyone else.

The main thing is I made it through practice and after we tied up the boat, I staggered up to where we would meet. I had started to feel like a River Rodent and belted out the cheer with the rest of them. More important, they gave me a River Rodent T-shirt. The shirt had a flame breathing dragon on it with the name of our team emblazoned on is side. I was very happy to get that shirt, feeling I now belonged to these crazed paddlers.

Sheldon came up to Hans afterwards and handed him a small, clear plastic bag. "I thought you might be interested in this."

Hans looked at the object in the bag. It was a yellow, human looking tooth the size of my thumb. "What is this?"

"Sasquatch tooth. Go on, take it. I have others. If you give it to a zoologist, they will tell you it has all the characteristics of a human tooth, except its size. Ask them to name the animal it came from."

Hans looked dumbfounded. "This is amazing."

"Of course it is. However, if you were to show it to the world there would be hoards of idiots trying to be the one that captured one. Right now, the Sasquatch is safe as being a myth. If the world truly believes they're out there, they'll be hunted down. Now you have a Sasquatch tooth. The best thing you can do for them is to keep it hidden in your house."

Hans looked up at Sheldon and handed back the tooth. "I'm sorry I doubted you. You best keep the tooth where it'll be safe."

Sheldon nodded. "Thank you, Hans. Now it's beer time, eh?" With a slap on Hans's shoulder that made the big man's knees buckle, Sheldon grinned broadly and began to head to the parking lot.

I looked at Hans and recognized the expression on his face; it's as if you're playing a game of bullshit poker and the other guy is claiming to have an extraordinary, almost impossible hand. You challenge him only to find he really did have the impossible hand. Sheldon tells outrageous stories but always has something to back him up. I felt for Hans; I have learned not to bet against Sheldon the storyteller. Sheldon always wins.

* * * *

Sheldon thought it odd I changed clothes in the car as I clumsily tried slipping my jeans on under the steering wheel. "Who are you trying to impress by putting on a change of clothes?"

"No one," I lied. I felt like telling him I didn't like stinking up my car but he doesn't take such hints easily. It would be a waste of breath.

Sheldon peered at me. "I bet there's someone you like on that boat." Then he gave one his deep laughs. "That's okay, they're all good people."

I was expecting to be stuck with his beer tab again but Hans generously picked it up. Sheldon made a show of reaching for his wallet but Hans insisted on paying.

I began to doubt Sheldon has a wallet, or if he has, if it ever has been opened. All the same, I was pleased I managed to sit next to Chelsea and shared a couple of laughs with her.

"So Harry, you're not married?"

I shook my head. "No, divorced. She now lives somewhere in the interior of BC. Thank God, that way I don't have to worry about running into her here. How about you? Boyfriend?" I felt my pulse speeding up.

"No. Just broke up a few weeks ago. He was spending too much time on his hobby, car racing." She shrugged. "Nice guy but a little too transfixed on machines."

I realized I was holding my breath. I smiled, picked up my beer glass and, touched her glass with mine. "To you, bench partner," and promptly dropped my glass. It bounced off the table, doing a lovely summersault, and then crashed on the floor. I stared at my empty hand as Chelsea and the others laughed. Then a couple of them went to get help from the bartender.

The table was wet, my pants were wet and my throat was dry. Nothing like making a good impression. Chelsea and the others laughed it off but I felt like a fool.

Then Sheldon raised his glass. "To Harry, who likes paddling so much he likes to get wet after practice is over as well."

The others all raised their glasses and saluted me. I felt better, especially after Chelsea leaned over and put her arm around my shoulder. She gave me the briefest of hugs and then pulled her arm away. Maybe Sheldon isn't such a bad guy after all.

Chapter Four

I was able to handle practice better as I learned a better technique of holding myself steady on the bench by locking my feet on the bench in front of me. I also learned to keep my back straight so I could breathe easier. This made me a better paddler but I paled in comparison to Sheldon. He was often used as an example by the coach to the rest of the crew on the right way to paddle. He not only had this great reach, but when he put his paddle deep into the water, he would accelerate the paddle back with such force I'm surprised his paddle didn't break. The dragon boat moved with his paddle alone.

Chelsea whispered to me, "He is absolutely amazing. I heard another dragon boat was trying to recruit him for their boat but he turned them down. I guess he's loyal to us Rodents."

I thought about what she said. As you may have picked up I have some issues with Sheldon, but he is loyal to his friends. Sometimes his ego, which is larger than a dragon boat, is hard to take. But if you need help, I have to say he would be one the guys you could count on. "Yes, he's certainly a strong paddler."

She gave me a studied look. "Are you jealous of him?"

"What? Good heavens, no." I looked into her questioning eyes. "I just find him hard to take sometimes. Always so full of himself. A nice guy but he can be overwhelming during the course of an evening."

"I think I know what you mean. Damn good looking man for his age, though."

"I suppose he might be. Want to take a guess how old he is?"

She looked at him for several seconds. "That's hard to say. Fifty? Sixty?" She frowned, not sure at all of his age.

"He might be. I've asked him and he never answered me. He could be seventy for all I know." I didn't add his nephew, Robert, thinks Sheldon is around two hundred years old. Robert claims to have found a photograph of Sheldon, dressed as a soldier during the War of 1812. "Try asking him his age, or better yet, what his full name is."

She looked puzzled. "You don't know his last name?"

"No, and I'll bet no one else on this boat does, either. The man is a mystery all by himself."

We continued to practice, and when we finally arrived at the dock I was exhausted, though it was a different kind of exhaustion. It wasn't my lungs, or heart, that was ready to implode, but my whole body. That was an improvement in a way as I was getting in better overall shape. A large bruise was forming on my hip as it banged against the gunnel with each stroke. This paddling was a lot harder that I first imagined. I limped my way up to where we would get some final instructions and do the team cheer.

Danielle spoke about how well we all did in the practice. "Really good performance. Our start is great and our finish is coming along. Our newbies are learning what it takes to be a dragon boat paddler. They're doing a great job of pulling water."

Chelsea gave me a small elbow at that last comment and a quick smile.

Danielle continued, "For our up coming festival in Kelowna there is some business to tidy up. One, we have obtained accommodation at the Victoria Hotel, though most of you will be sharing rooms.

"Harry and Sheldon, I need you to fill out these registration forms and return them to me for next practice. Okay River Rodents, lets bring it in."

We cried out River Rodents three times and then broke apart. I walked with Chelsea to the parking lot.

"So when Sheldon fills out that registration form we may find out his name and age after all. At least Danielle will know."

I frowned. "I'll believe that when I see it. Sheldon is very tricky about not revealing information he doesn't want to."

"You really don't trust him, do you?"

I thought about that. "I trust him as far as not cheating me in a poker game. He won't necessarily lie but still might not reveal the truth."

"A devious man, then?"

"Exactly. Are you going for a drink at DP?"

She shook her head. "No, I can't. I'm expecting company."

My first thought was she had a new boyfriend. My shoulders dropped.

She quickly added, "My mother and sister are coming over."

I smiled. "Perhaps after next practice then."

"Sure." She smiled back.

We stood by the driver's door of her car, a small white Nissan, for several seconds.

"I guess I better get going." She slowly opened her door and I backed away, wondering why I didn't take advantage of the time to ask her out or at least her phone number.

She pulled out of the parking lot and gave me a wave by curling and uncurling her fingers the way only women do. I waved back using my full arm and then headed to my car, only to see Sheldon standing by the door.

"Do you need a ride?"

He gave a toothy grin. "If you don't mind. There is something I need to tell you."

I nodded reluctantly and made a mental note to buy some more air freshener for the car. I drove out of the parking lot and waited for Sheldon to speak. As usual, it didn't take long.

"I'm glad you're going with us to Kelowna."

"Thanks. You mean the team needs more paddlers, I presume."

He laughed. "No, it's not the paddling I was thinking of. The area around Kelowna is a magical place and the people who live in the area have all heard tales of strange occurrences around there."

"In what way." I rolled down the window and tried to breath in the fresh air as much as possible.

"I best let you find out for yourself. Harry, fate has destined you to go there. You may find that paddling is inconsequential compared to what else may happen there."

I wasn't sure about fate pulling me along, but one thing I knew was wherever Sheldon went there was bound to be trouble.

Chapter Five

Two days later, I made my way to the storage shed that held the wood paddles and life vests or PFDs. Many of the veteran paddlers had their own PFDs and paddles. Some choose a wood paddle but often, like that show off Sheldon, opted for a carbon fibre model. It was lighter and could be cut to exact length for individual needs.

I tried to find one of "one size fits all" life vest that actually did fit and wasn't too wet from the previous user. Nothing like a wet life vest to made you comfortable. I then picked among the paddles, looking for one that was the right length and where the paddle edge wasn't too banged up.

The shed had a single light bulb hanging from the ceiling and the shadows inside made it tough to see the equipment. Other paddlers were working around me, either returning items or trying to find something like myself. A few minutes later, we walked as a group towards the dock, chatting on various topics.

There are some dragon boaters who live, sleep and eat dragon boating. Often they have a far away look in their eyes, something like the old man in the "Rime of the Ancient Mariner". A lot of them are single, devoting every spare moment on perfecting their technique. Reach for it, pull back, lengthen the stroke, getting wet, rotate, and finish it now! Means only one thing to these people; it's dragon boat season. Do not, on any condition, step between them and their paddle. Conversation is simple with focused dragon boaters.

Novice: "Nice weather."

Dragon Boater: "Great day to be on the water."

Novice: "What did you do on the weekend?"

Dragon Boater: "I was on the water."

Novice: "Have you read a good book lately?"

Dragon Boater: "I only read Dragon Boat Monthly, Paddler Weekly, and Focus in the Boat."

Those not infected with Dragon Boatlitis, can carry a normal conversation and have been known to even miss the odd practice. Of course, even those who are not affected when they are in the dragon boat there is a tendency to ignore there is a life outside of the boat. When you're sitting in a boat surrounded by nineteen other paddlers, all clutching their paddles protectively, it's hard to be thinking about what's going to be on TV later.

Danielle was standing at the dock, greeting everyone and I handed her my registration form.

"Thank you, Harry. I'll put it with Sheldon's and send it in tomorrow." She tucked my form next to an envelope attached to a clipboard.

"Sheldon put his form in an envelope?"

"Yeah, he said he wanted to make sure it didn't get accidentally wet. He's always so thoughtful." A mist appeared in her eyes.

Thoughtful! I think he was just trying to hide the information from prying eyes. Not that I would pry but what does he have to hide? Very suspicious indeed.

I climbed into the boat and talked to those around me, especially Chelsea. We all agreed it was a great day to be on the water. The sun was strong as we pushed off from the dock, carefully avoiding hitting the rocks along the shallow banks with our paddles. Soon we set out along the river cutting into a small breeze that helped keep us cool. A small dark cloud was starting to form along the horizon. The weather forecast was for seventy percent chance of showers and a fifty percent chance of a thunderstorm. My math is a bit weak but I guess that makes it one hundred and twenty per cent chance something bad is going to happen

I was getting more confident with paddling now, still learning some minor details. A good paddler knows how to rotate while sitting fixed on the bench and makes the effort, well, effortless. The start is very important, and different teams have their own way of accelerating during the start. Our team uses eighteen strokes to reach cruising speed, with each stroke increasing in strength. At the end of the eighteen strokes the stroke is changed slightly, becoming longer and with less force. This is where the coach is living in a fantasy world. Let me explain.

At the end of the start each paddler is suppose to have given all they have, pushed themselves to exhaustion. Then the stroke is lengthened, supposedly to allow the paddlers to recapture their breath and strength. It's called "active recovery". I call it "active exhaustion". Tell me how, if one is completely out of breath, one's heart is pounding so hard the ribs hurt, and your muscles have turned to jelly, how continuing on will allow one to become refreshed?

Somehow, I managed to carry on, out of total fear of being exposed as a wimp. It's unforgivable to stop paddling during a race. Last year a paddler in one of the festivals became too tired to paddle and stopped for few seconds to catch her breath. At the end of the race, she was forced to walk the plank and was never heard of since. Some sins are too great to forgive.

Thus, I was not going to be the one in the boat that stopped paddling. I would never be able to look at any of my team- mates in the eye again if I did. Of course, I was getting better handling the race piece. Sometimes within a few minutes after a race piece, I was able to speak again.

The race at most festivals is about five hundred metres, and can be completed in less than three minutes. That makes it average about ten kilometres an hour for a six hundred plus pounds boat. If one adds the weight of the paddlers, it brings the total weight to four thousand pounds. During the race, a good dragon boat team can reach a speed of fifteen to twenty kilometres per hour.

There are a couple of other positions on the dragon boat I have to talk about. First is the drummer who perches precariously at the front of the boat and pounds a large drum to help keep timing in the boat. The other thing the drummer has to do is to yell loud enough for the whole length of the boat to hear. The drummer usually works with the steersperson when different commands are issued. Because the drummer doesn't paddle, a major criteria is weight and thus often a small woman is chosen. To help maintain a strong voice she will often practice yelling at her husband and children.

The steersperson stands at the back of the boat, holding the twelve-foot paddle that pivots on a small stand. Its not an easy task maintaining balance, and still forcing the paddle to move against the water. As I mentioned the dragon is long and heavy and won't change direction easily so the steersperson has to plan ahead. Besides steering the boat, the steersperson also has to guide the pace of the race and yell commands. The other rule of thumb is no matter how well the paddlers are doing it's a given they are holding back some energy and must be yelled at to work harder.

I had a chance to observe other paddlers during practice. Occasionally the coach would have just part of the boat paddle while the others observed their technique and made their task even more difficult by holding their paddles stationary in the water.

I held on to my paddle tightly, feeling the force of the water press on it. I looked at some of the other paddlers, though I ignored Sheldon. He was too damn good; perfect rotation, the paddle sliding into the water instead of plunging, reaching forward instead of lunging, and then the great acceleration of paddle during the stroke. I could never reach that perfection and decided it would be easier to look at mere mortals instead.

Danielle called from the front of the boat, "It looks like it's going to start storming soon, so let's cut the practice off now."

We headed to shore, grumbling that we wanted to continue with our practice. That wasn't entirely a lie but let's face it. Who wants to paddle an oversized canoe when there's a cold beer waiting at the bar? That was a rhetorical question, no need to answer.

I climbed out of the boat and offered my hand to Chelsea, who gave me a smile and a "Thank you" as I pulled her up to the dock. The River Rodents are a social team, lots of encouragement and offering a helping hand with almost anything. I noticed Sheldon took charge of tying up the boat and then securing it with a padlock.

We moved up as a group to do our usual talk about the practice. Danielle also made sure we all had arranged for travel to Kelowna. Some had chosen drive to the festival while the majority of us were going to fly down.

"We have just one more practice but I think we're all ready to go. Let's bring her in."

We all closed ranks and did the River Rodent chant. It was a great feeling being part of the team. Despite being a newbie and still trying to master the technique of paddling, the River Rodents had made me feel welcome and a big part of the team.

"Harry, can I talk to you?"

I turned towards Danielle and approached her.

"What's up?" I was concerned she was going to say I hadn't made the team as a standby.

"Trina and David have a family emergency and can't make it to Kelowna. In addition, Robert hurt his back and won't be paddling. So you've been moved up from standby to paddler."

My jaw dropped. "I am?" I said weakly.

"You'll be fine. Chelsea will be your bench partner again. Don't worry, we wouldn't ask you if we didn't think you could do it."

"Thanks, I'll do my best." Now I was nervous. So far, in practice, I was assuming I was just along for the ride and was being pretty relaxed. Suddenly I found out I was going to be in an actual race.

I began to walk with Danielle to where the cars were parked. Chelsea was waiting for me several feet away and joined us.

"I just told Harry he's going to be a regular in Kelowna. As his bench partner you have to make sure he drinks enough beer the night before the race and otherwise be ready to go." She laughed.

Chelsea slipped her arm under mine. "Then we better get started practicing the beer training now."

When we were close to the cars, a thought came to my mind. "By the way, Danielle, since you have the registration forms can you tell me how Sheldon spells his last name? I need to look up his address for later."

"Sure." She opened a waterproof bag and pulled out her clipboard. I saw my registration form clipped there but when she looked underneath it, Sheldon's envelop wasn't there. "Now where could that have gotten to?"

She checked the clipboard again and then inside the bag. "That's odd, it seems to have disappeared."

Chelsea looked inside the bag and agreed there wasn't any sign of Sheldon's registration form.

"I'll look for it again later. It must be hiding somewhere." Danielle shook her head, looking puzzled.

We said we would meet Danielle at the bar and then I walked Chelsea to her car.

"See, I told you there was something strange about Sheldon."

The dark cloud flashed lightening.

She giggled. "Maybe Sheldon really can do magic."

Thunder boomed.

"I've heard rumours he's a warlock." I smiled as if I was joking.

Lightening lit up the sky.

"I hope not an evil one." She opened her car door.

The thunder rolled over us, warning us.

"See you at DP's." I hurried to my car as the first cold, large drops of rain fell.

I dashed to the bar, getting soaked from the short distance across the parking lot.

I sat down, cold water dripping down the back of my neck. We all agreed we ended practice in the nick of time. Erin and Tim, who gave Sheldon a ride to the bar, were the only ones not caught in the heavy rain.

Sheldon quickly consumed his second pint, looking dry, relaxed and not the least concerned about how he was going to get home in the thundershower. "This reminds me of the time I was in India during the monsoon season. I had just finished crossing a bridge when the river suddenly rose up and washed out the supports. The bridge crashed down and swept away in the torrent. I was stranded under this deluge of rainwater, considering my options, when I heard a deep growl coming from the green foliage that lined the edge of the road. I could not see the creature that hid under that green canopy because of the heavy rain, but I recognized the growl as that of a Bengal tiger."

The others at the table were listening in rapt attention, including the waitress, who had failed to see me arrive. I finally had to go up to the bar to obtain my own beer, and then decided to buy another pitcher of beer for the team.

I hadn't heard of Sheldon being in India before and thus wasn't familiar with the Bengal Tiger story, but after you've heard a dozen or so Sheldon stories you get immune to them.

"I held the ten inch knife in my hand, carefully moving towards the centre of the road. It was a tremendous dilemma for me. I didn't wish to be killed on that isolated road but I didn't want to hurt that magnificent cat, either. I pondered a way to protect myself and save the life of the tiger, knowing it must be extremely hungry to attack me."

I looked at Chelsea, who was listening carefully to Sheldon's story. She looked beautiful and I felt lucky to have met someone like her. True, any possible romance was going slow; part of the reason is that we both knew if things didn't work out, then being on the boat together might be awkward. So we wanted to be careful. At least that's what I told myself. Truth was I lacked the courage to ask her out. The fear of rejection was strong.

"I knew the Bengal tiger liked to pounce on their prey in a sudden leap. I wouldn't have much warning when the moment came. However, until that time came, I hoped to find a way to avert the attack. I would hate to have to kill it."

"But didn't you have only a knife?" This question was from Eric.

Sheldon took another drink, his third pint, and stared at Eric. "A knife is more than sufficient as a weapon. I learned how to use it effectively from Igibira Tribe in Africa. Only a knife you ask? I assure you I could use the knife to kill the tiger." He took another swallow of his beer and then returned to his story. "I carefully moved to where the road had been washed away and lowered myself over the edge, clinging to anything with my fingers as I dangled over the roaring river."

I only half listened to his story. How true it was I couldn't hazard a guess. I do know I've never caught him in a lie but that may mean just that he's a clever liar. He held everyone's attention with his tale. I have to admit he is a good speaker.

"The tiger became frustrated he couldn't reach me and after roaring his disapproval disappeared back into the jungle. I waited several minutes before I climbed back up. Eventually I began to make my way down the road to where I hoped I could find civilization again."

I was glad the story was finished. Maybe the waitress would return to serving drinks again.

Sheldon has an amazing ability to consume beer. He was now on his fourth pint without showing any effects of it. No one else was even trying keep up to him. What is even more amazing than his beer drinking is how he manages to avoid paying for it. I was interested to see how much he would pay for his drinks tonight.

"Harry would you mind giving me a ride home? It's still raining quite a bit and an old guy like me could get sick from it," Sheldon said that with a grin.

"Sure." I'm not sure who he was trying fool with the "old guy" stuff. He does stuff that would give a twenty-year-old trouble.

I turned to Chelsea. "Sheldon must live close to here as he never brings his car. How about you?"

"West end of downtown. It's a high-rise."

"Oh, I go past there on my way to the docks. Would you like to catch a ride for next practice and save using your car?"

"That would be great."

Chelsea gave me her address and phone number. I was elated and carefully placed the paper in my wallet.

A short time later Chelsea, Sheldon and I were the only ones left. Sheldon excused himself to go to the washroom and (of course) just as he left Jill bought the bill for our table, setting it in front of me. I picked it up and then counted the money left on the table from the rest of the team. The River Rodents are a generous bunch; most of them had added a few extra dollars on top of their share so the bill was already entirely covered. I threw in a twenty-dollar bill, covering the tip. It seemed ridiculous I was giving her a tip after I had to go and get my own beer when she became enthralled in Sheldon's story. Regardless of my opinion on the service, with Chelsea sitting at the table I was not about to look like a miser.

The end result was that when Sheldon returned the bill had been paid and taken away again. He made some sort of pretence of offering to pay but Chelsea told him his story was well worth the price of a few beers the others had paid.

"You can always buy us a beer another time, Sheldon," she said brightly.

Sheldon buy us a beer? Maybe when hell freezes over, but at least the beer will be cold.

The three of us walked to the entrance of the bar and watched the rain come down in buckets.

"This is awful." Chelsea peered out at the wave of water coming down.

"Give me your car keys. I'll bring your car around."

"You'll do that for me? You'll get soaked."

"I know, but I'll get wet going to my car anyway."

I dashed out to her car. It didn't really matter whether I walked or ran; I was going to get soaked. I had to move her car seat back after banging my knee on the steering column, and then cautiously moved the car across the parking lot. The avalanche of water made it difficult to see but I managed to stop directly in front of the bar entrance.

"Oh, Harry, you're soaked." Chelsea frowned as I entered the lobby.

I stood nobly. "It's nothing. The water won't hurt me."

"Thanks all the same. I owe you." She gave me a quick hug and then dashed to her car with one hand over her head as a form of protection. After a wave good-bye, she drove off.

I looked around for Sheldon and spotted him at the bar, conversing with the waitress. Jill laughed at something he said and then took out her pen. She wrote down something on a piece of paper, folded it and then handed it to him with a lovely smile.

Unbelievable. I can't even get her to serve me a drink and he gets her phone number. There is no justice.

"Come on, Sheldon, time to go." There was no way I was going to bring the car around the front for him. It would nice to see him get soaked too.

He said something to her, she giggled, and then Sheldon walked briskly to meet me at the front.

I stepped out the front doors, expecting the heavy rain again. I didn't mind; my clothes were already saturated with water but now Sheldon would suffer the same fate.

Or not.

The rain had slowed down to a drizzle and Sheldon barely got touched by the rain by the time we reached my car. Quietly cursing I drove out of the parking lot to the street when the rain began to pick up in intensity again.

I wasn't happy he managed to stay so dry but at least I figured I could find out where he lived. That was until Sheldon directed me in a confusing pattern of shortcuts to his house.

"Turn here. At these lights make a sharp left and then right at the next stop sign."

The rain was making it hard to see again and the car windows started to fog up. I could see well enough to drive but the street signs were a blur. I couldn't tell where I was and the streets looked unfamiliar. The homes looked well kept, though of an old-fashioned style using bricks with a grand entrance.

"This is good. Thanks for the ride, Harry. When you get to the end of the block, make a right and then a left at the stop sign. You'll see a set of lights. That's Whyte Avenue and you can find your home from there." He jumped out of the car and disappeared between the parked cars.

I wasn't sure which house he went to, the fog in the windows hid where he went. I drove slowly, trying to determine where I was but couldn't make out any street signs. I was lost. I followed his directions and ended up on Whyte Avenue, although I was still baffled how I arrived there. From the bar to where I now sat in my car was normally a good thirty-minute drive, yet Sheldon brought me here in only twenty minutes driving slowly.

I drove home wondering what was it about Sheldon that everything he did was mysterious. "This is a problem for Edwin Drood." I smiled as the rain poured down.

Chapter Six

I arrived to pick up Chelsea a few minutes earlier from her apartment than our agreed time but she was ready as soon as I called her from downstairs. I felt nervous, like I was a school kid going on a first date, but she seemed relaxed and happy. I opened the car door for her, trying to make a good impression. I had tuned the car radio to a station that played music for a younger generation, hoping that would make me appear more youthful.

"How long have you written for the Journal?"

"About six years. My column, News and Views, has been running for four years now."

"Do you like writing that sort of stuff? I mean the social stuff that's going on in the city?"

I shrugged. "It's alright, I guess. I prefer do heavier stuff but they pay me well enough to do it. It's pretty easy getting the information as well. People phone or email with the latest news around the city and I just put it together."

She looked over at me. "I've read your column a few times. You're not a bad writer but I think you'd do well going after bigger stuff. I don't mean to criticise but I get the feeling you're holding yourself back."

She was right. I did hold myself back. After my divorce, I lost a lot of confidence and was thankful for my social column. Shortly after my divorce is when Edwin Drood appeared. He was able do write about things where Harry Winston was out of bounds and out of character. "I have a plan to make my journalistic career more exciting and challenging. It's going to take a bit longer to get there, that's all."

"So what do you want to write about? Politics? Science?"

"Paranormal stuff. The boundaries of science."

She nodded. "That would be cool. That's like the Edwin Drood guy in your paper. He writes that weekend column about vampires and stuff. Do you know him? I guess no one knows his real name."

"I know who he is."

She held a question on her lips for a moment and then changed her mind. "I won't ask you to reveal his identity. But maybe someday you could take over from him."

I smiled. "Maybe I can."

We walked down from the parking lot and waved at some of the River Rodents waiting for the others to arrive.

Chelsea whispered to me, "You know they saw that we were the last leave the bar last time and now we show up together for practice. They may be getting the impression we're going out together."

I looked at her. She was smiling as if it were a joke. I liked the thought that we could going out with each other. "Let's give them something to talk about." I grabbed her hand.

She laughed and held on to my hand for a few seconds before breaking away. "You'll have them gossiping about us for sure now."

I grinned, feeling a victory of sorts.

I said hello to Danielle who was checking to make sure all the forms were completed for our up-coming festival.

"Harry, we have all your paperwork done. You'll be staying in a hotel room with Ted. How are you getting down there? Flying or by car?"

"Flying. I guess I had better make arrangements. By the way, did you find Sheldon's registration form?"

"That was really odd. When I got home, I pulled out my clipboard and there it was, right under yours. How I missed it earlier I haven't a clue."

"So you have it now?"

She shook her head. "No. I faxed his and yours to the festival and his form jammed in the machine. I had to rip it out. Fortunately the festival managed to receive all the information first."

It was more evidence that there was something peculiar with Sheldon. However, I had other things to be concerned about and that included our final practice.

The practice went well. I was coached to lean forward more and to drop my arm so my paddle went deeper. It was tough refining my technique but I wanted to make sure I didn't let down the team during the races. Chelsea encouraged me to keep trying and I began to understand that dragon boating is a lot more complicated than it looks.

At the end of the practice, we gave our customary cheer. Sheldon was as boisterous as usual, and I began to appreciate what he brought to the team—enthusiasm, strength and ability, fine qualities to be sure. Still, I didn't trust him.

I walked with Chelsea back to my car. "Do you want to go to the bar for a drink?"

"Sure, but just for one. Do the team thing. But I don't feel much like drinking tonight."

"Okay, fine with me. By the way are you flying or driving to Kelowna?"

Chelsea told me she was flying and gave me enough information about the flight that I would be able to take the same plane as her. I told her about Sheldon's missing registration form and described the peculiar route he used to his house.

She laughed. "You're just fixated on him. I'm sure there's a logical explanation for it all."

"Maybe. But here's something else. Since I've joined the River Rodents and gone to bar he has not put down a solitary dollar."

"Really?"

"Just watch. He never pays."

We each had a beer and then water as we chatted with the other members. Erin asked what was the story with us, commenting we show up together, sit on the boat together, drink together, and was there was something else we were doing together? The others laughed and Chelsea blushed a bit.

I stammered out we were just friends but that brought forth more comments. Sheldon saved us from trying to explain what friendship meant by proposing a toast to being friends. Sometimes even evil men do the right thing.

Jill, the waitress, provided great service to the table, especially those near Sheldon. She constantly had one hand on his shoulder, grinning away at him. When she returned, she held a tray full of pints of beer and a pitcher for Sheldon.

He acted surprised when she placed in front of him. "Jill, what is this? I ordered only a pint."

"I know. But you're always so nice, so the pitcher is on the house." She smiled happily that she was able do a small favour for him.

I whispered to Chelsea, "See, he never pays."

"You're jealous." She giggled but watched with interest how Jill behaved around Sheldon. Very friendly. The "I know you and we are close and I'll let everyone see" type of friendly.

I wasn't jealous of Jill lavishing undue attention to that old miser, but rather how things always went his way. "I'd rather pay for your beer than get a free beer from Jill."

She gave me a smile. "The way to a girl's heart is through beer theory?"

"If that's true I'll buy you a whole pitcher."

She looked at me for a second before replying, "Maybe after dragon boat season is over. I gotta stay in shape."

After our drink, I drove Chelsea back to her apartment. She was quiet during the trip but as we neared her place, she quickly asked if I would like to come up for a drink. In less than a microsecond, I agreed.

During the elevator ride up to the eighteenth floor, she gave me a short history of her life.

"I like to party, drink and do fun stuff, but I decided I had to establish priorities early if I wanted to have success at school. I'm careful how much time I spend away from my studies and can't afford to drink too much. Dragon boating gives me a nice social outlet and I don't feel pressured to drink too much. The other thing is my old boyfriends didn't seem to understand I needed to work hard on my courses and were always trying to drag me away from my studies. They tried to make me feel guilty."

I followed her into her apartment. It looked like a student's apartment with slightly mismatched furniture. It was clean with the usual bit of junk lying around. She went down the short hallway and closed a door.

"I don't want you to see my messy bedroom."

"That's fine. Maybe another time." As soon as I said it, I mentally kicked myself.

She laughed and blushed.

"Sorry, that didn't come out right."

She shook her head. "That's okay." She went to her fridge and handed me a can of beer. "But along that line I don't want to get into a heavy relationship right now. I'm still hurt from the last one and don't have the energy for another one. Okay?" She looked at me with those lovely green eyes.

"I think what we have right now is great. I'm a bit nervous about dating and relationships myself."

She let out a sigh and touched her beer can with mine. "To slow and easy then."

"To one step at a time."

I learned about her family and how close she was to her mother and sister. They both lived in a small town only a half hour away from the city but that still made it difficult to get together often. Her father had died about five years ago and the small family drew even closer together.

"I find it pretty impressive that you're studying math in university. You must be pretty smart."

"I don't know about that but I do work hard to get my good marks." She took a drink of her beer. "I felt a little intimidated that you were a journalist and wrote for the local paper. I thought here is a guy who has made his mark in the world."

Taken aback by that revelation, I said, "Really? I thought you found me uninteresting."

"Oh no. I even Googled your name."

I was dumbfounded. A pretty, intelligent woman found me interesting. I guess you never know what others are thinking about you. "So you know then I'm an axe murderer?"

"Yeah but I think you've had your quota for the year already so I guess I'm safe."

I finished my beer. "Thanks for the drink and letting me see your place but I guess you need to do some work."

"I do." She stood and walked me to the door.

I tried to linger a bit and then asked her if she wanted to ride with me to the airport. She agreed after a moment of hesitation.

"Sure. I think that would be great."

I stood at the doorway, not wanting to leave but knew I had to.

She gave me a smile and put her hands on her hips. "Look, just because we're going to go slow on the relationship doesn't mean you can't kiss me."

I put my hands on her waist and pulled her close. Her lips were soft and I felt my heart race. It wasn't a deep kiss but I kissed her until I ran out of air.

She gave me a smile. "Alright dragon boater, we'll see you in a few days time."

I left the apartment building feeling giddy and drove home quickly. As soon as I got home, I phoned the airline to get a reservation on the same plane as Chelsea's. I felt fantastic and not the least bit jealous of Sheldon and all his luck.

Chapter Seven

I don't really care for airports. It's hard to find a place to park your car and you have to walk six miles to the air terminal. Then you fight the crowds with slow line-ups everywhere. The counter people look bored as they stamp your ticket and tell you to proceed to gate seven hundred and twelve.

Then there is security with their magic wands that they pass over your body. On a random basis, the wands beep and the poor traveler will have to undo zippers and stand with their arms spread like a windmill. The carry on baggage that was so carefully packed is spilled out after the x-ray machine operator decides a ballpoint pen looked suspicious.

After that, the happy traveller is allowed to wait by the gate in lovely hard plastic chairs carefully designed to put pressure on the kidneys. Seats are spaced so that no matter where you sit you face a wall with an abstract painting on it titled "Birds in Flight". I think it looks more like "Birds in Flight Hitting a Glass Skyscraper".

As you wait, a loudspeaker will make announcements, the voice usually sounding as if the speaker has stuffed her mouth with a peanut butter sandwich. No matter that you can't make out "This Important Announcement" done in six languages. All you have to do is watch the monitor that is updated constantly about arriving and departing flights. This will give a sense of security that all is under control. Don't be fooled by this. The monitor is actually controlled by a bored high school dropout. His qualifications are that he knows the difference between the number 3 and the letter E.

Despite all that I was happy as a pickle in a jar (this is a Saskatchewan saying and I have absolutely no idea what it means but it sounds kinda rustic so I'll use it). Chelsea was with me and we waited on the bright orange chairs for the hostess to announce that the passengers could board. Our plane was a small one, perhaps holding only thirty passengers. That didn't stop the hostess from directing the proper loading procedure. First the handicapped, then those with small children, then first class passengers, then those passengers scared of heights, then those with red hair, and finally the regular coach passengers. Then all four of us made our way to the plane, squeezing past all the other passengers.

The usual description of what to do in an emergency was brought to our attention. Then we received our delicious meal of crackers and cheese in a plastic package. We also had a choice of water or pop in a five-ounce cup. I settled into my seat, trying to avoid a hard lump in the seat that had worked its way past the half-inch foam rubber used in economy airline seats. Flying is so glamorous.

Chelsea made the short flight something special for me all the same. I don't know what we talked about exactly, but before I knew it, the plane landed and we went to the terminal to collect our luggage. Why is it so difficult to unload the luggage from a plane to the luggage carousel? How do they mange to lose something as big as a suitcase? Careful planning I suppose. Two hours later, we retrieved our luggage and caught a cab to our hotel.

"Harry, Chelsea! How was your flight?"

I looked across the hotel lobby and saw Sheldon stepping out of the elevator. I meekly waved back. "Hello Sheldon."

Chelsea was friendlier. "It was fine. How are you doing?"

"I'm doing great. The rest of the team is meeting for drinks at the Blue Wave down the street. Come join us after you get settled in."

"Thanks, Sheldon. We'll be down later." She gave him a warm smile.

We registered at the hotel and then went up to our rooms, which were on different floors unfortunately. The rooms were standard fare, economical in space with two double beds. The pastel painted walls held the usual prints of sailing ships and flowered gardens. I washed up and then went to the lobby to wait for Chelsea.

I walked around the lobby, looking at the folded pamphlets that showed the various attractions around the city. It seemed Kelowna was situated along a string of lakes that all offered various entertainments such as trails, houseboats and festivals. Of course, to make it all a little more exciting there were rumours of a monster in one of the lakes called Ogopogo and in the forests, the legendary big foot monster called Sasquatch.

Chelsea came down to the lobby, looking great. She had changed out of her jeans into a pair of shorts and a short fitted top. I took a gulp and waved.

"Hi, Harry. Sorry if you were waiting but I needed to change."

"That's okay. You're worth the wait." I took her hand and we walked down the street to the Blue Wave where other River Rodents greeted us. I looked around the bar and saw the T-shirts of other dragon boat teams. The Racing Serpents, Smoke and Water, Lake Slime, and H H P.

Sheldon was there, talking in that loud voice of his, probably about another of his wild adventures.

"The pizzas were very good at Plato's and it's located just up the street here."

I found two chairs for Chelsea and myself. I looked questioningly at Erin and then at Sheldon.

Erin informed me, "Oh Sheldon is just telling us the best places to eat here. He really knows this city."

I nodded to Chelsea. "Ask Sheldon anything. He'll know the answer."

Chelsea grinned as she smacked me on the shoulder.

Sheldon was oblivious to my comment. Once Sheldon started to talk, he was like a freight train of conversation. Nothing was going to deter him and soon he was on another favourite topic of his, strange creatures. "The lakes here are all well known for their fishing, and the lakes are well isolated in the interior of British Columbia. However, in the far past, the lakes were connected to the Pacific Ocean. Geological changes occurred slowly and the creatures that lived in them were cut off from the ocean and adapted to live in the lake. Occasionally one of the primitive creatures is spotted."

"Are you talking about the Ogopogo monster?" Neil, a blond hair young man, posed this question. Besides being tall and thin, he had blue eyes, making him a target for some of the ladies on the boat.

"That is one of them. Ogopogo is actually a primitive whale and feeds on small fish."

Neil didn't want to let it go at that. "I thought Ogopogo was made up to attract tourists?"

Sheldon shook his head and smiled. "Oh no, my young friend. The natives here knew Ogopogo before any white man stepped in the area. Reports of the monster go back to the eighteen hundreds."

Neil didn't look convinced. "I've heard of people claiming to see the creature but where is the actual proof?"

Sheldon looked annoyed. "You want me to prove it to you?"

"If you can show me anything more than someone's eye witness report I'll buy you your beer and lunch you just had."

Sheldon frowned. "Well, I didn't want to do this but scepticism is a healthy tool in science." He reached into his jacket pocket and produced a photo. He passed it to Neil. "I took the picture myself and you can see clearly that it is a monster of some sort."

Neil raised his eyebrows and passed the picture around.

I have to say it looked like a monster, with a horse like head and a long serpent body that showed only parts above the water. It was a dark blue or grey in colour and the skin looked shiny. I looked at Sheldon. "When did you take this picture?"

"A few years ago."

Typical Sheldon, vague on time lines. The thing is it looked like a sea monster in a lake. It could be any lake and there wasn't any perspective; there wasn't anything else in the picture to give any indication of its size.

I passed the picture on, not sure what I was looking at and I had too many questions to say that was the Ogopogo monster. I didn't bring up those concerns to Sheldon, not wanting to encourage him to keep talking. The others were more impressed and acted excited at the photo.

Sheldon carried on. "Of course, I never showed the picture to the press. I was concerned that a real hunt for the poor beast would occur. They should be left in peace. Also I don't want the publicity it would bring to me as I'm a modest man."

I choked on my beer as Chelsea pounded my back.

Neil took defeat graciously. "You're right Sheldon, the monster seems to exist. I'll buy your lunch and beer."

I croaked out a whisper to Chelsea, "See? Sheldon never pays."

She laughed and then whispered back at me, "Smart guy then."

The conversation drifted around the table on monsters in general and I could see the gleam in Sheldon's eyes. I know he has many monster stories; he's told me a few of them. Right now, he was holding back from saying much, perhaps figuring one monster tale was enough for one day.

But my mind wasn't entirely on monsters and strange creatures. Casually I rested my hand on Chelsea's thigh. She gave me a quick glance but didn't otherwise react.

The conversation gradually went back to dragon boating itself, and as my fingers gently stroked her leg Sheldon reminded everyone about the upcoming ceremony by the lake where the dragon boats were docked.

"Let's all go down and watch. We can check out the lake and our tent at the same time."

"What is he talking about?" I partially whispered to Chelsea.

Sheldon can catch any whisper and the question allowed him to show off again his knowledge.

"The awakening of the dragons is a ceremony performed by the monks. The Chinese believed the dragons to be both real and mystical. The dragons could bring good luck and prosperity in the coming year and so they were honoured and revered. The ceremony includes music, chants and dancing of symbolic dragons. The monks at the end of the ceremony open the eyes of the dragon boats. It is a ritual we should observe as it may bring us the luck we need to race well."

The others at the table nodded at Sheldon's explanation.

"What about the tent? I thought we were staying in the hotel."

Chelsea laughed. "We are. The tent is where we hang out between races. We have food and drink there. It's just a place to relax. Most of the dragon boat teams have a tent and they're all side by side."

We paid for our bill, except that scoundrel Sheldon who had Kevin pay, and headed to the waterfront.

There was a sizable crowd around the docks. A lot were dragon boaters dressed in casual clothes and a team T-shirt. Some of the River Rodents knew the different teams and said hello to some individuals. The competition between the teams appeared to be friendly and wishes of good luck were common.

We settled around the dock area and a watched as two teenaged boys began to play what looked like red Bongo drums. Then two dragons appeared, men under a colourful blanket with the lead man holding a large dragonhead. The two dragons danced and moved to the drums.

I was enjoying the show as I reached over and touched Chelsea's hand. A second later, she turned her hand to hold mine. I felt elated and looked around to see if anyone was watching us. No one was but I noticed Sheldon was looking at the top of the mountains that sat behind the city. A white cloud had settled between two peaks and looked like it was ready to pour rain down the mountainside. A flash of blue-white lightening lit up the cloud as it jumped from one edge to another.

I looked back at Sheldon who was rubbing his chin, looking deep in thought.

I didn't think too much of it. Right now most of my thoughts were on Chelsea, and how excited I felt as I held her hand.

The ceremony continued for several minutes until the dragons stopped dancing. Then a monk walked to end of the dock and brushed at the eyes of the dragon figureheads mounted to front of the dragon boats. After he was done, applause broke out, signifying the ceremony was completed.

I was still happy holding Chelsea's hand but Sheldon looked troubled.

Chapter Eight

We made our way down a wide brick sidewalk that ran along the lake. Normally there would be green grass along the sides to create a park like setting. Now, vendor tables, filled with goods for sale and food, edged the sidewalk. Chelsea stopped to look at some of the tables selling T-shirts and other tops, all of them with a dragon boat theme printed on them. She held up a pink tank top in front of her with a fire-breathing dragon curled around a dragon boat with people furiously paddling.

"What do you think?"

I thought the tank top looked a bit small and would be rather revealing. The art on the shirt looked good but I wondered about her wearing it in public. It would certainly attract attention to a pair of her assets. What I said was, "I think it would look great on you." That wasn't a lie; it would great on her. It's just that I could picture all the guys staring her.

She paid for the top and stopped at another table selling necklaces, inexpensive dragon shaped symbols with a leather string. She bought one, slipping it over her neck and we continued our slow walk down the sidewalk.

Chelsea wanted to stop at every table and check out the different merchandise. I was content just to be with her, though I found some of the goods interesting. I ended up buying a couple of pink lemonade drinks for us and after that, we continued our handholding stroll.

At another table, she picked up a carved wood dragon. "Isn't that nice? Lots of detail on it."

"It looks pretty good."

The vendor saw a possible sale. "It's only twenty four dollars."

She shook her head. "Maybe later."

"I'll buy it for you."

"No Harry, I don't want you buying stuff for me." She gave me a smile. "Drinks are fine but I don't want to feel I owe you anything, okay?"

"Sure, I understand. You wouldn't owe me anything, though. I just wanted to do something nice for you."

"Harry, you're being nice enough to me already." She squeezed my hand. "Come on, let's look at our tent."

The tents were all in one area near the lake and we wandered between the duplicate tents looking for ours. Each tent was about ten feet square with a high centre peak. The tents had been filled with tables, coolers, and other essential items for the weekend of dragon boat races.

Our tent was facing the lake and some team members were already arranging items inside. Some small folding chairs were set up along with a table. A couple of paddlers were setting up a clothesline and then hanged a sheet over it, making a small corner a changing room.

Sheldon carried in two large flats of plastic water bottles and set them on the table. Soon packages of fruit and trail mix appeared as other paddlers brought in stuff. Two coolers appeared and suddenly the tent looked lived in.

"It looks like a lot of food is coming in here." I looked at the large quantities of food. Most of it healthy, though there were a couple bags of junk food too.

"You can get pretty hungry between races." Chelsea took some trail mix. "You have to keep your carbs up otherwise you don't have any energy for the next race."

I looked out at the lake and watched the sailboats and other watercraft. "It looks rather calm out there."

"It is right now. It doesn't usually get too rough but sometimes the waves make it difficult for the boat."

Chelsea stood right next to me, our bodies were barely touching but I felt even closer to her than that.

"You seem deep in thought, Harry. Thinking about lake monsters?"

I grinned. "No, not even Sheldon has me convinced of them."

"What then?"

"I was thinking how nice it is to be with you. A few weeks ago I never heard of a dragon boat and here I am in Kelowna with you." I wanted to put my arm around her but wasn't sure about the reaction from the rest of the dragon boat team if I were to do so. I suppose the rest of team figured out there was something going on between us but I didn't want to make her feel uncomfortable.

She nodded. "I'm really glad you're here too. Especially if there are lake monsters."

Sheldon's voice shattered the peace and quiet. "Everyone, lets meet at the Rose and Crown for dinner and drinks."

I whispered to Chelsea, "I'd rather stay here by the lake with you."

She laughed. "And do what? Go skinny dipping? We do have to eat you know." She took my hand. "I'll let you buy me a drink at the Rose and Crown."

The Rose and Crown was like all the pubs with English sounding names. The decor consisted of dark furniture with token old English pictures hanging on the walls. The menus usually have some sort of food that might pass as English cuisine, such as nachos. Okay, the nachos really are Mexican food but so many English pubs serve them that they have been adopted as a standard food item. The pubs try their best to have old English charm with modern Canadian prices. It must work because the pub was busy by the time we got there.

Of course, Chelsea had to change before we went there. Some women feel that to wear the same clothes longer than four hours is a fashion sin. Chelsea is better than that; she lasted six hours since her last change. Meanwhile I was wearing the same jeans I arrived in but decided I had some time to kill before I met her. I went to my room and put on a fresh shirt.

I was becoming very familiar with the lobby as I waited and sat in one of the cushioned chairs. I picked up a newspaper lying on table and read news I could care less about, but at least it was better that staring at a wall with a print of a schooner with all its sails bellowing out.

Chelsea came downstairs and waltzed into the lobby. I stood up and stared as she approached.

Okay, maybe I was being a little too critical when I said women want to change their clothes, because what I saw was well worth the wait. I stared at bare legs under a short, black flared skirt and the hot pink top she bought earlier. It didn't quite meet the skirt and the top had a scooped neckline that gave a hint of what was underneath. Chelsea had also redone her make-up and hair, making me feel suddenly underdressed and grubby. She walked up to me smiling and I noticed she was also taller, thanks to the shoes she was wearing.

"You look great."

She grinned, knowing that she did. "Thanks. I like that shirt, it looks good on you."

I'll give her credit for finding something to compliment me on, that wasn't easy to do. I doubt anyone else would notice my shirt with her walking next to me. She looked gorgeous and I began to have doubts how long she would be going out with me. I pushed that thought out of my head and walked with her to the bar, occasionally sneaking an arm around her waist.

"Did you hear about Sheldon's problem with the hotel?"

"No, what happened?" My hopes went up that there was justice after all.

"The hotel screwed up his registration; basically they didn't have him as a guest. After a few minutes of conversation at the front desk they called the hotel manager. Turns out the manager knew Sheldon years ago and gave him a top floor suite without a charge." She looked up at me. "You're not upset about that, are you?"

I exhaled slowly. "No, he can have all the free drinks and rooms. I got something better than that."

"What's that?"

"You."

She laughed. "Oh you're so full of it." She put her arm around me and gave me a hug. "But thank you anyway."

We made it to the Rose and Crown and quickly found our table with Sheldon's loud voice acting like a beacon. As we approached the table a woman's voice called out my name. I slowly turned to the familiar sound and spotted her. She waved at me and I gave a small wave back.

"I'll be back. Save me a chair," I reluctantly told Chelsea.

Ex's. Everyone has thoughts about them, some good, some bad, some revengeful. Divorces can bring out the worse in couples. Dirty, dark secrets used as weapons against former lovers. It can be ugly for friends trying to maintain relations with both.

Some divorces can also end amicably, like mine, but there is still tension when the two meet. As I walked over to Sheila, a lot of thoughts raced around in my mind, some lapping others in the whirlwind of confusion.

She actually divorced me; her argument was that I didn't satisfy her. She quickly amended that to meaning in life, not sexual. Apparently, I didn't add enough excitement in her life. I wish she had discovered that in the two years we were dating and not during the one year of marriage.

I said we departed amicably. Close enough to the truth. She made it clear I wasted three years of her life while I felt I wasted a year's pay on the divorce settlement.

"Hello, Sheila." She had died her hair blonde and it was longer as well. She looked about the same weight, one hundred and twenty pounds of fake and bake, on a five foot seven frame with high heels on. Always wore high heels. She had added a couple of new features to herself as well. Her breasts had gone from a size B to a generous C, which she'd proudly displaced from a push up bra.

"Hello, Harry." She smiled, white capped teeth showing. "This is Richard Cummings. Richard, this is Harry."

Richard reached across the table to shake my hand. "How're ya doing, sport?"

Sport? I grinned back and shook his hand. He wasn't much taller than Sheila was, though quite a bit heavier. Black, shiny hair with curls combed back. He was also well tanned and wore an open, colourful shirt that revealed a gold necklace resting in the forest of black chest hair. He looked very fashionable. Unfortunately, for him it wasn't 1974.

"Nice to meet you, Richard." I looked at Sheila. "How have you been?"

She giggled and grabbed Richard's hand. "Oh, let's just say I'm a very busy woman. With Richard it's always something new."

I smiled. Always something new with Richard? No doubt, he was going to surprise her with a digital watch, the very latest thing thirty years ago.

I felt a hand on my shoulder, turned and saw Chelsea. She was smiling sweetly at me as she put her arm around me. Introductions were made and she positively glowed as she chatted with us. I looked at Sheila, who no longer had a constant smile, and at Richard, who was trying to look down Chelsea's shirt. Take a good look, my primitive friend. Those are real and not blemished by too many UV rays.

Chelsea was clinging to me like we were ready to jump in bed. I could tell it was making Sheila a bit annoyed as she squeezed Richard's hand and laughed too hard at a weak joke.

"Well, I have to drag Harry back to the table. We need him to settle some of the dragon boat issues. It was nice to meet you, Sheila, and you too, sir."

Richard closed his eyes for a brief second. Nothing like being call "Sir" by a sweet young thing to make you feel old.

We walked hand in hand to our table.

"Thank you for that."

"That's alright. Sheldon told me she was your ex and I know how difficult that can be."

I wondered how Sheldon knew Sheila was my ex. I don't think he ever met her but I might have shown a picture of her to him at one time. Still it seems Sheldon knows everything. This time I didn't mind at all.

I gulped down my first beer, feeling pretty good as I stroked Chelsea's leg for a few seconds. I didn't push my luck with her by too many touches but she was hard to resist. After I finished my beer, I casually looked to where Sheila and Richard were sitting. They were gone.

"You were married to her how long?"

"Only ten months."

Chelsea digested the information for a few seconds. "She looked older than you."

I didn't hesitate. I kissed her.

Chelsea laughed. "One compliment and you get all excited."

"Almost as excited as Richard when he was trying to look down your shirt."

"That was funny. I saw him trying to sneak a look so I leaned forward a bit to give him a better look. He stared, thinking he was getting away with it. What he didn't know was that Sheila was quite aware of his eyeballing and was going to get it later. Typical guy, thinking women don't know what they're staring at."

I immediately averted my eyes from below her shoulders. Women, Chelsea in particular, know what my lustful eyes are looking at? I throw myself at the mercy of the court. Can I truly be held responsible for what my eyes do on their own accord?

She whispered, "That's okay. You can look at me. I didn't wear this shirt to hide myself from you. As far as other women are concerned, look, but don't stare."

"What other women?"

She grinned. "Very smooth Harry, very smooth."

We didn't drink too much and together with dinner, we were all quite sober as the evening progressed. The River Rodents were aware tomorrow was race day and alcohol was not something of which we needed to indulge.

A small band started up, playing the blues. Lex Justice was the bass guitarist and lead singer. He was a big man, not fat, but muscle big. There was lots of dark hair done in dread knots and tattoos inscribed on his big arms. He was not the type of guy you wanted to meet in a dark alley.

Lex and the band played well, very well actually, and he had a great voice. After the third song, he stopped and pointed at our table. "I see a good drinking buddy of mine is here. Sheldon, how are you doing, my friend?"

I couldn't believe it as Sheldon greeted him back. Does Sheldon have friends everywhere?

"Sheldon, why don't you come up here and do a couple of songs with us? I know you play a mean bass guitar."

Sheldon held up his hands in a modest protest, but our table and the crowd around us refused to give in. We clapped our hands and chanted his name. Sheldon reluctantly went to the stage.

I never knew Sheldon played any musical instrument but there he was playing bass like he had practiced with the band for years. He was good, damn it.

"Are you going to stare at Sheldon all night or are you going to ask me to dance?"

"Sorry. It was just a shock to see him up there."

I took her to the dance floor and she soon moved her hips to the music. She looked great. I watched her and tried not to move too much. Some guys can dance really well. The other ninety percent of us best not try to draw attention to ourselves.

The music was good and easy for dancing. Then a slow song came up and I nervously put my arm around her waist. She drew closer to me as we made a small circle and then she rested her head on my chest. I was in heaven as I breathed in her fragrance. I kissed the top of her head and then a few seconds later she looked up at me.

I don't pick up hints that well, but even I knew the next step to our dance. I bent down and kissed her on her lips. They slowly parted and I continued to kiss her after the song had ended. The rest of the bar disappeared as I fell in love.

We danced the next song, a much faster one, and then retreated to our table.

Love is not always reciprocated, especially early in a relationship. Thus, I didn't tell her my feelings, in case that honesty scared her off. She looked happy and relaxed. I tried to act relaxed and happy myself, ignoring the feeling that someone had punched me in the stomach.

"That was some dance you two did." Erin laughed as we sat down. "I hope you have the same passion tomorrow during the dragon boat race."

Chelsea blushed a bit and because I was in love with her, I thought that made her look even more desirable. If she had decided to smear mustard on her face, I would still think she looked great. Love isn't blind; it just sees everything through rose coloured glasses. I sat down, trying to stop myself from grinning at everything.

A few minutes later Sheldon and Lex Justice came to our table. Lex was laughing at something Sheldon had said and then clapped him on the back.

"I gotta get ready for the next set, Sheldon, but thanks for coming up on stage. Just like the old days. You never missed a beat."

"I just tried to keep it simple. An old guy like me gets forgetful how to play sometimes."

"Quit bullshitting me, man. You never age." Lex gave a deep, hardy laugh.

I notice all the women at our table were looking at Lex, smiling as they gave him that dreamy eyed schoolgirl look. It must be the tattoos.

"Anyway Sheldon, I've taken care of your bar tab as way of payment for your help." Lex walked away and the ladies at our table began to return to normal, though some of them quickly whispered comments to one another.

Chelsea leaned towards me. "You're right, Sheldon never pays."

"That's okay. If Lex hadn't paid, I'm sure I would've been stuck with it somehow."

She laughed. "Optimism."

I walked back slowly to the hotel with her and escorted her to her room. I can't remember what we talked about. It was small stuff, like what colours she liked, that I had dog when I was a kid and maybe her favourite fragrance was mentioned. I just really enjoyed holding her hand and listening to her talk and it's been a long time since I enjoyed listening to a woman talk.

"I'd invite you in but one of my roomies likes to strip down in the room and not get dressed again right away."

"Your roomies are female, I hope."

She laughed and punched me on the shoulder. "What kind of girl do you think I am?"

"One that knows how to punch." I rubbed my shoulder.

"Well, I don't want to damage you before the races. I'll be easy on you for a while."

We had enough small talk I figured. I put my hands on her hips and pulled her close. She wrapped her arms around my neck and we kissed long and hard. Twice. Then I reluctantly went to my room three floors below where my roommate was watching a movie.

I had seen the movie before but Ted had the remote control, so he got to pick the show. That's the rule, first one to the remote controls the TV. Besides, it was a Die Hard movie and you never switch channels on a Die Hard movie. We didn't talk much, guys sharing rooms usually don't, but we each had a can of beer and made the odd comment about the show. A short time later, I decided to get some sleep. Of course, that was difficult as I was thinking about Chelsea.

Chapter Nine

The team was to meet in the hotel lobby. When I arrived, a bit on the early side, some River Rodents were drinking coffee or tea while others shuffled about chatting. Sheldon was, of course, making his presence known. He was talking about his carbon fibre paddle to one of the team members, showing it off as he paddled the air with it.

I looked around but Chelsea had not made it down yet, so I walked over to him.

"Good morning, Sheldon."

He held his paddle in mid stroke and turned to look at me. "Good morning, Harry. Great day to be on the water."

"I guess, though I thought maybe I'll grab some breakfast first."

"I suggest Hawkshead Bistro about two blocks west of here. I went there this morning after my run."

"After your run? What time did you get up?"

"A bit before six, as usual."

I shook my head. Trust Sheldon to get up early for a run. I have serious doubts he is human. What human gets up early for a run before a dragon boat race? I looked towards the elevator, hoping Chelsea would arrive. Instead, other hotel guests spilled out chattering away like excited monkeys.

"Looking for Chelsea?" Sheldon chuckled. "Don't worry my friend; she has made it clear you are hers."

"Really? How do you know this?"

"Harry, remember in the bar last night when she went over to where you and your ex were talking?"

"Yeah, she turned the tables on her."

"Harry, women are very protective of those they consider their own. She would not have gone over if she didn't consider you hers."

That was a surprise to me; I never thought of the possibility of a woman defending me. The elevator made a pinging sound and then it stopped. Chelsea came out of the elevator with four other women that were on our dragon boat team. Within a minute, everyone was greeting one another while I quickly moved over to Chelsea.

"Hey, there." She gave me a warm smile.

"Hi, all set for the big day?"

"Maybe after breakfast. I'm starving."

Danielle called attention to the River Rodents. "I have wrist bands for everyone so we can enter the dragon boating area. Please don't lose them; it's difficult to get replacements."

After a short discussion among the team Chelsea and I left the hotel to have breakfast, going to Hawkshead Bistro that Sheldon suggested earlier. I held her hand as we walked, feeling content about life.

"So how long ago were you married to Sheila?" Chelsea asked casually, which is a sure sign that it wasn't a casual question.

"About two years ago."

"Can I ask why you two split apart?" Her voice was quiet, with a hint of hesitation in the words.

"In a nutshell she wanted more than I could give her."

"That's strange. You have a lot to offer. What more did she want?"

"I'm not sure. More excitement in her life I suppose."

"I find dragon boating pretty exciting. Maybe she should have tried that instead of divorce."

I chuckled at the thought of Sheila trying to paddle a dragon boat. "I don't think she's the type."

"No children then?"

"No."

She remained quiet and I took that as a hint my answer was incomplete. "Doesn't mean I don't want kids, just she wasn't the one to have them with."

She nodded. "I want to have kids some day but not now. University studies are a priority right now."

We sat at a table and I showed a great interest in the single page, plastic covered menu. But it seemed the personal questions were over, much to my relief, and we talked about other things.

Paddlers are usually social people. That makes sense when you consider that you're jammed into a boat with nineteen other paddlers, so you better not be the unfriendly type. As we walked to the dragon boats and said hello to other paddlers. Most of the paddlers wore shirts that identified their teams and while we would be racing against them later, for now there was a sense of being comrades.

By tradition, most of the women when they recognize another woman paddler exchange hugs. Men have a different tradition. They lift their paddles to their shoulder in a kind of salute. In the middle ages, they would have used swords.

Regardless of gender most of the conversation contains the comment, "It's a great day to be on the water."

We joined a group of other paddlers who stood along a rail that bordered a brick walkway. The walkway ran along the length of the lake and provided a good view of the dragon boat races.

I didn't know any of the teams but there were six boats racing down their lanes. One boat surged ahead of the rest and two other boats soon lagged behind the rest. The other three boats were close to each other without a clear leader for second place. At the three hundred metre point, one of the boats started to slide from lane five towards the boat in lane four. We could see the steersperson in the fifth lane frantically leaning on the paddle to try to correct their direction, but to no avail. The boat in lane four moved over as far as it could but the nose of the fifth lane boat crashed into the middle of the boat.

The paddlers in the fifth lane were dragging their paddles, trying desperately to hold the boat. The collision was not at high impact thanks to their efforts and the boats broke free from each other again.

By then it was too late for both boats. The boat in the first lane that was neck and neck with the other two boats took a large lead and secured second place.

Crashes between boats do occur but it is rare, especially with the number of experienced teams at the festival.

"What happened there, Chelsea?"

"I'm not sure. The boat seemed to slide sideways like something was pushing it."

We discussed the collision with those around us but nothing new could be determined.

Chelsea saw some of the other female paddlers on our boat and turned to give me a kiss.

"Hey, I want to talk to the girls. I'll see you later at the tent."

I watched her joined the others and waited a few minutes before starting behind them. A couple of them gave a quick glance behind, looking at me, and then continued to do the talk and walk with the others.

That is one of the amazing things I find about women. The five of them all seem to be talking about the same time and no doubt, all of them were able to listen to the others while still speaking. In technical terms, I think it's called multiplexing.

I had little doubt I was one of the subjects in that conversation but what was being said was impossible to guess. To say I was uncomfortable about that would be an understatement.

"Harry!"

I turned at the sound of the voice, recognizing Sheldon's blast immediately. "Hi, Sheldon. Did you see that last race?"

Sheldon nodded. "It was very strange."

"Did the steersperson lose control?"

"No, that wasn't the case. I believe there was something in the water."

"What do you mean?"

"Let me investigate a bit more on that. Come, let's get ready for our race."

I walked with him, puzzled by what he meant by something in the water.

Chapter Ten

There is a ritual before a dragon boat race. Though every team goes about it a bit different, the River Rodents share a common routine. First, there is a gathering at the tent. There is small talk and a few of the paddlers went behind the makeshift curtain to change. Most guys didn't worry about any screening; they changed their shirts and shorts at the back of the tent. I'm sure the women noticed them but they were discrete in their glances. Some of the women went behind the curtain and you could see the dance of bare feet as they put on their dragon boat uniforms.

Another popular tradition is the final meal, usually consisting of fruit, trail mix or a granola bar. I was new to the dragon boating and though I took a couple drinks of water, I felt too keyed up to eat.

Chelsea came up to me after changing into the River Rodent racing jersey, a stretch material with short sleeves. The team shirt was black with a colourful dragon printed on the back with "River Rodents" on the front.

"That's a nice shirt." It followed the curves of her body nicely and I was envious of the dragon that got to cling to her.

"Yeah, we had to order them a few weeks before you joined the team. But I'll talk to the lady who did the ordering and see if there are any left. I think they're about forty bucks and we should get you one."

I like that she used the term we as in like we were a couple. "That sounds good to me."

"How're you doing, Harry?" She gave me a puzzled look.

I grimaced. "I may be a little nervous about this race." I was beginning to have doubts I should even be on the boat. I wondered if they would be better off with nineteen paddlers or someone from another team.

She put her hand on my shoulder and smiled. "You'll be fine." Then she squinted her eyes at me. "God, your muscles are all bunched up."

"Like I said, I'm a little nervous."

"It's a race, not an execution." She gave me one of those sweet, sexy, understanding, 'I care' smiles. "Come."

She took my hand and led me to an open area just outside the tent.

"Take off your shirt and lie down."

I hesitated and then pulled off my shirt before lying down on the grass. I wished my muscles were bigger, and that I had done push ups this morning.

Chelsea climbed on my back and began to massage my neck and shoulders.

"Just relax. Think of nothing."

I nodded. However, here was a beautiful woman rubbing my back and I was suppose to think of nothing? I felt her warm hands on my skin and her fingers pressing into my muscles. It was wonderful.

Not just because of the massage but also because I knew she cared about me. I began to relax, my muscles yielding to her manipulations. At least my shoulders and back began to relax. Below my waist, something else was anything but relaxed. Unlike my shoulders, it was not going limp.

She finally stopped. "How was that? Are you feeling bit more relaxed?"

I turned to face her. "Yes, thank you very much. I feel much better. How about you take off your shirt and I give you a back massage?"

She laughed. "Right. Maybe later when we're alone." She gave me a meaningful look, only for the mood to be interrupted by Sheldon's booming voice.

"River Rodents, it's time for our warm up."

I sighed and we followed the rest to an open area outside of the tent area. The River Rodents assembled in a large circle where we did arm and leg stretches. This was followed by arm pulls by partnering up with another team member. I quickly chose Chelsea, even though we had a difference in weight. She was still giving me a smile and my mind was on anything but the race ahead.

Women are very good at playing hard to get and ignoring men interested in them. When a woman becomes interested in you there isn't any mistake when they turn on the charm. Everything becomes different; how they look at you, how they act and even their voice. I was feeling light headed from her attention when we began a short run as part of our warm up.

I did the run without thinking about anything but her and my mind was still in vacant mode when we lined up for our first race. I then began to remember why we were here. I was one of team members who didn't own his own paddle and PFD. I looked for a paddle that didn't look like it was used to break rocks and then searched for a PFD that was dry and was a size large. I ended up with one that was soaking wet on the left side and only damp on the right. It was also marked size medium but fitted extra large, which averaged out to a size large.

I stood waiting for the others to enter the dock. There was little talking as the paddlers prepared themselves mentally for the race. My earlier doubts about my paddling ability began to return when I felt a big hand on my shoulder.

For the first time since I met him, Sheldon spoke in a soft voice. "Harry, all you have to do is to be the best you can. We are a team and not one of us is going to make us win or lose a race. You know what to do, just focus on one stroke at a time."

He walked away, leaving me to reflect on his words. I have to admit Sheldon surprises me now and then, doing something really thoughtful. It's probably just a ruse.

We were loaded into the boat and I took my place next to Chelsea. A few minutes later, we pushed off from the dock and made our way to the start. The River Rodents, like all the boats, did a practice start as we approached the start line. The six dragon boats were jockeyed so that all of them were as close as possible to the start line, with a dock official, called a referee, ordering some boats to move forward or back a few strokes. Then he announced, "Starter has the race."

"Attention, please!"

I raised my paddle just above the water with my arms outstretched and my body twisted above the guttle. I was so full of adrenaline that my paddle was vibrating. Only a second or two passed but in that time I managed to glance at Chelsea who was focused on her own paddle, the boat next to us, the lapping water, back to look at Chelsea's legs, the paddler in front of me and finally back to my own paddle. I know one is supposed to stay focused on the task but I was just too jumpy to stay still. Then the air horn sounded.

"Tooooot!"

In unison, the River Rodents exploded their paddles deep into the water, trying to propel the dragon boat up and forward. In eighteen strokes, the boat had to reach a speed where it glided at the top of the water and reducing the resistance to it. In practice, my arms were tired after the start, but now in the race I was surprised at how soon the steer person yelled "Lengthen!"

I changed my stroke, reaching further into the water, as I watched the front of the boat to keep in timing with the rest of the boat. I heard our drummer repeat the command to lengthen as she pounded on the large drum in front of her.

"Boom…boom, Boom…boom, Boom…boom."

It sounded like an echo, and then I realized the second "boom" was coming from the drummer on a boat right next to us. It was either slightly ahead or behind us and I resisted the urge to glance to see where it was, concentrating on my own timing.

I realized the race was half way done when we passed the orange buoys, even though I felt the race had just started. The sound of the drum from the other boat had faded away and it seemed we were temporarily alone in the water.

"Hey!" a distant male voice called out in surprise, followed by the sound of a body falling into the water.

We kept paddling, focused on completing the race. Still, in the back of my mind I wondered what had caused the splash in the water.

We continued to paddle through the water, though we definitely were not alone. Off to my side I heard the voices from another boat as well as the pounding of their drum. I stole a glance and saw their boat, two lanes away, and about a half boat length ahead of us.

"Finish it! Finish it now!"

I jumped into action, pouring every once of energy I had into my paddle. I concentrated on the timing of my strokes by looking forward and ignored the temptation to take one more look at the other boat. The voices and the drum on the other boat became louder.

I could feel the surge in our boat as we sprinted towards the finish line. Then suddenly a new command was issued.

"Hold the boat!"

We dug our paddles into the water, trying to brake the huge boat. It slowed down as our steersperson turned the boat away from the cement wall that marked the end of the lake.

We congratulated ourselves on our race, even though we didn't know where we finished. We had done the best we could and had left nothing behind in our efforts. I was exhausted and I still hadn't caught my breath. Even so, we began the slow paddle back to the docks and there we would find out how well we did in our race. People standing above us on the walkway applauded the boats as they went by, and we heard a couple of shouts directed at our boat for a great finish.

The unloading at the docks was busy. As we left, another team was ready to come and take over our boat. We made our way to a large display boat that listed the teams and the results of each race. I took Chelsea's hand and tried to peer through the crowd to see how we did.

Sheldon had elbowed his way to the front and called out the result. "We got second place! We edged out that other boat by less that a tenth of a second. Great race River Rodents!"

The team assembled off to the side where the coach gave a summary of our race.

"Overall, very good. A much better result than we expected for our first race. We had a good start but lost a bit in the middle of the race but what a fantastic finish we had. We were almost a boat length behind with a hundred metres to go and we caught them. If we can improve the middle portion of our race, we'll be in good shape.

"Now one other issue is that one of the boats lost there steersperson during the race. He claimed everything was fine and his boat was on course when something hit his steering paddle so hard it knocked him over. Earlier in the day, another boat seemed to be pushed across its lane causing a crash. The race officials are speculating that one or more tree logs are drifting just below the surface and are causing the problem." She gave a pause and then continued. "Of course some people claim it's Ogopogo but so far it hasn't been seen. I suppose we'll stick to the floating log theory until we know more."

Everyone smiled at the last statement by her. I suppose people like the thought of a lake monster, unless we meet one face to face, but it seemed more likely lake monsters were more imagination than substance.

I walked with Chelsea to our tent area and saw Sheldon staring out at the lake.

"Sheldon, are you looking for lake monsters?"

He turned slowly back towards us with a slight smile on his face. "Well, I don't expect to see any logs, that's for darn sure." He began to walk with us.

Chelsea looked up at him. "What do you think it is then?"

Sheldon frowned. "The trouble is we have a tendency to dismiss all kinds of creatures as fables, mistaken identity or fraud. The simple fact is we don't know what's out there or even what our universe is made of. The explanation of log just under water is stretching things a bit I would say. If it wasn't a log, then there could really be a creature of some sort under the water."

I looked over at the lake where another race had begun. "So you think it may be Otopogo?"

"Perhaps, or something even stranger."

We reached the tent and Sheldon took an orange to eat, leaving Chelsea and I to wonder what he meant by something even stranger. I suppose I had enough clues in front of me to figure out what may be going on, but my thoughts were on Chelsea. If I had been paying closer attention, I'd know there was something in the lake that wasn't your average sea monster.

Chapter Eleven

It was great walking around with Chelsea. When you're happy with the person next to you, everyone seems friendlier, the grass is greener, and the air smells fresher. I was in love with her and wanted to tell her or show her, but I was scared I'd frighten her off. I kept my feelings to myself, but tried to sneak in comments to let her know I cared a lot about her.

"You made my life fun again."

"I did?"

"Absolutely. The dragon boating, the beer drinking, Kelowna, and kissing a pretty girl. Actually it's mostly kissing the pretty girl."

She laughed. "I think it's nice kissing you too." She put her hands behind my neck and gave me a long kiss. I was in heaven as we generally ignored the world around us.

I had my arm around her waist as we stood watching a large fountain spewing water around stone dolphins that were leaping in the air.

"We should head back to the village and meet up with the rest of the team, Harry."

"I'd rather stand here with you. But I guess we better get going." We started back to the tent site. "Do you want a drink or anything?"

She shook her head. "No thanks." Chelsea appeared to appraise me. "The girls all agreed you were a great guy and I should be nice to you so you'd stay on the boat." She gave a grin.

"They really said that?"

"More or less. We discussed a few other things about you as well, but that was just girl talk."

That is something all men learn sooner or later in life, usually later. Women talk about everything and if you are going out with one of them, details about you will be revealed. Men talk about women in general, but usually don't give out much detail about our girlfriends. There is an archaic saying "Gentlemen don't tell". Obviously that isn't strictly followed but I'm not one to tell one of buddies how Chelsea is in bed, what her body is like – they can see that for themselves – or what her favourite colour is.

On the other hand, I'll bet all of Chelsea's girlfriends know what kind of kisser I am. It makes for interesting introductions when I meet one of her friends for the first time. I'll know her name and she'll already know what kind of shorts I wear.

I guess that is as good a reason as any to be on good terms with your girlfriend; one doesn't want all of her friends to be mad at you at the same time.

The tent was busy with people walking about. Eating, drinking, stretching exercises and meditation all going on at the same time. A few comments were directed towards Chelsea and me asking what we had been up to.

She blushed slightly and smiled that we were just walking around. That was met with challenges with what she meant by "Just walking around". I kept my mouth closed, not wanting to draw any more attention to ourselves and what I considered a private matter. Foolish me. See the above paragraphs that women share details.

Danielle soon called for our attention and then led us to an open area to do our warm up exercises. I was feeling good about everything. I was even friendly towards Sheldon and couldn't care less the women were all fighting for a position next to him. After the exercises, we made our way to the loading area. Several paddlers went to the port-a-potties for the first of the nervous pees. Some paddlers will go two or three times in the space of thirty minutes just prior to the race.

I wasn't nervous yet. I stood relaxed next to Chelsea with a dumb smile on my face. I wasn't exactly focusing on the race. I began to realize there was indeed a race coming up when I had to look for a paddle the right length and in decent shape to use. The PFD I ended up with was soaked with water and too loose but that was preferable to one too tight.

We were loaded into the boat a few minutes and another potty break later. Unlike the first race in the morning when the lake was calm, there were some small waves lapping against the side of the boat.

We lined up with the other boats in lane four. When all the boats lined up the call went out, "Starter has the race."

I tensed up, squeezing my paddle so hard the wood on the shaft shrunk in size. I held the paddle just above the shifting water waiting for the next command.

"Attention please!"

My paddle shook in my hand.

"Tooooot."

In unison, our paddles dove into the water. Water splashed around us as the huge boat attempted to surge out of the lake. I counted the strokes mentally and was ready when the steersperson yelled "Lengthen, lengthen now!"

A few stokes later he yelled, "Timing, time it up."

Someone, or some paddlers, was off on their strokes, and I hoped that that didn't include me. All the same, I concentrated on the lead paddler to make sure my timing was as close as I could get. Timing doesn't just mean putting your paddle in the water at the same time. One also has to pull back the water at the same rate and exit at the same time. If you pull your paddle too far back, it will make your return too slow and that will affect the paddler behind you as they reach forward. When paddles collide, you know there's a problem.

Despite our timing perhaps being off, I sensed our boat was doing better than the last race. It seemed faster and there wasn't the rocking, surging motion in the boat when we are out of sync present.

Thus I was surprised when the steersperson yelled, "Focus in the boat. Focus in the boat!"

I was focused and wondered why the new command. Then suddenly, off to my side another dragon boat was moving towards us.

A few seconds later, the broadside of the dragon boat invaded our water. The two boats continued to pace each other as the paddlers tried to keep the boats moving.

Paddles clashed between the two boats and it looked like both boats would lose valuable time until we separated. I looked up towards the front of the boat and saw Sheldon reach forward and pull back with his paddle. The paddler in the next boat, a good size young man, tried to position his paddle just behind Sheldon's. For a brief moment, there was a contest of strength, and then Sheldon's paddle swept the other paddle backward. Sheldon rotated and reached forward again. Once more, he pulled back the other paddle with his own.

I heard the other paddler curse as he gave up paddling and used his paddle to try to push our boat away. Thanks to Sheldon the rest of the paddlers behind the young man lost their timing as well, as Sheldon used his strength to power our boat forward. A few seconds later, we pulled away from the other boat and resumed our race.

It was a great feeling to have won the clash of paddles. In a way, it was like a scene from a movie where two ships full of buccaneers battled for supremacy. Okay, we used paddles instead of swords and guns, and none of us wore eye patches, but it was exciting all the same. Of course, I'll have to give credit to Sheldon, who almost single-handed disrupted the timing of the other boat and allowed us to pull away. Let me rephrase that. I'll give him the credit but damn if I'll actually say so to the others. No need to feed his ego.

The race ended for us rather successfully. We achieved another second place finish and we congratulated ourselves on our ability to recover from the boat collision. We were lucky; a small difference in the way the two boats collided could have left us out of the race. In our excitement, we didn't learn until later that another boat in the race also suffered a mishap.

Chapter Twelve

Danielle gathered us around in the tent. "Look, I have some announcements to make and let me go through all of them before answering any questions. First, we are now in the top thirty."

Cheers erupted. That was good news. There were a hundred and fifty teams in the competition and so far, our times had been better than we expected. We were also roughly defined as a recreational team, as opposed to the competitive teams. The competitive teams took training to another level, living and breathing dragon boating. Then there are the corporate teams, made up of paddlers from specific groups. Now some of the corporate teams can be very good and some competitive teams can run into difficulties during the competition. All things considered, we were quite happy how high we had finished.

Danielle gave a small smile. "The boat we collided with in the last race has filed a protest against us. They claimed we interfered with them. If the protest is upheld we could be disqualified or penalized."

The drummer yelled, and believe me when she yells you can't hear yourself think, "What the hell are they talking about? They came into our lane. Our lane! Are they on drugs or something?"

Danielle held up her hands. "Please, calm down. I'm sure the protest won't work. We'll know within the hour. During that race, another boat had a problem. According to those who saw it, it looked liked the boated lifted up a foot and then when it came down was swamped. The paddlers tried to continue but had to be rescued as it appeared the boat might sink."

The tent was quiet on the news. We all felt bad for the team that had their race cut short. That could have happened to any of us.

"Because of that, and a few other unexplained incidents, the rest of the races are being postponed until the cause has been established. They are looking for submerged logs and other possible culprits. It has become a safety issue."

As you might expect there was a lot of questions, opinions and talking afterwards. I stood next to Chelsea and reached for her hand. She looked up at me, her eyes showing the frustration of the news.

"Don't worry, things will be resolved and we'll be back racing soon enough."

She sighed. "Thanks, but we were doing so well, then this happens."

Before I could reply, I felt a heavy hand on my shoulder. I turned and saw Sheldon.

He whispered to me, causing several heads to turn in our direction, "Harry, can I speak to you in private?" So much for the element of secrecy.

I reluctantly let go of Chelsea's hand and followed Sheldon out to a secluded area near the lake. I looked back at Chelsea and she was watching us leave, her lips slightly parted as if she wanted to say something.

"What is it Sheldon?"

He pursed his lips as he looked around for anyone within hearing distance. "Harry, I have some suspicions on what is causing the disturbance in the water. I would like to have your help, or more specifically, as your shadow character Edwin Drood."

I was a little shocked that Sheldon wanted my help, at least for something more than paying for his bar tab. I was also starting to piece together that would account for the dragon boats tipping, though that explanation I kept to myself for the time being. It still sounded outrageous to me. "What do you need me to do?"

"Could you meet me in my hotel room? It is best I explain the matter there."

"Okay, but I think I should tell Chelsea where I'm going."

"Are you sure? She may want to come along to the hotel."

"I'm sure. I don't want to hide things from her."

"Including that you're also Edwin Drood? Very well, meet me in ten minutes."

Since this was Sheldon, I automatically adjusted that time to fifteen minutes. There's no point at seeing him any sounder than I had to. I went back into the tent, going up to Chelsea.

"What was that all about?"

"Come with me. I need to explain something to you."

Once we got outside of the tent and hearing distance of the others, I began to speak. "Sheldon thinks he knows what's going on in the lake, what is causing the boats to collide."

"Really? What is it?"

"He didn't tell me, but said he would explain in his hotel room. I guess he needs my help."

"Your help?" She stopped walking and turned to face me. "Why you? You're not telling me everything, are you?"

I closed my eyes for a moment, hoping she wouldn't storm off mad at me for not saying anything earlier. "He needs someone that he believes is familiar with the paranormal."

"The paranormal. You're an expert on that?"

I nodded. "I also write a column as Edwin Drood."

Her expression changed and she put her hands on her hips. "You're also Edwin Drood?"

"Yes, sorry. I should have told you earlier."

She grinned. "You're full of surprises." She gave me a shove on my chest.

"You won't tell anyone will you?"

"No, but you better not be hiding any more big secrets like that from me."

I tried to remember if I ever had been in prison or elected Prime Minister. Unless I had suffered amnesia, there were no other big events in my life.

"I'm not. We need to meet Sheldon in his hotel room."

"Hmm, one girl and two men in a hotel room. Will I be safe?"

"Only from him."

We rode the elevator to the top floor, emerging on a much nicer hallway than the ones on the lower floors. The carpet was even clean. We knocked on Sheldon's door and it swung open.

"Come on in my friends." Sheldon was in a boisterous mood as he held a beer can in one hand and map in the other.

The living room was spacious with French doors at one wall leading to the bedroom. The other side of the room featured the mini kitchen and, in front of us, glass doors that led to a balcony. I walked over to the glass doors and noted it had a great view of the lake and the surrounding mountains. Sheldon sure had lucked out in getting this room. Sheldon gave me a beer and Chelsea a glass of wine; don't ask me how he just happened to have a bottle of her favourite wine, Soljan's Sauvignon Blanc, on hand.

Chelsea relaxed on the couch and looked at Sheldon. "So what is the secret of what's happening in the lake?"

He smiled. "Well I don't think it's a submerged log."

I sat next to Chelsea. "What then? Ogopogo?" I decided to play along with him but I guessed it wasn't any ordinary sea monster.

He laughed. "I wish it was so. That would make it easier to fix. No, I'm afraid we have a much more serious issue here."

Chelsea smiled. "So what would be more serious than a lake monster?"

Sheldon held up his index finger on his right hand. "A lake monster that is also a spirit."

I was confused. "You mean a dead Ogopogo?"

Sheldon shook his head and laughed. "No, Ogopogo has nothing to do with this. The spirits I'm referring to are those that belong to dragons."

Chelsea leaned forward. "You mean real dragons, fire breathing dragons that fly?"

"Yes, I believe the spirit of a dragon is causing the problem we are seeing."

I took a drink of my beer, and then another one. "Are you serious? What could we do about a dragon spirit even if it was the culprit?"

"I'm very serious about this, Harry."

I was about to say he was nuttier than a fruitcake but then Edwin Drood took over my thinking. Sheldon has proven to me on more than one occasion he knows something about the supernatural world and I have to admit I've seen some things I thought before were only fables. So what was it that Sheldon knew?

I recalled he noticed a cloud and a bolt of lightning during the awaking of the dragon ceremony by monks. Okay, so we have a religious event of sorts at the same time a freak lightning bolt hits a mountain. I began to speak aloud my thoughts.

"So during the awaking of the dragons a lightning bolt strikes the mountain."

Sheldon nodded.

I leaned back on the couch and closed my eyes, my voice changing pitch slightly, "The lightning is actually an intense form of energy from a flow of electrons. But that energy is not limited mere electricity, there are also radio waves generated and possibly harmonics that extend into the realm of quantum mechanics." I opened my eyes. "The monks' prayer, which is more than words but also mental thoughts of their beliefs, was amplified by the lightning bolt's spillage of energy and transferred to a domain where dragons do exist."

Chelsea looked between Sheldon and me. "Seriously? This really happened?"

Sheldon nodded. "Yes, it is the best explanation I can come up with. Harry has filled in the logical part of it. I just knew the end result."

"I think I need more wine. How come you don't believe it's a floating log or Ogopogo?"

Sheldon refilled her glass, "A submerged log could not have caused what we have seen so far, boats being pushed or lifted without leaving any marks on the hull. As far as Ogopogo is concerned, no one has seen part of it which would be unusual if it was coming into contact with a boat."

"Alright. But a dragon? Aren't they supposed to fly with big wings in the air and not swim under water?"

I stood and walked over to the balcony and then turned to speak to her. "If was a real dragon, you would be right. As Sheldon said earlier this is a spirit of a dragon and thus doesn't have boundaries. A spirit can go though solid walls or rock if it so chooses, or in this case, fly through water."

"So just where is this dragon and what do we do about it?"

I looked at Sheldon. Obviously, he had to have some plan or he wouldn't have asked me to meet him in his room. Truth was I was worried about his answer; I don't know what he planned but it probably wasn't safe.

"Harry and I are going on a little hike to where we saw that lightning bolt hit. I believe that will lead us to where the real dragon is. Once we find the dragon we will do what we can to stop its spirit from roaming on our world."

I was right, it wasn't safe. It also confirmed that Sheldon was nuttier than a fruitcake.

Chelsea looked at me. "Are you really going to do this? Climb up a mountain and search out a dragon?"

I nodded, trying to look brave and give the look, 'Men have to do what men have to do'. I hoped she could make a good argument why it would be stupid for us to do so and talk us out of it.

"That sounds exciting. Count me in."

Well that sure didn't sound like an argument for not going. Maybe she was drinking too much wine.

Sheldon shook his head. "No, my dear, it would be too dangerous for you to go."

Exactly my argument for staying put here, only she should have said it.

"Why, because I'm a woman? I'm in good shape and can keep up with either of you on a hike up a mountain. If you two can face a dragon, so can I. Besides I know first aid if one of you got hurt. If Harry is going, so am I."

Sheldon looked at me and I gave a small nod.

"Alright then. I'll make the arrangements for three people." He walked over to the phone and punched in a series of numbers.

"Hello Pete? I need to add to my previous order."

I half listened to Sheldon on the phone, wondering how my life had suddenly taken such a bizarre turn of going to search for a dragon.

Chelsea walked over to me and took my hand. "What are you thinking about?"

"Just that the sooner we head out and find this dragon the better."

"You're not scared in the least are you? I guess you've seen lots of strange things as Edwin Drood and this is just one more."

I looked upward. "After a few adventures you learn not to fear the unknown but to accept it as part of life's experiences." I felt a bit guilty feeding her that line but she gave me a hug.

"You're very brave."

The line was worth it, the guilt feelings disappeared.

Sheldon's voice disturbed my role of being brave.

"Okay, we better get going. We have to make a stop at a sporting goods store and a grocery store."

"How do we get there? Did you rent a car?" I knew that a couple of dragon boaters rented vehicles but I didn't know about Sheldon, or even if he had brought his own car down here. Come to think of it, maybe he bicycled here.

"I obtained use of a modest SUV."

The modest SUV turned out to be a Lincoln Navigator, big, expensive and with more interior comforts than a five star hotel. I sat in the back giving the front passenger seat to Chelsea, and was smothered by the leather seats.

Sheldon guided the monster out of the parking lot and on to the street. He didn't drive fast, keeping the vehicle a constant fifty kilometres an hour. I do mean constant. He hit every green light, other vehicles that were in front of us melted out of the way. Traffic wasn't light but it seemed by divine intervention we had a lane to ourselves at all times. He made a couple of turns and parked the SUV right in front of a sporting goods store.

"Okay, I'll introduce you to "Double Speak" Pete and you can give him the proper sizes for your boots and coats. I'll then go over and get some food supplies."

I followed Chelsea and Sheldon into the store. "Sheldon, why did you call him Double Speak Pete?"

Sheldon just gave me a grin and continued to walk to the counter set in the centre of the store. "Pete, I want you to meet my two friends here."

Pete was an older, white hair man with a bit of a paunch. He had a small beard as well, making him look like an out of work Santa Claus.

"Sheldon, so good to see you, so good to see you."

"This is Chelsea and Harry. They need you to finish up our supplies."

"Can do, Sheldon, can do."

Sheldon left us and Pete led us to where the outdoor shoes were kept.

"Right this way, right this way." It was dreadfully apparent how Pete got his nickname. If Sheldon hadn't said anything, I don't know if I would have really noticed; but, now I found myself listening to every twice spoken sentence out of Pete's mouth.

We selected a pair boots and jackets and carried them to the front counter where Sheldon's earlier order waited. I looked at some of the items, waterproof matches, compass and flashlights. He also had several containers of bear spray, which made me a bit nervous and a couple of Swiss army knives. Men generally love these knives, and I'm no different. Twenty-seven different blades and tools tucked inside a bright red handle. I'm sure I could build a two-bedroom log cabin and the furniture inside. I held the beautiful tool in my hand, relishing a time I could use it.

Chelsea picked up the other knife. "What do we need these for? They're kind of useless as far as I'm concerned."

That's the difference between men and women. Men want red knives and women want red lipstick.

Chelsea looked concerned as she studied the price tag of the jackets. "These are a bit expensive. Maybe I don't need one."

I realized Chelsea would insist on paying for her own, and on her student income couldn't afford it. "Don't worry about it. Sheldon has a special deal with the store and they're donating most of this stuff. Could you check to see if Sheldon is back yet?"

"Sure." She gave me a sweet smile and hurried out.

I felt guilty lying to her but I didn't want her to go broke because of our hiking trip.

Pete put all the items in a couple of bags and then looked at me. "The total is four hundred and fifty six dollars, that's the total. How do you want to pay? You can pay by debit or charge. How do you want to pay?"

I groaned. I knew I would never see a dollar from Sheldon. I slowly passed my Visa card over.

Pete gleefully took it. "Sheldon is such a great guy, a great guy. That's why I gave a thirty percent discount, a thirty percent discount."

I signed the bill reluctantly. I know you can make the argument that with the discount Sheldon in a way paid for his one-third share of the expenses by getting the discount, but I won't accept that. That "great guy" costs me money at every turn.

I lugged our stuff out the door, just in time to see Sheldon load up the food supplies in the back of the SUV.

I swung the bags into the back. "We've got a lot of supplies here. They were a bit expensive," I whispered so Chelsea wouldn't hear.

Sheldon dropped a case of water bottles into remaining open spot. "Oh, don't worry about the groceries. I'll cover their cost. You can pay for the gas."

It turns out the Navigator has a gas tank the same size Lake Huron and uses premium gas. I had to increase the credit limit on my card. The Navigator had one of those GPS devices built into the dash. It showed our location, where we were, where we were going and just for good measure, locations of the nearest gas station. Apparently, it knew what kind of gas mileage this "modest SUV" got.

Sheldon didn't worry about the GPS unit but followed his own instincts as we drove on a perfectly good highway up a mountain, only to turn off on to a smaller asphalt road and then on to a gravel road. A yellow diamond shaped sign warned of logging trucks on the road. A logging truck picked that moment to challenge a portion of our road, sweeping down the road towards us. Sheldon barely reacted as he calmly moved the Navigator to the right, missing the log monster by inches. The logging truck, maybe a hundred metres long and as wide as a house, lumbered past us. I held my breath as the SUV shook in the wind currents, bits of tree bark, leaves and dirt swirling around us. I heard Chelsea gasp, and then we were past the tail end of the truck. A ridiculously small red flag waved at the end of the longest log.

Sheldon didn't act upset or concerned at the least. He reached over to air controls and adjusted the fan speed slightly. "That will help clear out the dust a bit."

"That was a close call," Chelsea commented.

"Oh we had plenty of room still on the shoulder. No worries, those truck drivers know how big their loads are."

Chelsea turned back and looked at me. "Next time you're riding up in the front."

"Next time I'm walking."

Sheldon ignored us and after a few kilometres turned off on to an even smaller road sparsely gravelled with plants trying to grow in the centre. I'm not sure what we would do if came across another vehicle. Fortunately, that never happened. He did stop the Navigator in a small clearing off the road.

"Okay, we walk from here," Sheldon announced in a voice too loud for the confines of the SUV.

I wouldn't mind walking at all, as long as we didn't come across any logging trucks wandering around in the woods.

From the back of the Navigator, we slipped on our windbreakers and then the backpacks containing food, water, bear spray and other assorted items. A sleeping bag hung at the bottom of the backpack. We changed into our hiking boots and began our journey.

The backpack wasn't too heavy and we were able to make good time on our hike. Sheldon seemed oblivious to the backpack and the fact we were climbing up a mountain. I had to ask him to slow down. The truth was Chelsea was doing better than I was, and she had taken extra clothes along as well that were jammed in her backpack, but she nodded at me when I complained to Sheldon and added her own comment.

"These are new boots and I would like to break them in a bit more slowly."

I love the smell of a forest, but it was hard to enjoy it when you're gasping for air. I trailed behind Chelsea with Sheldon leading the way. He finally took a break to drink some water and eat an energy bar. I sat against a tree and gulped water down my parched throat.

"Sheldon, do we need to get out the bear spray?" I recalled it was near the bottom of my backpack.

He shook his head. "No, we're not likely to come across any bears around here. We're making enough noise they'll stay away. The bear spray isn't for here."

"What do you mean it's not for around here?"

He grinned. "It's not even for bears. Let's get going before the sun disappears."

We climbed upward, the trail getting easier as the trees thinned out. My feet were getting a bit sore from the hiking boots but I daren't complain about that, or my aching legs, or how the backpack was getting heavy, the lack of oxygen or how hungry I was. Chelsea was moving along without complaint or any sign she needed a break and damn if I was going to be the weak link in our group.

Sheldon turned around. "Let's stop for a bite to eat."

"If you need a break, that's fine with me," I croaked out.

We had a good view of the lake and the city of Kelowna. The lake looked beautiful with the white sailing boats skimming along the surface. I didn't see any dragon boats on the water and presumed the races were still being held up for safety reasons. Judging by the view we had of the lake I guessed we were close to where we say the lightning bolt hit.

We continued our journey and soon came across a strange blemish on the mountainside. Black marks streaked the rock around the outside of the cave. Stones were scattered around the entrance, as if something too big had pushed its way out of the cave. I tried to peer inside the cave, an irregular shaped semi-circle opening slightly taller than myself. I could see only a dozen feet in, and it looked pretty much what I thought a cave should look like.

Sheldon looked around as well and picked up a rock. "Well, this looks like the spot where the lightning bolt hit."

Chelsea turned on her flashlight and shined it inside the cave. "It does. What do we do next? Look for a dragon?"

"Of course, but we have a journey to make first."

I was almost scared to ask. "Where do we go to find this dragon?"

Sheldon smiled. "I believe at the other end of this cave."

Chapter Thirteen

There are people who enjoy crawling through caves. Spelunking they call it. I call it you gotta be crazy if you enjoy that. To be fair there wasn't any crawling involved in this cave. One had to be careful of the rocks on the ground and anything hanging from above like stalactites. Or is that stalagmites? I can't remember which hangs from the ceiling and which builds up from the floor, but both are something to avoid.

The cave was dark, except where our flashlights made beams of light dance in front of us. The air smelled like wet fungus.

Sheldon, of course, led the way. Chelsea followed him as we made our way deeper into the cave.

"Watch out for the stalactites hanging down," Sheldon called out.

I immediately added, "And the stalagmites below."

The cave became narrower as we progressed and soon we were twisting along a tunnel, maybe wide enough to drive a small car through. It seemed to me the tunnel was also dropping slightly, but after a few turns I lost my sense of direction.

Sheldon stopped to shine his flashlight on the ceiling. "Do you see those stalactites? They've been broken off sometime in the past."

Chelsea looked where the light was glinting off the end of one of the mineral deposits and then on the cave floor where broken pieces of the stalactites were scattered. "How long ago did this happen and what could have done that?"

I studied the ceiling, noticing the broken ends were not sharp but rounded. "That had to have happen some time ago for the ends to be reforming. As for what caused it, I don't have a clue."

Sheldon continued to look at the ceiling and then at the floor. "Both the stalactites and the stalagmites have been broken. I would guess that something large was moving through here."

Chelsea looked around nervously. "Like a bear?"

Sheldon shook his head. "No, I don't think so. It would have to be bigger than that."

With that happy thought, we continued our journey. I lost track on how far we travelled and began to wonder where the cave led to, if it actually led anywhere but a dead end. So far, there had been only one route to follow and there wasn't a danger of getting lost. All the same, Sheldon had been scraping the wall of the cave at regular intervals with his knife, marking the rock with an X.

We continued to follow the cave's path, which was more like a tunnel. I noticed the temperature was rising slightly and air had an odd quality to it, slightly higher in humidity but with an odour in it. The smell became slightly stronger as we walked.

Chelsea finally made the comment we were all thinking, "It smells like there's a garbage bin close by."

Sheldon added his own inspiring message. "I do believe it'll get even stronger in a few minutes."

Chelsea responded, "Sheldon, what do you know that you're not telling us?"

"Nothing much more for certain, but I'm speculating that we're getting close to the source of the smell."

Chelsea continued to pester Sheldon with questions. "What do you think is causing that smell? Have you been here before? Are we in danger?"

I smiled to myself. Chelsea asked good questions, but she was going to learn Sheldon never revealed much information to direct questions, especially those that concerned him.

"That smell can be caused by a number of things. I suspect we will understand its source when we arrive there. I have not been here before but have been in similar situations. As far as danger is concern, of course there is some risk. To what extent I suppose we will find that out together."

I heard Chelsea sigh. "Sheldon?"

"Yes?"

"You're full of it."

Now I have thought the same thing on many occasion, but never voiced it. I'm not scared of Sheldon but he does have a quick temper. He's a big man, strong and I would guess knows how to fight. I've seen him angry on occasion. His face gets red, providing a contrast to white hair, and his eyes bulge out. Frightening is a good term to describe him. He didn't get angry this time, merely making that loud "har, har, har" laugh of his.

Twenty minutes later, or it might have been forty—who can tell when you're walking behind beams of light—we arrived at an open pit.

We looked down at a huge cavern, perhaps as big around as a hockey arena, without the seats. It was deep, maybe a story above us, and a couple below with jagged rocks sticking along the walls. I could see the details quite easily because at the bottom of the cavern was a large hole where sunlight was streaming through. I studied the walls of the cavern and saw a path that wound its way down to the floor. There was a way down to the bottom and I had no doubt that's where we were heading.

As Sheldon dug out a rope from his bag, I breathed in the air. The stench of rotting vegetation assaulted me. I looked at Chelsea and she wrinkled her nose at the smell.

"It doesn't smell so good in here."

I nodded. "Worse than Sheldon's cologne."

She laughed and then looked serious. "I guess we're going down there."

"It would seem to be the next step." I wanted to tell her she could wait here while Sheldon and I went down, but she would have felt insulted by that.

Sheldon proceeded to tie a rope around our waists, the theory being that if one of us slipped off the edge of the path along the cavern wall, the others would be able to prevent a fall all the way to the bottom. That was fine if Chelsea slipped, or me. We weren't so heavy the others couldn't save us. But if Sheldon slipped he would likely pull all three of us down. He should go on a diet before securing a rope to the three of us.

We made our way cautiously along the uneven path. Rocks along the path made sure we were paying attention to every step and occasionally the path got rather narrow. I have to admit I wanted to embellish the story here and tell how Chelsea slipped from the path and only my quick thinking saved her as she dangled from my outstretched hands. Or how I saved Sheldon by using my great strength to hold the rope as he struggled to climb back up on the path. Alas, I decided to stay to the truth; as you will soon read it was even stranger than you can imagine. Okay, I don't know you personally but most people couldn't guess what will happen to us. If they did, it's because they jumped ahead a few chapters. Cheaters.

The light improved as we made our way downward on the path, though we kept our flashlights on. There were many shadows around the dark rock and we needed to make sure we didn't fall off the path (see above paragraph). Occasionally the path dipped inside another cave and we followed the sloping trail until we emerged back into the cavern. There were many small caves, and some larger ones, that led deep within the mountain. We didn't go into all the caves; some were just openings by our path. Other caves had the path go inside them and there we had to be careful about choosing which of the forked paths to choose. When we did come to a forked path Sheldon would study the two paths. It appeared he was either trying to remember which route to take or calling upon divine intervention to give him the correct answer. Then again, if he was a warlock maybe he was using a magical spell to guide him. No matter what method he used, he didn't make a wrong turn and got us down to the bottom of the cavern. Maybe it was just dumb luck but he made it look like he actually knew what he was doing. Again, Sheldon did his X scraping of the rock walls.

Bats, I have to mention those. We saw a few thousand of them in different parts of the cavern but they simply clung to the walls, waiting for nighttime to come. There were a few more in the caves as well but for the most part we didn't get very close to them. Which was fine by me and I could tell Chelsea had changed her walk when she quietly went past a group of them. By the way, the bats seem to add their own smell to the increasing odour of the cavern. It was a like the smell of wet fur. The bat dung didn't help either.

With the bats around us we didn't want to stick around, but the way down was leading to the unknown source of the rotting vegetation stench, not precisely an incentive to hurry either.

So far, I've indicated our journey was dark, smelly and uneasy feeling of danger. There was one positive in all this. I got to watch Chelsea walk in her tight jeans and I hope it wasn't too obvious to her where I trained my flashlight beam, but she had a nice walk even in hiking boots.

We made it to the bottom of the cavern, the path ending in a sharp edged, broad slope. We stopped there, looking around. We turned off our flashlights as the sunlight coming in from the opening was strong enough to illuminate most of the floor. The area of the smell was coming from a pile of brown and green plants heaped on top of each other to form a six foot circle about three feet high. It looked like a hideous nest.

Chelsea pointed at the ugly circle of plants. "I guess we should check what that is all about. It really stinks."

That it did and I knew we really should investigate it. "Sheldon, why don't you take a look? You're closer."

Sheldon looked back at me and then signalled for us to follow him. Not that we had a choice; there was still the rope attached to us. I was hoping he'd detach the rope and go by himself. We slowly ventured forth to the stinking circle. Sheldon began to lift up the edges of the plants and there we found an egg. An egg nearly the size of a basketball and was yellow in colour with brown spots. He went to a different spot of the nest and after a couple minutes of digging found another egg.

Chelsea asked, "What are these?"

Sheldon answered quickly. "What I suspect is what we have found is a dragon's nest."

"Maybe we shouldn't hang around here." She touched the egg. "It feels kinda rubbery, and warm."

I looked around the cavern. "Sheldon, she has a point. Something has been adding these plants to act like an incubator and could return any minute with more plants."

Chelsea looked at me. "You mean the plants are providing the warmth, like a compost heap does?"

"Exactly. If it were a dragon, it would let the plants do most of the work of keeping the eggs warm. Many animals bury their eggs and let the sun heat the ground but inside a cave, another method had to be used to warm the eggs. But the plants have to be added at regular intervals to keep the process going."

We headed towards the exit and were within ten feet of leaving when we heard a flapping sound and then a soft wind blew into the opening.

I pointed back at the ramp where we entered the cavern floor. "Sheldon, something is coming in here! Let's get the hell away from the nest."

We ran to the ramp, slipping on the surface slightly just as the light in the cavern dropped.

We lay flat on our stomachs as we watched a black shadow enter the cavern. I couldn't make out many details but it was big. I tried to breathe quietly and not move a muscle as the creature entered the cavern, making a slow circle around the nest as it emitted a moaning sound. The sunlight came back as the dragon moved away from the entrance and I could see it in its entirety. The simplest way to describe is to call it a striking looking monster.

The body was the size of a horse, supported by two thick, long rear legs and two thinner front limbs. All four limbs ended in paws with six long black claws, though the front paws also had a thumb. A tail twice the size of the body seemed to have a mind of its own as it whipped around. A long but thin neck supported a cone shaped head that was currently holding a mouthful of vegetation by too many three-inch long teeth. The teeth were curved and pointed and I felt sorry for the plants. The eyes were large and brown, set apart over a long snout, with a pair of small ears with fluffy hair sitting on top of the head. In addition, on the head, were two backward curving horns. The upper jaw had long whiskers protruding along its length. Yellow and red scales with patches of fluffy white feathers covered the whole dragon. Folded over the body were wings, black with yellow and red spots. The over all impression was a graceful looking monster and it looked quite exotic. It also scared the hell out of me.

It dropped the mound of plants on the nest and then pushed it around with its snout. Then gently, so carefully it looked ridiculous for such a monster, it went on top of the nest. We watched. There wasn't anything else we could do, and hoped it didn't detect us.

Gradually the big eyes began to close. Still we didn't move. It's funny how when you don't dare move you realize that your leg desperately needs to be scratched and that you need to pee. These sensations invade your thoughts, demanding attention. Thus, the time it took for that damn dragon to close its eyes seem to take an eternity. When it did close its eyes we still didn't move, waiting for a sign it was asleep.

That sign was deep breathing it made, a low humming noise emanated from the throat. It sounded like a giant cat purring. Sheldon slowly sat up and began to remove his boots. We did likewise and when we had accomplished that task without a sound Sheldon pointed back up the path. We slowly rose and began to tip toe back up the ramp. Occasionally one of us bent down to keep our balance on the slope and not slide down on the loose dirt.

I managed to hold my breath the ten minutes it took to reach an opening to another cave. At that point, Sheldon took over as lead again. We also stopped to put our boots back on and, as quietly as possible, made our way deep into the new cave.

It was an unremarkable cave, compared to the other caves in which we'd wandered; rocky sides, a few bats, tricky footing and a little smelly. We used our flashlights, though the cave wasn't completely dark. There was light coming from somewhere up ahead but there were too many shadows to walk confidently without our beams of light. The cave began to split into a multiple of routes and Sheldon had to stop to work out the best path.

"I don't know if it makes a difference because I see light coming from several of these tunnels, but this path looks a little wider so we might as well use that." Sheldon scratched another X into the rock and then looked at me. "I hope we don't get lost when we go back. Even with these marks to guide us a return route can look very different in these tunnels."

I suddenly became worried. It was going to be up to Sheldon to find our way back through the caves and tunnels. I wasn't paying enough attention to our route during the journey down. I had been too busy watching Chelsea.

Sheldon was right about which path to pick. At least we had a glimpse of the outside. The way was partially blocked by stalactites and stalagmites, looking a bit like a set of giant teeth. The teeth looked a bit dangerous, but as we made it past the last row of stalactites, we could see some of them were broken off.

Chelsea pointed out a difference from the broken stalactites and stalagmites we saw earlier. "These edges where they broke off are sharp, like this happened more recently."

I looked the floor of the cave and saw a couple of broken ends. "You're right. Whatever broke these off though stopped about here. Couldn't be pleasant pushing past these things." I picked up a broken end. It was hard and rather sharp. It would make a good spear if you could attach it to a stick.

Twenty minutes, more or less, we made it out of the cave into the bright sunlight.

* * * *

The outside turned out to be what you expect the side of a mountain to look like; rocks, scrawny evergreens, more rocks and tricky footing. We scrambled down the mountainside and this where the rope finally did come in handy. Chelsea lost her footing, but I pulled hard on the rope to prevent her from tumbling down the mountain. I heard her give a gasp as the rope pulled taunt and she looked up at me.

"Thanks," she whispered.

I smiled a hero's smile back at her, feeling very important.

We continued our downward journey and when the trees were of decent size and density, we stopped to drink water and have a power bar. I also went behind a tree for other reasons.

Chelsea and I later sat next to each other against a tree, facing Sheldon as he leaned against another tree that was bending under his weight.

"Sheldon, where are we?" I didn't recall any caves that hid dragons around Kelowna and assumed we were somewhere else.

"It's another world, a parallel world to ours. Similar in a lot of ways but as you saw there are significant differences as well."

"I see the differences. We arrived here just by following a cave in a mountain? Why haven't I heard of someone else doing the same before?"

"Because it's more than just following a path. It also requires the appropriate application of quantum mechanics, specifically the Heisenberg uncertainty principle."

"The Heisenberg uncertainty principle?"

Sheldon shrugged. "Some refer to it as magic."

Chelsea pointed a finger at him. "You used a magic spell to get us here? Don't you think you should have told us that before we went on this journey?"

Sheldon paused to think a moment. "No, I don't see how telling you ahead of time would have been beneficial. Either you would go or you wouldn't. If you refused to go I would have lost your help."

Well I have to give him credit for being honest there. Also for the first time he admitted to knowing how to use magic. Now I wonder what else he was willing to telling us. "So what now, Sheldon? Are we supposed to go and kill the dragon that is responsible for attacking our boats?"

Sheldon looked upset. "Kill a dragon? Even if we could accomplish such a task, why would we want to murder such a magnificent creature? No, no, no. We need to find the dragon that is causing our problem and get it to stop."

Sheldon must be on drugs. Negotiate with a dragon to stop bothering us? We would need a high priced lobbyist to help us there.

We resumed our trek down the mountain but after a point, we decided the danger of slipping was remote enough to remove the rope joining us.

Shortly after that, we heard an awful screech above us. I looked up at the sky and saw two dragons flying above us. From below the dragons had colourful bodies of brown, red, and bright green and blue covering their wings. They floated above us, gliding on their large wings. You might think that would make them look graceful, but I was remembering those three inch teeth and that made the dragon more dangerous than anything else.

We looked at the dragons for another second or two before we realized they were circulating back towards us. As those large heads dipped down to see us better we took off running towards the trees.

I was scared out of my wits but stayed behind Chelsea in case she came into difficulty. Sheldon was spreading the gap between us when he stopped to take off his backpack. At first, I thought he was trying to lighten his load but he reached into the zippered compartment and pulled out the cans of bear spray. He immediately began to spray the air above him.

"Keep running for the trees!" he bellowed.

I didn't need any more encouragement than that. Chelsea and I hurried past him and reached the first of the scraggly trees. Moments later Sheldon caught up with us.

"The dragons are not likely to try to land among the trees as their wings may get entangled with the branches. But they also have a very sensitive sense of smell and the bear spray will discourage them as well." Sheldon watched them do a circle above us as he spoke.

Now instead of a screech one of the dragons growled; a deep throated sound that vibrated into our bones.

I caught a whiff of the bear spray as it floated through the air towards us, actually a pepper spray spread in a fog like pattern. Fortunately, the effect was weak, otherwise, we would have been in more trouble than the dragons. Whether it was the pepper spray or the close proximity of the trees the dragons turned away from us and left us alone.

We continued our descent down the mountain, weaving among the trees and large rocks.

The sun was strong and the air humid and we began to take frequent drinks of water. In fact, it was getting a bit too warm. At our last break, Chelsea disappeared behind a few trees and changed into her shorts. Women like to change clothes and I wasn't surprised she had brought along a change of clothing. I'm fairly certain she didn't pack a dress as well but maybe she did slip a skirt into the backpack.

We reached the bottom of the mountain and the temperature was now more than warm. I had tucked my jacket into my backpack and now unbuttoned my shirt. Sheldon had taken off his shirt but was wearing a white T-shirt underneath. Still, you could see his muscles under the fabric and I wondered what he did for exercise to get a build like that. Chelsea wore a loose T-shirt, though I could perceive her figure underneath. Part was the body as it touched the shirt and the other was my imagination, which filled in details I had no right to fill in. As I found out shortly, it turned out that my imagination was spot on with the details.

Our progress was interrupted as we approached an open area. A hissing noise; high pitched enough that it sounded like a long, slow whistle. Sheldon immediately held up his arm and we stopped.

Chapter Fourteen

"Sasquatch," he whispered.

I looked at Chelsea. Well, to be truthful I was looking at her a lot. But in this case it was to confirm Sheldon had said something strange.

"What do you mean Sasquatch?" I whispered back.

"There is a Sasquatch, or possibly a family of them, ahead of us. The hissing is a warning. I suggest we make a sharp turn away from here."

I looked at the trees but couldn't see anything that resembled a Sasquatch. All the same, I followed Sheldon along a new route. Another round of hissing started as we walked. Sheldon stopped and slowly removed a can of bear spray from his backpack. Chelsea and I followed suit.

A Sasquatch appeared from the among the trees. He and it was definitely a he, stood with his long arms away from his body. He was over seven feet tall, probably weighed over six hundred pounds and covered with reddish-brown hair. The face was remarkably human looking, though with more hair than a member of ZZ Top. His eyes showed intelligence. It looked like the Sasquatch wasn't threatening us but rather giving us warning to not approach any closer. We didn't linger but kept the bear spray ready, though I'm not sure how effective it would be.

"Sheldon, just how many Sasquatches are there around here?" I looked at the trees around us but couldn't see much.

"That is a good question. I doubt more than a couple of hundred in the area. This fellow might be the head of a family of maybe a dozen. They are shy and therefore it is hard to accurately estimate their numbers. They are also very family-orientated. So what we see is the male protector and gives the impression there is just one Sasquatch standing there. Right behind him there will the others in his family. He would have at least one female and several offspring."

I frowned. "You mean to say there are whole bunches of Sasquatches behind the trees?"

Chelsea broke in. "What do you mean at least one female? You mean that big brute has more than one lady? Typical male, wanting to have more than one female." She turned towards me. "Do all men think like that? Do you think like that?"

I looked at her and calmly explained to her that wasn't true. "No. No, no! I don't think that. I just asked a question, that's all. Honest, I don't think at all about such things."

"Well, maybe you should." She walked away, leaving me to look at Sheldon for answers. I'd be better off looking at the Sasquatch.

I'm not sure what made her upset, but it may have been something from her past, or something I said, or something the Sasquatch did. It didn't matter. I was at fault.

I caught up with her. "Look, I'm sorry if I did anything to upset you."

She looked at me. "Don't apologize, you didn't do anything wrong. Let's drop it." She gave me a smile.

Now I was worried. You don't have to be a rocket scientist to know that any time a woman tells you to drop it and then smiles at you, it isn't over. It's like a wave that washes up on the shore and then retreats. But you know there's another wave coming, maybe even stronger than the first.

We continued to hike through the more open areas along the mountain, though as we travelled down to lower parts along the mountainside the trees and bushes became denser. It also became warmer, though the trees around us hid the sun. When we finally came across a river, it was refreshing to splash some water on our faces and relax a minute. I took the opportunity to talk to Sheldon.

"Do you have a clue exactly what we're supposed to be doing?"

"To find the dragon that caused the problem with the boats. Unfortunately, the location of the dragon is really only known by the Sasquatch."

"The Sasquatch knows where the dragon is?"

"Yes, but it is difficult to ask them directly. I don't really speak their language well enough to help us."

"I gathered that. I didn't even know they had a language."

Sheldon narrowed his eyes at me. "Of course they do. Granted, much of it is grunts, whistles and hand signs, but it is a language."

That sounded to me like how some men communicate in a bar. Maybe we should have brought a waitress with us as an interpreter. "Okay, so how we do go about getting the needed information from the Sasquatch?"

"We will need to find the local humans here who know how to talk to them."

That seemed logical, but I wondered how Sheldon knew all this. I didn't bother asking how he did know; his answer wouldn't have told me anything.

We followed the river, which was gradually getting wider so its banks became easier to walk. The rocks that were so prevalent earlier had disappeared and left a mixture of sand, gravel and mud to walk on. That made the walking easier but we weren't in any hurry, under the theory we weren't exactly sure where we were going.

Chelsea touched my arm and whispered to me. "Harry, I think we're being followed."

"Sasquatch?"

She shook her head. "I don't think so. I mean whatever is following us is being rather quiet and I think a Sasquatch is a little too big to be stalking us." She hooked her thumb towards our right.

I looked to the right and detected the slightest movement a dozen feet into the forest. The trees weren't that thick but the shadows hid any detail. Something smaller than a Sasquatch was trailing us.

Sheldon was aware of being followed and called a halt a few minutes later. He sat on a log and gestured us to join him.

"This may take a few minutes until they're sure who we are. Be sure to stay relaxed at all times until they trust us."

"Who are they?" Chelsea asked.

"Native humans for this region. They're actually oriental in appearance."

Finally, a group of male humans approached us carefully along the riverbank we were walking on. They were slightly on the small size and as Sheldon indicated, they appeared to be oriental. They wore clothes made from the skins of animals with a pattern dyed on part of it. Their hair was long but didn't look unkempt. That about sums up my initial impression of them other than they also carried spears. Fortunately, none of them was pointed at us.

One of the men stepped forward and chattered gibberish at us, and then smiled.

Sheldon bowed his head slightly and responded to him, in slower gibberish. He then smiled back.

I stood next to Chelsea and exchanged looks with her.

Chelsea frowned. "Why do I have the feeling Sheldon has been here before and hasn't told us everything?"

That was as true a statement as you'll ever hear about Sheldon.

The village consisted of various sized buildings, all made of small vertical logs arranged in a circle with pointed roofs. The cone topped huts seemed to be randomly placed except for the centre of the village which was left open. There were perhaps a couple of hundred people in the village, which Sheldon pronounced as Gibber-Ish.

The people were friendly, though only conversed with Sheldon. The women were all pretty, with long hair and wore decorated animal skins. The villagers wore enough clothing for coverage but didn't appear to be too concerned about some skin showing, especially the younger ladies. The men were bare-chested for the most part but usually had an animal skin draped over their shoulder.

After we stood a few minutes smiling away at the smiling villagers, we were led to the open area that seemed to be a place of some importance. The ground was bare as if it was well used and benches were placed in a semi-circle. There weren't very many of the benches, and truth be told, weren't very comfortable to sit on. The benches consisted of thin tree branches roped together and small knots were left on to poke upward against those sitting down.

They prepared a wonderful feast for us. Well not just for us for us, as the villagers ate too. We ate, drank a tasty fruit drink and after the food was done we listened to some of the people singing songs to a drumbeat. When the entertainment began we sat on the benches, at least the men did. The women sat on the men's laps, a rather nice custom since none of the women were overweight. I watched as one of the men gently took Chelsea's hand and pulled her down to his lap. As I watched her, a young lady sat on my lap. I looked at Chelsea and she returned my expression, "When in Rome do as the other visitors do."

I kept drinking the tasty fruit drink and after a while it occurred to me it was slightly fermented. That may have contributed to the minor problem later.

The pretty lady sitting on my lap tried to talk to me but soon gave up on words. We did exchange names and she tried to pronounce my name, coming up with "Arry." I tried to say her name. It was something like "Olala". Instead of words, she smiled at me and ran her fingers along my chest, just being friendly. My fingers grazed along her bare hip in the same friendly manner.

Sheldon meanwhile conversed with the village leaders. I won't give you details of the conversation, as I didn't understand a word he said.

Meanwhile the pretty lady was getting very friendly sitting on my lap as she laughed and sang along with the main singers. I didn't resist her advances; I didn't want to appear rude. She continued to touch me with her hands and then kissed me on my cheek. Very sweet I thought. These people sure were friendly and nice to their visitors. One of the smiling women continually refilled my cup of the tasty fruit drink.

I looked over at Chelsea, who was not being near as friendly to the man whose lap she was sitting on, and it didn't appear she was looking very friendly at me either. This was not good, I thought, as I drank more of that tasty fruit juice. Not good at all as my hand that was around Olala's hip slipped down to squeeze her thigh. I honestly didn't consciously put my hand anywhere on her, it did so on its own. But I would be the one be held responsible for that.

Then the singing changed and we all got up at did this strange hand waving dance. It was fun but I nearly spilled my tasty fruit drink. Olala stayed close to me and tried to help learn the dance moves, and I thought I was doing a great job dancing. I did find the dancing rather strenuous and I was sweating when the lovely Olala kindly took off my shirt. I think she must have thought I was doing a great job dancing because she also gave me a hug and a kiss.

Chelsea was also learning the dance and had moved quite close to us when the music stopped for the final time. She didn't look pleased with my dancing techniques, or how friendly Olala was with me, not understanding it was their culture to be close with each other.

Sheldon approached us. "I have spoken to the elders and they have agreed to help us with our problem. We will be leaving in the morning with them and I suggest we enjoy their hospitality in the meantime." He looked at me. "Are you alright?"

"Sures I ams," I said brightly, though Sheldon looked like he was weaving. It's hard to focus on a person who weaves back and forth.

Chelsea pried the tasty fruit drink from my hand.

"He won't be if he continues to drink and enjoys their hospitality." She looked at Olala. "Especially her hospitality."

I wasn't happy. I was given water to drink and Chelsea made me walk with her the length of the village and then to the river. It wasn't a romantic walk. Not only didn't she want to hold hands, she kept her arms crossed in front of her. When we arrived at the river, she splashed water at my face and chest.

The cold water did help me see things a bit better.

Chelsea handed me my shirt and I looked at it questioningly.

"Maybe you should put it back on before you get all the women excited."

I put my shirt back on but couldn't find any of the buttons to do it up.

"You have your shirt on inside out." She almost smiled at me.

"Oh. I was worried someone had stolen all the buttons to my shirt." I took off my shirt and put it back on the right way.

"You do know you're completely drunk, don't you?" This time she did smile at me.

I blinked at her. "I guess I do now."

"I forgive you for acting the way you did but next time you better take it easy on that fruit drink. Come on, it's time to go to bed and sleep it off."

That sounded promising. Sleeping with Chelsea was a great way to end the night. Unfortunately, it turned out I had to share sleeping quarters with Sheldon that night, not with Chelsea or with the charming Olala. This was unfair and I sure wanted some more of that fruit drink.

* * * *

All that hiking and fresh air I did the day before caught up with me the next morning, because I woke up tired and with a headache. I stumbled outside to a morning with the sun far too bright, and needing water to drink. I vaguely remember having a good time the night before and suddenly felt worried that I might have done something wrong.

Fortunately, Olala wasn't angry with me and gave me a warm smile as she handed me a fruit drink. Alas, it wasn't fermented but it did help quench my thirst. She refilled my cup and gave me a quick hug and kiss.

Sheldon had been up early, probably went for a run up the mountain and back, but was now talking to one of the village elders. I assumed it was a village elder as she had grey hair, appeared stern and looked like my Aunt Milda. I was always respectful to my Aunt Milda, who could make you feel guilty with one look from her black eyes.

I slowly managed to disengage myself from Olala and the other smiling and friendly women and went to search for Chelsea. I found her sitting under a tree relaxing.

"Hi." I gave her the best smile I could come up with.

She looked up at me and gave me one of those half smiles. You know the type; a smile she didn't want to extend to me but felt rude not to respond to my smile.

"I'm sorry about last night."

"Which part? Your hand roaming around that half undressed woman that sat on your lap, being drunk or trying to teach everyone how to dance?"

"Was I trying to teach them how to sing, too?"

She rolled her eyes and then gave me a smile, this time a full one. "If you had tried to teach them how to sing they likely would've thrown you in the river. How many glasses of that fruit punch did you drink anyway?"

"I'm not sure but they were very tasty." I sat next to her. "I'm sorry for what I did, in particular the parts I don't remember."

"Okay, apology accepted. It was interesting watching you dance. It looked like someone had put itching powder down your pants."

That may have not been a compliment but at least she noticed me. I felt bad what I did the night before though my memories weren't exactly clear on what I did, so I accepted the dancing observation without comment.

I took her hand. "Come on; let's see what Sheldon is up to."

It turned out Sheldon had arranged for us, and several of the Gibber-Ish people to go with us to talk to the Sasquatch.

"They are very kind to do this," he boomed, "but they feel they owe me a favour. We will travel to an area that the Sasquatch accept as a meeting place and explain what we need."

I was still feeling tired but Chelsea picked up on Sheldon's comment.

"Sheldon, what do you mean they owed you a favour? Have you been to this village before?"

Sheldon's jaw dropped slightly and then he spoke. "I believe the words were they feel they owe me a favour; I have no idea why in all due modesty."

Chelsea persisted. "Alright, but have you been to this village before?"

Sheldon sighed. "I won't lie to you. I did know of this village before, but I will not discuss details right now. It is far too complex to explain."

"Alright, but I will be asking again later."

I was shocked. Sheldon actually admitted to something he didn't want to admit. Maybe it was too much of that tasty fruit juice.

We started off on our journey with five villagers, one of them being Olala. She seemed quite happy and eager to go. She gave me another unfermented fruit drink and a hug just before we started out. I didn't expect the hug and quickly looked around to see if Chelsea saw us. As far as I could tell, her back was turned.

We walked along a trail upward at a pace that had me drinking lots of water. It was tiring walking around trees and watching out for loose rocks while carrying a backpack. One of the older male villagers led the way with a small group of villagers and us following him. At one point Chelsea gave Olala a glare but didn't say anything. Chelsea did walk close to me during our hike and that seemed to keep Olala away, at least for a while.

The trail was a long one and we then started a descent, more dodging trees and rocks until we finally came to a flat area near a river. Obviously, it had been flooded occasionally because there were still pockets of mud and water about. Yellow and green grass covered the area but not any trees. It seemed to be an acceptable area for the villagers because they finally stopped, took out the drums and placed them in the tall grass.

We sat down around the two drummers and waited. Sheldon was near the front with the drummers while I sat a bit behind with the others. Chelsea was near my right and Olala at my left, both only inches away.

I was nervous at the close proximity of the two women. With Chelsea, I wasn't sure how she was feeling towards me, and with Olala, I couldn't quite remember what I did the previous night. I also found the day too warm but didn't dare take off my shirt, recalling vaguely that being a problem last night with missing buttons. Insects buzzed around my head as I contemplated how life could get so complicated when you hang around with Sheldon.

The men pounded the drums slowly, matching perfectly with my throbbing headache. I closed my eyes wishing something would happen. It did.

I felt Olala place her hand on mine. I took a quick glance at her and she smiled. I looked at Chelsea and she turned to smile at me. Did I mention before how life can get complicated?

The drumming stopped and I looked to see several Sasquatch appear from the edge of the field. They slowly approached. There were three males and two females but one older male led the way. He had white hair mixed with his brown and seemed to be slightly hunched over. When he was a dozen feet away, he did a few hand gestures, like a traffic cop in Italy without the white gloves, and then a short toneless whistle.

Our guides reciprocated. Olala slowly walked over to the front and added a few gestures of her own. The lead Sasquatch focused on her and did more hand waving and a kind of hissing and clicking noise. After another couple of minutes of conversation, Olala turned to our oldest male guide and spoke gibberish to him in a whisper. He in turn spoke to Sheldon.

Sheldon nodded and twisted around to speak to us, in what he must have considered a whisper. The Sasquatch took a step backwards in alarm but then relaxed again.

"They know where a family of dragons inhabit a series of hills. Likely, that family has the dragon we seek. They described the location to our friends here who have agreed to show us the location."

I thought of us trooping through the forest to find a family of dragons. Great news. I'm sure we'll end up as dinner. "I suppose that is good news."

"It is, but there is a small detail that I'll have to go into later."

We watched as Olala and one of the men produced a colourful strand of pebbles and a pair of clay pots. They carried them slowly and carefully to within a few feet of the Sasquatch, placing them on the ground before retreating to our group. Olala sat next to me again looking very pleased.

The Sasquatch waited several seconds and then quickly took the items lying on the ground. All of the Sasquatch turned away from us and disappeared into the woods again.

We stood up, stretching our legs as Sheldon conversed with the Gibber-Ish leader. Then he gave a forced smile towards Chelsea and me.

"It seems the villagers have done us a great favour in getting information from the Sasquatch where the dragons live. They had to pay for that information by giving them some items that the Sasquatch consider valuable. The villagers have also agreed to guide us to the exact location."

I suppose, if you think going to where dragons live a good thing, then they did do us a favour. "That was very nice of them."

"Yes, well, I suppose we do owe them a small favour in reciprocation."

I felt puzzled. Sheldon was acting nervous and not his usual boisterous self. I have to admit that was a nice change but I was definitely suspicious on the why. But then, I was usually suspicious of

Sheldon, though in most cases it didn't have a direct impact on me. This time it did.

The villagers led the way. I couldn't quite pronounce their names, much less spell them. I tried to come as close as I could.

The oldest villager in our group was a male, named Theolguy, who was the leader of the expedition. Grininman was a young fellow who was always in a good mood. The last male was middle aged and rather serious in nature. His name, best I can pronounce, was Ovrthehil. The other female was a young lady, slightly older than Olala, named Welndowd.

I didn't mind the walk too much. My headache had disappeared and I was able to enjoy the sights and smells of the forest around us. The canopy of trees kept the direct sunlight from us, making the air much more pleasant as we travelled. Olala occasionally would walk next to me, looking up at me with bright eyes and a big grin. I would have responded to her but I was going out with Chelsea, and she was all I wanted. Last night I got a bit out of control and in my drunken state, I suppose Olala might have gotten the wrong impression that I was available.

That was likely the reason why Olala tentatively reached for my hand and then locked her fingers within mine. I really didn't know what to do. Let me explain.

I was taught and brought up to be polite, especially to ladies. So if a lady asks me to dance, I will always dance with her. If a lady needs help opening a pickle jar, I will do my best to twist off the top. Therefore, when Olala grabbed my hand, I froze. I didn't want to be rude by yanking my hand away, nor did I want to encourage her. I continued to hold her hand and looked frantically around for Chelsea, hoping she didn't notice what was going on. Fat chance of that.

Chelsea came up behind us and rather firmly separated our hands. In fact, after she separated our hands she stepped in between us, giving Olala a bit of push as she did so. Chelsea grabbed my hand and glared at Olala.

"Better get away before you get hurt," she hissed.

Chapter Fifteen

Olala looked at Chelsea and then at me. She pursed her lips and ran ahead.

I felt bad about her being upset. I even felt worse for myself as Chelsea squeezed my hand and began to interrogate me.

"What the hell are you doing holding her hand? Why are you letting her get so cutesy with you? Do you prefer her over me?"

I wasn't sure which question to answer first. Somehow, I knew explaining that I was being polite wasn't going to be an effective excuse. Women can be so illogical. I said the first thing that came to my mind. "I'm sorry. I'm very sorry. I didn't mean to be holding her hand."

"Then what did you mean to be doing?"

That had to be a trick question and there never is a good answer for trick questions. My jaw worked but a sound didn't come out.

"Well?"

"I don't know what to say. I admit I was being friendly to Olala but…"

"Who?"

"Olala."

"Her name is Ohwanwana. How in the world did you come up with Olala?"

"I think I was drunk when she told me her name."

Chelsea shook her head. "You're hopeless. Do you see what your flirting caused?"

"I know and I'm sorry. I didn't know what to do when she came over to me."

"For crying out loud you could have shook your head and pointed at me. Maybe she would have understood that, stupid spoiled brat."

"I'm not a brat."

"She is. Her daddy is the big Kahonna in the village."

"She is?"

"A brat?"

"No, being the big Kahonna's daughter."

"Of course she is. Weren't you paying any attention during the ceremony?"

"What ceremony?"

She gave a sigh and then continued, "The ceremony after the music where she sat on your lap and before the dancing began."

I didn't recall that part. I wonder if the tasty fruit drink was the cause. "I don't remember that part."

"Of course not. You were too drunk to even notice she had picked you as a partner for more than just someone to dance with."

The tasty fruit drink hypothesis was confirmed. "I'm really sorry Chelsea. I don't know what to say. I'm sorry I was too drunk to notice what was happening and have caused this problem."

"Okay, enough sorry already. You're forgiven. But just remember if you go to another world with a girl, you should leave with her, too."

I walked happily with Chelsea following the others. I saw Olala talk to Theolguy rather excitedly and use various hand gestures. I saw him rub his forehead with his hand and then pat her on her arm. Slightly mollified she dropped back to the rest of the group with her arms crossed.

Sheldon then walked up to Theolguy. They began to converse with much hand movement and head shaking.

We walked back towards the river to where the tall grass weaved in the air. The ground was muddy in places but without trees in our way, we made better time. At least until we stopped. Two of our guides, Grininman and Ovrthehil, went to refill water containers.

Sheldon slowly made his way towards us where we sat on a small rise on the ground. I noticed Olala was watching us closely a few dozen feet away.

"Hi, Sheldon. What's up?" I looked up at his face, his forehead creased as his hand rubbed his chin.

"We have a bit of a situation and I'm not sure how to address it."

Chelsea crossed her arms. "I assume this is about Miss Princess."

Sheldon nodded. "Ohwanwana has a great deal of influence, being the oldest daughter of the village ruler, Chief Mstpwrfl. What she wants, she often gets."

Chelsea frowned. "I told you she was a spoiled brat."

Sheldon nodded. "That much is obvious. However, the village did negotiate with the Sasquatch to find where the current home of the dragons and have agreed to lead us there. I want to say that Chief Mstpwrfl did not ask for any compensation in return for helping us. However, I did tell him if we could return a favour to him, we would. Later Chief Mstpwrfl asked me politely if we would grant Ohwanwana a desire."

Chelsea rolled her eyes upward. "So what did she desire? A gift card to shop at West Edmonton Mall?"

Sheldon actually blushed a bit. "She requested that Harry be the father of her first born by spending time alone with her in her hut. I didn't know how to approach this rather delicate matter to you, Harry, and felt I had to share this information with Chelsea as well as you."

Chelsea stood up. "Why that little witch. She thinks all she has to do is ask for a man and she can have him? I think I'll put things straight to her right now and believe me, there won't be a language barrier problem between us."

I stood up as well, though I didn't know what to say or do.

Sheldon stood in front of her and held up his hands. "Please, Chelsea, that won't help matters any. I will talk to her and explain how you and Harry are a couple and that he cannot spend time alone with her."

"I'll bet I could explain it better." Chelsea let the air out of her lungs. "Alright, just keep her out of my space."

Sheldon walked away. I noticed my opinion wasn't really asked for and maybe it was just as well I didn't say anything. I haven't done too well saying or doing anything since we arrived at the village. "Chelsea, I don't want to spend any time with any woman but you. I don't know why Olala, I mean Ohwanwana, wants me but it's you I want."

She gave me a smile. "You're so clueless about women, aren't you? You're tall, good looking and new in the village. Unlike Sheldon, you're also fairly young. So when Ohwanwana saw you, she immediately thought of you as desirable as a mate. But I'm not going to let you get away that easy, understand?" She gave me a kiss.

I kissed her back, wrapping my arms around her back. We broke apart and looked over to where Sheldon was receiving some high-pitched gibberish from Ohwanwana. She rested her fists on her hips and shrieked demands at him. It wasn't pleasant to hear and I felt sorry for him as he took the onslaught of unhappy feelings. After saying that, better him than me.

She continued to blast at him and then her hands dropped to her sides and her voice lessened. Sheldon stepped forward and placed his hands on her shoulders. She fell against him sobbing.

I have to admit I felt rather guilty for getting her so upset. On the other hand I wasn't about to do anything about it.

Ten minutes later, we continued our journey. We moved away from the easy to walk through grasses and to where the trees became an obstacle path. I was going to ask Sheldon about the choice of routes when I heard a nasty sounding growl above us. I looked up and saw four dragons sailing over the river. The dragons appeared to be in two pairs with the second pair a bit behind the first set. The roar had come from the first pair and suddenly one of the dragons folded its wings and dived towards the riverbank. At the last moment, the wings unfolded and it swooped just above the ground at a frightening speed. Its giant mouth opened and a yellow flame shot out. I saw a group of deer suddenly flushed out from a small grove of trees frantically rush in the opposite direction towards the river.

What happened next was the execution of a planned hunt. Another dragon landed, between the forest and the running deer. It kept its wings widespread and advanced towards the deer, shrieking as it did so. The deer panicked, swerving away from the latest predator, running parallel to the river. Then the third dragon landed, also keeping its wings spread apart, in front of the deer. The deer turned to the last open direction, the river. The dragons roared and sent yellow flames towards the panicked deer. The deer squeezed together and ran tightly together towards the river. That's when the fourth dragon landed with its rear legs in the river, its tail splashing water as it waved back and forth.

The deer froze in a circle, prancing around, unable to find an escape route as the four dragons advanced in slow steps. First one dragon and then the others sent flames to the frightened deer. Finally, the dragons lunged towards them with their open jaws, full of teeth and dripping with saliva.

The dragons were not just feeding; they were in a killing mode. As soon as one dragon killed a deer, it released the limp and torn body and attacked another. Of the fifteen or so deer attacked, I saw only two escape death, racing for the safety of the woods.

We watched the aftermath of the slaughter, all of us silent. The dragons gorged themselves on the deer, their bellies noticeably swelling. Two of the dragons finally flew off, looking lazy as they returned the same direction they came. The other two dragons remained and appeared to be guarding the deer.

We continued our journey but our conversation was subdued. The dragons showed great planning and skill in trapping the deer, but the hunger they showed in killing them left me shaken. I wondered how

Sheldon was planning to stop the dragon that was causing our boats to crash. They were not a creature I wanted to get close to.

Chelsea walked next to me as we manoeuvred around the trees and rocks. She finally spoke what I had been feeling.

"That was a bit unnerving how the dragons attacked."

"It certainly was effective." I reached for her hand. "I guess we now know what we're dealing with and better be careful." A low-pitched growl caused us to look up again. More dragons approached the area where the deer were killed but this time the monsters were in a loose group of different sizes. "It looks like the rest have come to feed."

"The way they eat there won't be even bones left."

She was right about that. It was hard to believe that anything could stop those massive jaws from devouring whatever was between them.

We took a break and I hoped to spend some alone time with Chelsea. Sheldon came up to us where we were sitting by a tree, not looking like he needed to have a break at all.

"I wanted to talk to both of you about Ohwanwana. I hope her wishes haven't caused any problems."

Chelsea shook her head. "I think we straightened her out."

"Well, that's a bit of a concern. She isn't used to her wants being denied and I'm sure she'll make another attempt at getting what she wants. I have to warn you she can be stubborn and devious."

"Sheldon, don't I have say in this? I mean I want Chelsea and I'm not interested in Ohwanwana." I didn't bother to add unless I'm drunk.

"I suppose your opinion would ordinarily matter but we are not on our world. The customs here are different and Ohwanwana has a lot of power in her village."

Chelsea didn't look pleased. "Maybe she needs to understand a different kind of power, like a pissed off dragon boater."

I needed to divert the attention away from Ohwanwana and her wants. "Sheldon how do those dragons breathe fire? I have to admit they look pretty terrifying."

"The dragon's fire is actually a chemical reaction. The dragon releases two chemicals, hydrochloric acid and potassium permanganate. When they combine, there is a spontaneous fire plus a corrosive gas. Any prey that is hit is often rendered blind and helpless for any subsequent attack."

"That's a pretty vicious method to attack, as if those jaws weren't enough." I thought how terrible it had been for the deer to take blasts of that dragon fire and not having anywhere to escape.

"The dragons are efficient when it comes to killing. They usually coordinate their attack with several dragons. If there is more than they can eat, they invite the rest of their colony to consume the kill. Dragons are intelligent and quite social. They don't kill unless they feel the need to eat and share the food with other dragons."

"You said a colony of dragons?" I didn't like the thought of a large group of dragons.

"Yes, perhaps thirty dragons will live together. The exception is the parents of a nest, who take turns protecting the eggs in a cave or an isolated area. The dragons migrate as a group, usually following the coastline of a large body of water or a river. They like to use a flat area to be able to attack their prey. Because of their wings, they have trouble entering a forest, though they will chase prey along the ground a short distance into the trees. For a large creature they can actually run quite fast."

Wonderful news—a fast moving fire-breathing monster. "So exactly what is our plan when we find this colony of dragons?"

"We figure out which of the dragons is interfering with our boats naturally."

"Okay, then what? How do we get it to stop?"

Sheldon grinned. "That's where you come in."

"Me?" I didn't like that thought.

"Of course, why else do you think I had you come along? I knew I could find the dragons but how to stop the one causing our difficulties was something I wasn't sure about. You're a smart man, Harry, and have dealt with the paranormal before, so I thought you could provide the solution."

He had to be kidding. It was nice to have a vote of confidence from him but I didn't know anything about dragon behaviour. In fact, I was fairly certain I wasn't going to be any help at all. "How is that a plan? I didn't even know dragons existed before yesterday. Why would I know what to do?"

"It's simple, Harry. Why else would a series of circumstance place you here if you weren't meant to stop the dragon? Fate has brought you here and now it's up to you find a solution."

"And what would that solution be?"

Sheldon shrugged. "I'm sure you'll know what it is at the right time."

I began to have a bad feeling about this fate thing. On the other hand, I did meet Chelsea so maybe fate wasn't all bad.

* * * *

Normally I don't mind the rain. It had been a hot day and then suddenly the dark clouds moved in. There was blue sky one minute and a zap of lightning the next. The rain wasn't cold but it came hard and fast. Ten minutes later we were drenched as the sun began to peek through the clouds.

As I said, I don't mind the rain but when you're carrying a backpack with your clothes soaked the fun ends rather quickly. We grumped along, hoping our clothes would dry off. Grininman didn't seem to mind the wetness around him and kept smiling away as he talked gibberish to Theolguy. I was under the impression Theolguy wasn't enthused to be conversing with Grininman and generally ignored him, other than to cover his ears once or twice. Ohwanwana also talked to Theolguy but he definitely paid attention to her. At one point, he turned to look at Chelsea and me, giving us a bit of a scowl. Theolguy wasn't calming her down; in fact, she seemed to be getting more upset all the time.

Grininman later said something to her and the smile on his face that vanished faster than a cold beer in front of a dragon boater when she made a retort back. I began to suspect Sheldon was right when he told us she was used to having her way.

Grininman was looking a little crestfallen until Welndowd came over and consoled him. His grin became bigger than ever.

Chapter Sixteen

Ovrthehil was the next victim of Grininman, who chatted away without bothering to see if anyone listened. Ovrthehil kept plodding forward and generally ignored his companion. Meanwhile Theolguy continued to the lead with Sheldon next to him, though they weren't talking other than the odd comment in gibberish. Right behind them was Welndowd, who was looking around the forest at everything. She was rather pleasant to look. Best not let Chelsea me staring at her or there could be trouble, I decided. But she did show off her assets rather well with her loosely secured skins.

That left Ohwanwana, who was trailing behind us by herself occasionally and other times just in front of us. She didn't look or act upset but was quiet and seemed to rove around us.

Chelsea stayed close to me, not giving Ohwanwana an opportunity to near me. It was like a game of cat and mouse with me being the cheese. Okay, that didn't sound right but you know what I mean.

Despite the amount of rain that fell on us, we needed to refill our water containers. Theolguy led us out of the forest after carefully scanning the sky for dragons. I took Chelsea's canteen so she didn't have to get wet and went to the river to refill them. Grininman jabbered at me with a big smile on his face and gave me a wink.

I smiled back but I didn't want to encourage him to continue to try to have a conversation. I refilled the canteens and then dropped the purification tablets in them, just in case the water from the mountains wasn't so fresh.

I blame Grininman for distracting me as I made my way back. Suddenly Ohwanwana grabbed me and began to kiss me.

"No, Olala, no," I said between kisses. I didn't know if Chelsea was watching as I tried to pry her fingers off the back of my neck, but I should have guessed she was.

Chelsea grasped Ohwanwana by her waist and pulled her away. She then swung her around and left her tumbling to the ground.

For a moment, I thought Ohwanwana was going to cry, but then she stood and snarled something gibberish at Chelsea before charging her.

Then it was on, the two women began to fight as they rolled on the muddy ground. The guides, Sheldon and I stood around in a semicircle and watched. You may wonder why none of intervened. Well to answer that, I suppose it didn't really look like they were hurting each other and there's something fascinating about watching an evenly matched fight. Especially between two beautiful women.

It began to get very interesting when Ohwanwana pulled off Chelsea's T-shirt as they rolled into some muddy water. Chelsea didn't seem to care and pulled on Ohwanwana's hair to try to gain the upper hand.

Sheldon turned to me. "You know that they're fighting over you."

"I do."

"You know that no matter what happens you're going to pay dearly."

"I do." He was right, and I hoped I could afford the aftermath of the altercation. I looked scornfully at my hand. It was what got us into trouble during that drunken night.

Ohwanwana fell backwards with Chelsea tumbling on top of her. A moment later, I saw a muddy yellow bra tossed away. The two women rolled with Chelsea now on the bottom and then they rolled again with their arms and legs entangled and their bodies covered in mud and pieces of grass.

Welendowd shouted something and a moment later Ohwanwana's top came off. Welendowd shouted again, maybe words of encouragement for Ohwanwana. Then again, maybe she didn't like Ohwanwana. It's hard to interpret gibberish.

Sheldon seemed to be observing the wrestling match without emotion, perhaps weighing when he should intervene. Theolguy seemed to have his eyes closed as he slowly shook his bowed head mumbling something. Ovrthehil had a small smile on his face and was enjoying the show, though nothing compared to Grininman. He looked ecstatic, almost jumping up and down with excitement. He also shouted words of encouragement, though whether that was for one woman or the other it was hard to say. Maybe he was just trying to get more clothes to be ripped off.

Ohwanwana was now on the bottom again. She tried tearing at Chelsea's shorts but the material held against her efforts. Meanwhile Chelsea began to try to shred the leather ties that held Ohwanwana's skirt together. Ohwanwana twisted to stop her and for a moment, the fight was at a stalemate.

Then with a shout, Chelsea began to tear off the skirt.

Ohwanwana stopped trying to save her skirt and tried desperately to dig her fingers at Chelsea's shorts. Suddenly she pulled out a small white fabric, making Chelsea yelp in surprise.

Ohwanwana tossed the panties to the side. Then the two women sat on the ground facing each other, each grappling for a hold on the other as they yelled.

I can't tell you what Ohwanwana said but Chelsea said, "That hurt, you stupid bitch and they were expensive."

That may have inspired Chelsea because the fight ended a moment later. Chelsea stopped trying to pull Ohwanwana down and instead followed through with a great right fist punch to the chin.

Ohwanwana fell backwards and her limbs went limp. Fight over, knockout in the fifth round.

Chelsea stood up and looked down at Ohwanwana who was now slowly moving her hand to her head. Satisfied that Ohwanwana was either still alive or that she was in pain, Chelsea walked over to where I stood.

I tried to avert my eyes from her mud-covered body but failed miserable. Along with my hand, my eyes were always getting me into trouble. I have to admit Chelsea looked really good dirt aside. In fact, another body part of mine, that also could get me into trouble, was really appreciating her figure.

Chelsea jabbed a muddy finger into my chest. "This was the last straw. If she wants you, she can have you."

I watched her stalk away, back to where Welendowd was consoling a sobbing Ohwanwana. Chelsea picked up her shirt and then her bra, looked at the ends of the bra and threw it away before continuing towards the river. At the river, she edge, removed her boots and socks, and then waded into river, dunking herself under several times to wash off the mud. Chelsea looked even better with the water pouring off her. She also washed her shirt, vigorously shaking it in the water.

"Well, Harry, I'd say your life just became a whole lot more complicated."

I looked at Sheldon. "Thanks for the obvious. Any good advice?"

"Go and offer her your shirt. I wouldn't say a whole lot right now if I were you."

I nodded and made my way to the river just as she was making her way out. She was squeezing either the water or the life out of her T-shirt, making me rather nervous.

I took off my shirt and held it out toward her.

She stared at it.

"Please, Chelsea. Wear it at least until your shirt dries."

She snatched it from my hand. "I'm not forgiving you." She put it on and walked past me to her boots.

I stood like an idiot as she laced up her boots and Ohwanwana went by us with Welendowd holding her arm. Ohwanwana gave me a tearful look and then proceeded into the river to wash up.

I followed Chelsea back to where Sheldon sat, where we joined him in silent observation of the riverbank. Ohwanwana looked very sexy as Welendowd helped her wash off the mud. I tried to pretend I was looking at the distant hills, but damn it's hard not to watch a naked woman washing in a river.

"You can watch her all you want. I don't care anymore." Her voice was quiet and sad.

"I never wanted her. I don't know why she wants me but it's only you I'm interested in."

"You have a funny way of showing that."

"It's because I don't know how to say no in gibberish."

"Gibberish?"

"What the villagers speak."

She gave a half smile. "It's pronounced Givernich. You never learned to speak a foreign language, did you?"

I smiled hopefully. "Je désolé suis vraiment. That means I'm very sorry."

She smiled. "I know, but that is the worse French I ever heard. Better stick to Givernich. At least no one will know if you're saying it right."

We watched as the lovely naked Ohwanwana looked at her ruined clothing, shaking her head. Welendowd took the torn garments from her and folded them and they slowly walked back to where Theolguy stood waiting, his gaze averted towards the ground. He may have been the only one not looking at Ohwanwana. Certainly, Ovrthehil was carefully watching and Grininman looked overjoyed as he stared.

Chelsea turned towards me. "You have a t-shirt in your backpack?"

I nodded. I thought she was going to say put it on and cover up in case my bare chest drove all the women to distraction but that wasn't the case. Darn.

"Better give it to Ohwanabitch. We shouldn't leave her walking around naked."

I pulled my T-shirt out of my backpack and walked over to the very curvy Ohwanwana. She stared at me with wide eyes and a partially open mouth. I slowly extended my hand holding the shirt.

"Here, some people think it would be better if you wore something, though I disagree with that."

She answered me in quiet Givernich, which still sounded like gibberish to me, and took the shirt. She slipped it on and smiled gratefully at me. An Edmonton Oilers shirt never looked so good, which fitted her like a loose and very short dress.

I smiled back at her and retreated to where Chelsea eyed the proceedings carefully.

"Chelsea, I hope you forgive for the mess I caused. I don't even remember exactly what I did but I'll never drink so much fermented fruit juice again. I didn't know she was going to kiss me ..."

"Shut up Harry." This was from Sheldon who tried to whisper to me. "I think she knows."

Chelsea smiled. "Yeah, shut up, Harry. I don't want to talk about it any more."

Eventually we continued our journey. Two women were wearing my shirts, both looking sexy in them. Okay, a whole lot sexy.

I carefully took Chelsea's hand in mine and after a few seconds, she tightened the grip.

I felt relieved and enjoyed the silence as we walked between the trees.

* * * *

An hour later, we heard the first sounds; growling, screeching and yelping accompanied by flapping noises. You didn't have to be James Bond to know we were heading into danger.

We reached the open area where we saw at least two dozen dragons played around. The ground was near the river and we stayed behind a few large rocks located amongst the trees. I wondered how such monsters could look like they were having fun. The smaller dragons were the most active, running around, looking to playing a sort of chase game. They would bump their head into one of the other young dragons on the side and then run away. Occasionally one of the small dragons would take flight for a few seconds to jump over another. It seemed to be a complex game on who was 'it' at any particular time. Some of the other older dragons sat on their back legs watching the youngsters play. A couple of others were holding objects in their big hands, examining them with interest. One of the objects was a large pink and gray rock that the dragon slowly turned around.

The dragons were of different colours as well, including their eyes. Some were pure white while most were a mixture of various bright colours. I did notice one pure black dragon as well, that gave it an evil look with its yellow eyes.

Sheldon nudged my shoulder and pointed to an area near the river edge. A large dragon of brown and green was sleeping. It didn't look right. The large wings weren't held tightly against its body but lay limp against the ground.

"That be the one we're looking for. I think it's dying, in a dream state right now, and its spirit has invaded our world." Sheldon's whisper didn't attract the attention of the dragons so at least I knew their hearing wasn't perfect.

"Okay. Now what do we do?"

Sheldon smiled; it wasn't a smile that made me feel warm and fuzzy. "This is where you come in. You must stop him, or her, from interfering with our boats."

Me. Somehow, this seemed rather unfair. I was going to tell him that I wasn't able to do that and won't even try when Chelsea spoke.

"Harry, you're so brave to volunteer to do this. You're a hero to do this for all dragon boaters." She gave me a big kiss on the lips. "Just be careful, I don't want to lose you."

I was planning to be more than just careful, but it looked like I was going to be the one risking my neck. Damn I hate being a hero.

This is when Edwin Drood has to make an appearance. I whispered to Sheldon, "I need to ask our guides some questions. Can we move back a little so there is no chance the dragons will hear us?"

He nodded and motioned the rest of us to follow him. Once we were a good distance away, we sat in a circle. Sheldon spoke to the others carefully in Givernich and then turned to me. "What do you want to know?"

Edwin Drood took over. "The dragons, they seem pretty smart and I saw them using their front paws as hands. What else can they tell me about that?"

Sheldon repeated the question to them and they responded all at once. Ohwanwana shouted something and all the guides suddenly became quiet. She then spoke quietly to Sheldon, going on at length. At the end, Ovrthehil added a comment and then Sheldon repeated what was said to him, in English, not Givernich.

"The dragons are considered sacred creatures by the villagers. When they are seen flying overhead, it is considered a sign of good luck. According to legend, the dragons existed before people, and took care of the world. They allow people to exist as long as we don't upset the balance of nature.

The dragons used to visit our world by going through the tunnels, but were attacked by the people there who didn't understand the dragons were intelligent and benevolent. So the dragons left our world, not daring to return. The dragons weren't angry, just sad we didn't understand."

"Do the dragons ever attack the village?"

More Givernich was spoken back and forth. Ohwanwana had the most to say though the Theolguy also added a few words.

"They said they have never heard of a dragon attacking a person or even a Sasquatch, though it is also true the dragons are left alone as much as possible. Apparently the people fear the dragons as well as revere them."

I, or rather Edwin Drood, considered the information. Certainly, it would have been easy for the dragons to attack the village. It was flat and without many trees around it making it straightforward to land and attack but they never did.

"I have a theory on the dragon that is attacking our boats." I waited for Sheldon and Chelsea to look at me. "It's not really attacking to damage them. The dragon sees the dragonhead on the boat, perhaps thinking of the boats as dragons, and decides to play with them. It's what the young dragons are doing, lightly ramming the side of another dragon with its head."

Sheldon nodded. "That makes sense. It is why the dragon boats are bumped only occasionally and then only once."

To me it also meant the dragons were not the vicious creatures they first appeared to be. Certainly, they lived socially together and they showed intelligence. Now what to do with that information was another step. I decided I needed to observe the dragons a bit more. Our guides had enough of the dragons. Sheldon explained to me that they were superstitious about being so close to them. Maybe it was superstition but my reluctance to get closer to the dragons was strictly due to fear.

Chelsea and Sheldon went with me. It was nice to have their company but I was a bit worried about Chelsea's safety. I wasn't worried about Sheldon's safety. He got me into this mess after all.

The dragons acted much the same as before. Small dragons playing, older dragons watching and the medium size dragons were doing their own thing. That included a different kind of playing as a pair of dragons would fly off together to be alone. It was interesting watching the dragons wrap their necks around each other and then stare at each other, occasionally doing a bit of nibbling. To tell you the truth I couldn't tell the differences between the sexes but I presume the dragons knew, otherwise we wouldn't have the small dragons.

We crept a bit closer on our stomachs and watched. I didn't see anything new initially, but then I saw one of the largest dragons slowly cross the field. The small dragons scurried out of its path and the medium sized ones slowly but definitely moved out of the way. The large dragon made its way to the sleeping dragon and stood looking at the still form. There was quietness about the dragons as they watched that large dragon lower its substantial head, almost touching the other dragon. I could only see the back and the side of that large dragon but there appeared to be an immense sadness in its posture.

Chelsea whispered to me, "Do you have a plan yet?"

I didn't really but that didn't stop me from making one up as I spoke. I spoke with quiet confidence and smoothly laid out my plan.

"Well, that is, I thought that we could…uh, we're going to sneak down, or at least I am, to where the dying dragon is."

"Go on."

Oh, she wanted more details. "Well, we, that is, I, will try to find what I can do to pull its restless spirit back."

Sheldon whispered as well and it was fortunate the dragons didn't hear him. "I have a crystal that will call the spirit back to the body. Of course the crystal has to be placed as close to the heart as possible."

Chelsea looked at me. "Isn't that dangerous to be creeping around a dragon?"

I replied with courage resonating in my voice. She would have swooned but she was already lying down. "Yes, but I will do so at dark."

A new voice spoke, in Givernich.

I looked over and past Sheldon's bulk, not an easy thing to do, and saw Ohwanwana. I also saw that my shirt was even shorter on her lying down than standing.

Sheldon turned to me. "She decided she had to warn us that the dragons get more active at night than the daytime. She is worried you are going get yourself hurt."

Chelsea raised her voice a tad above a whisper. "She's the one who should be worried about getting hurt."

* * * *

We crept close to the sleeping dragon. We huddled together maybe a couple of hundred yards away looking for any more information about the dragons. Unfortunately, especially for me, there weren't any more clues. The "wait until dark plan" was out. If I was going to plant the crystal, it had to be now when there was daylight. I thought I was better off without Sheldon helping me, especially if he started using that whispering shout of his. As far as Chelsea and Ohwanwana were concerned, I didn't want to put them in any danger, so it was going to be me and me alone that had to make the journey to the dragon.

Sheldon handed me a large, flat, oval shaped crystal. It was bigger than my hand and reflected a rainbow of colours. "Remember to place it as near to the heart as possible and orient in a north-south direction."

I held the crystal, which was heavier than I expected. "I have a few questions. Where is the dragon's heart, which way is north and how certain are you this crystal will work?"

"I think the dragon's heart is located a bit lower than where the wings are mounted. North, let me see now." He looked up at the sun and then pointed vaguely in one direction. "More or less that way."

Great. I'm placing a crystal in an approximate location and maybe placing it in the right direction.

"As far as the crystal actually working, I'm pretty sure it will. The person I obtained it from indicated it would be useful." He gave a hopeful smile.

I looked at the slightly used crystal that was probably bought at a garage sale. I took off my backpack and dropped it on the ground. It looked like I wouldn't need it any more.

Chelsea put her arms around my neck. "Let me go with you."

I shook my head. "No, it'll be more dangerous for two people. One person has a better chance of not being seen."

A tear formed at the corner of her eye and she gave me a long kiss. "You better make it back dragon boater or I'll be so mad at you." She gave me another kiss, which was almost worth dying for.

Sheldon shook my hand, crushing my fingers in the process. "I know you can do it, Harry. It's why you're here. I believe in you, old boy."

Ohwanwana stepped forward and gave me a quick kiss on the cheek, saying a few quiet words in Givernich. Chelsea watched the exchange carefully, but didn't interfere, of which I was grateful. I really didn't want to see them get into another fight. I was running out of clothes to give them.

* * * *

I left the security of the trees reluctantly and, one-step at a time, made my way to the sleeping dragon. I noticed the end of the tail twitched a couple of times as I went by. I noticed something else. Dragons don't have a pleasant odour. In fact, I would have to say they really stink. I suppose when you consider the size of the dragons and the lack of washing facilities for them it was natural for them to smell; kind of like if you stuck your head inside an aquarium full of iguanas. I don't actually recommend that you do that of course.

I stepped lightly around to the side of the dragon, and close enough I could run my hand around the flank. I was feeling just a tad more relaxed that I made it this far. I felt like placing the crystal almost anywhere on the dragon but something was troubling me. I stopped near where the great wings were mounted on top of the beast and gripped the crystal tightly.

This was near where I was suppose to place the crystal and it would have been easy to quickly stick the crystal there and scurry away. There was something bothering me and it wasn't just the smell of the dragon.

Somehow, I knew that the crystal wasn't going to work. Maybe it was Edwin Drood, who was suddenly speaking to me but whatever it was, I was certain the crystal was not the answer for stopping the dragon's spirit from wandering.

Maybe that was the reason I decided to continue my slow march to the front of the dragon. The head of the dragon was rather ugly close up with the horns, scales and sneaking out of its lips, some rather nasty looking teeth. I looked at where the pair of horns rose from the skull and bent back to the neck. The horns weren't smooth but had a series of rings, as if they could telescope down. I looked at the point where the horns stopped and noticed something odd. Okay, granted the whole dragon thing is odd. But I saw something else that looked like even more horns sprouting out of its heck. As I leaned forward to take a closer look, a yapping sound made me jump. One of those small dragons that were running all over the place had seen me and sounded the alarm. Within seconds, the medium sized dragons came running over.

I might have made it back to the forest if I'd moved at the first sound of the small dragon, but I froze for the first precious seconds and suddenly it was too late. The medium sized dragons came within a dozen feet where I stood, staring at me. I give myself credit that I didn't wet my pants.

They didn't exactly threaten me, but growled, screeched and yapped at each other and at me. The small dragons would sometimes appear between their legs but stayed quiet. I didn't know what to do, other than to say "Nice dragons, nice dragons."

A minute later, the largest dragon came wandering up and the other dragons parted the way for it. It lowered its head and peered at me. Surprisingly, my pants still stayed dry.

I figured I had to do something, and slowly extended my hand holding the crystal. "Nice dragon, please take the pretty crystal as a peace offering."

It grunted and then changed its posture, reaching out with its clawed hand to take the crystal from me. The black claws actually were gentle as it lifted the crystal in the air. It looked impressed and might have even given a dragon equivalent of "Oooo."

It was maybe the thought of facing death that made my mind focus better. I suddenly knew why the dragon next to me was dying and how it happened. The dragon wanted to explore the caves and tunnels we used to arrive here, perhaps to travel to our world. But it couldn't use the easiest route for that was used by a nesting pair of dragons. Therefore, it found another entrance, the same one we had to use to exit the mountains. When it tried to move forward, it came across the stalactites, causing them to break. Unfortunately two of them penetrated and broke in its neck. The dragon must have been in considerable pain but made it back to its group before succumbing to a coma.

I turned and reached up to the neck of the dragon. I hoped the other dragons didn't think I was going to try to hurt it but the crystal seemed to have made them trusting of my intentions. I worked at the two embedded ends of the stalactites. First one and then the other came out; one was only about three inches long but the other was nearly eight inches long and near the vertebrates. Blood, brightly red, came slowly oozing out of the wounds.

I turned back to the other dragons and held up the broken stalactites for them. They stared intently on me and then back at the sleeping dragon. I looked back at the wounds on its neck. The blood was now flowing freely and as I watched it began to increase in volume, pulsing at the same rate of a slow heartbeat. I looked at its head, and saw the eyelid flutter. Then a large green eye came into view. It looked unfocused and cloudy but it was open. Several dragons made a hooting noise.

Seconds passed and suddenly the cloudiness of the eye disappeared; the spirit had returned to the body. Slowly the bright green eye focused as the giant head lifted up. The dragons roared their approval, deafening this close but it sounded like a song of joy. I took that moment to make my retreat.

Once I made it to the tail that was now swishing around with great energy I ran the rest of the way back to the others.

Sheldon crushed my hand again with another vigorous handshake while Ohwanwana gave me a hug and a kiss on the lips. The best was from Chelsea who wrapped her arms around me and while her body was welded to mine gave me a ten-minute kiss.

"My hero, Sir Harry the dragon saver."

Chapter Seventeen

It was a grand feast with much singing and dancing. The men all pounded my back and in broad smiles said something in Givernich. The women, bless them, gave me hugs and kisses—very affectionate kisses. I wish I knew what they said to me.

Chelsea didn't leave my side, accepting the accolades I received without acting jealous. Ohwanwana tried to return my T-shirt but I refused. She looked so much better in it than I ever could; I figured she should keep it. I wouldn't be surprised if I had started a new fashion trend in the village and I could make money selling shirts to the villagers.

The tasty fomented fruit drink went down especially easily. I remember few details of the latter part of the night. I recall Chelsea helping me stand up and taking me to one of the funny round buildings. I even remember Chelsea kissing me as she took off my shirt. Then the room began to spin in circles and there seemed to be several Chelseas around me. There my memories ended.

I woke up with wet cotton batten stuffed inside my head. The room was too warm and I rolled on my side to get more comfortable and fell off the bed. The floor was at least cooler than the bed and I stayed there for a while, wondering if there was any point in getting up. Ever.

Slowly I got to hands and knees. It took a valiant effort but I managed to stand up. Groaning, I staggered to the door with my hand covering my eyes from a sun ten times brighter than a sun needed to be. I stopped at the doorway; I was literally blind from the sunlight. I heard the sound of people and then some giggles. I took inventory of my situation and discovered I was naked. Oops.

I made a fast retreat back to the confines of the hut and searched for my clothes. This was not how one wants to start the day.

Chelsea came in as I finished dressing, carrying a mug of water for me.

"Here. I think you might have had a bit too much last night."

I nodded and gulped down the water. "I feel horrible. Any drugstores open around here? I need some aspirin."

She grinned. "Here. I had some in my backpack."

Smart woman. Pack something for every occasion.

"I don't remember much of last night."

"That may be a good thing. The villagers may not be ready to learn the twist, or the polka. On the other hand they did like the tune, We All Live in a Yellow Submarine."

"I almost walked outside naked. Can you tell me what happened?"

"Yes, the young ladies preparing food and were somewhat surprised at the sight of you. Men aren't normally naked in the village."

"No, I mean how did I get naked and what happened…that is…between us."

"Well, we were getting rather serious. Our clothes came off and I was going to reward you for your bravery. Unfortunately, the demon alcohol had other ideas. You passed out before we could finish."

"Oh God, no." I felt like crying. "Honest, I don't normally pass out."

"I hope not. It would put a crimp in any relationship." She smiled at me and then kissed my cheek. "See you outside. I need to get something to eat."

I sat there collecting my thoughts and then went back outside in search of more water. The women giggled again as I left the hut and I gave them an embarrassed wave. I found more water and kept drinking, finishing a gallon in less than a minute.

Gradually my brain returned to normal and I actually had some fruit to eat. Chelsea stayed close to me, though whether it was because she enjoyed my company, or to make sure Ohwanwana didn't enjoy my company, I couldn't really say. It didn't matter to me; I loved being around her.

Sheldon came up to me and I immediately put the cup in my right hand so he wouldn't attempt to shake it.

"Nice to see you up and about Harry. Our friends here are going to have a farewell lunch for us. They believe the gods sent you to save the dragon and that you are man of great healing power."

I wished my great healing power extended to my crushed fingers and my head. "That's very nice of them. Does this start in a few hours then?"

"Harry, it's already past noon." He pointed at the sun in the sky. "You may have slept in a bit."

That was an understatement and three-quarters. But I smiled and replied sincerely, "That's good. I'm looking forward to going back home."

Once again, there was food, drink, dancing and song. My appetite had retuned enough I could consume food again though the fruit drink I had was not fermented. This time I watched the dancing and did not participate. The villagers did a fine job of chanting out songs and singing. At the end, they did a final tribute to me. They attempted to do the twist while singing their rendition of "Yellow Submarine." In Givernich it sounded a lot different but I give them an A for effort.

Then we heard a noise high in the sky. A screeching sound heralded the arrival of six dragons flying low above us. The lead dragon was huge and was definitely the one I saw earlier at the field and took the crystal from me. The dragons swooped over the village. I gave the villagers credit; they didn't run or panic. I wasn't certain what to do but remained where I was because Chelsea clung to my arm as she watched them fly overhead. The last dragon looked like it was straining a bit and, as it went by, I saw glint of its green eye. Then it dropped a pink and grey object from its front paw that landed in an open area of the village. With a final screech the dragons disappeared the way they came.

Chelsea looked at me. "I guess they came by to say thank you."

Theolguy came up to me with the dropped object. It was a piece of granite that had been formed into more or less a ball of almost a foot in diameter. He extended it towards me, saying something I didn't understand.

Sheldon came up to me. "He's saying it's yours. A special gift from the dragons."

I took the granite from him. I could tell it had been worked to make it into its present shape. How the dragons did it, I don't know. Maybe their claws or maybe they used a type of tool. Regardless it was impressive they could do that. It was a unique gift but it also weighed a ton. How was I supposed to carry that all the way back through the mountain?

* * * *

The journey back was uneventful, other than getting the hissing sounds from hidden Sasquatch. I got several pats on the back from the village men and kisses from the ladies. Ohwanwana bowed her head to Chelsea in a nice gesture before she gave me a kiss that left me no doubt I could call her next time I was in town.

That granite ball was making my hiking difficult, weighting down my backpack. After an hour or so of our journey, Sheldon offered to carry it for me, no doubt, because I was slowing down our walk to a crawl. I was only to glad to let him carry it and see how he managed with it.

Much to my annoyance, he didn't appear to suffer at all, maintaining a brisk pace. The man just wasn't human.

* * * *

We didn't get lost in the caves, and didn't need Sheldon's markings along the wall. We made it safely out of the mountain again and I breathed in the fresh air. Unfortunately, it was late evening and we had to make our way carefully back to our parked SUV. Chelsea insisted that I sit up in the front and enjoy the spectacular view of logging trucks approaching us at a hundred miles an hour.

"Sheldon, what day is it? I'm wondering how the team did in the race or if they were all cancelled." I spoke as I tightened my seat belt and crossed myself.

"It's the same day we left; we haven't missed a single race."

I didn't argue or ask any more questions. For one thing, his answers would lead to too many more questions. Moreover, for another, his driving had a tendency to shut everyone up.

We arrived without incident back to the town site and I looked forward to sleeping on a real bed again. Chelsea gave me a wonderful kiss goodnight and announced she was going to take a long shower and then go to bed.

I nodded my approval and carried my hundred-pound granite ball to my room. My roommate wasn't in and I placed the ball on the table that supported the TV in the room. I was going to leave it on the floor but if my roommate tripped over it, we would have one less paddler for the next race. In the morning I figured when I wake up, it would be proof our adventure actually happened and wasn't just a dream.

* * * *

Morning came early and I jerked awake from a dream of dragons chasing me. I sat up in the bed and tried to figure out just how real the dream was. It was a little too vivid for my liking. Then reality descended on me.

I got out of bed and saw my roommate still sleeping and I looked over at the table where the TV sat. There wasn't any granite ball to be seen. I walked around the small room and there wasn't any place where it could have been hiding.

I washed up and dressed quickly. I looked at my watch and at half past seven, it was too early to start waking up people, except for one. I punched in Sheldon's room number on the phone and listened to the ring. The evil part of me hoped to wake him up but I was disappointed when I only received the electronic voice requesting to leave a message.

I was agitated and decided to head downstairs rather than sit in the small room. Thoughts raced through my mind that the whole adventure was just part of a dream. If so, my relationship with Chelsea might also be an illusion.

I saw a few people in the lobby but didn't recognize anyone on the River Rodent team. I tried to calm myself, going over the possibilities. No granite ball, thus a figment of my imagination. Therefore, my visit to another world never happened. Thus, my time with Chelsea never happened. Did even Sheldon exist?

The loud voice answered that question.

"Good morning, Harry! What are you doing up so early?" Sheldon strode across the lobby floor in his green jogging outfit.

I was so happy to see Sheldon I almost hugged him. "Sheldon, I gotta ask you something."

He looked at me strangely. "Sure, what is it?"

"I had a strange dream last night and I'm not sure what's real. Tell me, did we go climbing on a mountain yesterday with Chelsea?"

He grinned. "Yes, Harry, we really did climb a mountain and save a dragon."

I released my breath. "Thank God. I remember leaving a granite ball on a table last night and this morning it was gone. I was wondering if I dreamt the whole thing."

"Oh that. Your roommate saw it on the table last night and took it with him to a party I held in my suite. I told them you found it during our hike and they were all impressed by its beauty and how you managed to carry it all the way back to the hotel. You really shouldn't jump to conclusions so easily. Life can be stranger than dreams."

So it would seem. I waited for Sheldon to change and then went to breakfast with him at another small restaurant he had found during his run.

"You don't give yourself enough credit for what you accomplish Harry. You go on a marvellous adventure, save the dragon boat races, save a dragon's life and get a pretty girl to fall in love with you. Then you think you must have been dreaming all that." Sheldon shoved another piece of a waffle in his mouth.

"You're right. I guess I thought it was all too good to be true. So you think Chelsea has fallen in love with me?"

"Of course. Isn't it obvious? Why else did she want to go with us? She wanted to be with you. She also got into a fight with another woman over you and never once stopped caring about you, even when you were drunk."

"She never said she loved me."

"Actions speak louder than words. Have you told her you love her?"

"No."

"But you do, I can see it plain as day. You're willing to wade among the dragons but frightened to utter three little words."

"I was worried I would scare her away."

"If you're not honest with her now, when will you be? By not saying anything you cause her to wonder more about you and Ohwanwana and any other woman."

I nodded. Sheldon was right. Fear was holding me back. Then Sheldon said something to me I'll never forget, shocking the hell out of me.

"Come, let's go back to the hotel. I'll pay for the breakfast."

Chapter Eighteen

There was frenzy of activity at our tent as we prepared for our next race. Despite my efforts, I was never alone with Chelsea. I was wondering when I was going to get the chance to tell her how I felt.

I held her hand as we walked with the others to the dock. We talked about the up coming race, avoiding any topic that would take away the focus of being in the boat. I lined up and found a life vest that was a bit too big but at least somewhat dry. The paddle I had to use was the right length but a bit rough along one edge. Compromises sometimes have to be made and I figured being able to reach deeper was better than a perfect blade.

I joined Chelsea and the others along the ramp that led to the dock. The nervousness returned and several team members hurried to the port-a-potties. One of the team members walked up and down our line and spoke quietly.

"Focus in the boat. Picture yourself making that perfect stroke." He gave each paddler a tap with his black paddle.

After what seemed to take an eternity, we were finally allowed to go the dock and climb into our boat. I sat next to Chelsea as usual, giving her a smile as I clutched my paddle tightly.

We paddled slowly to the start line, practicing a start along the way. As usual, it took a few minutes to line up all six boats but the officials finally became satisfied with the alignment.

Then the horn sounded. I jumped at its sound and then jammed my paddle into the water. I reached deep into the water and pulled back as hard as I could. As I twisted, I could see the backs of my follow paddlers, all of them giving everything they had to launch our boat. I knew they were concentrating on making each stroke perfect. The outcome of the race depended on everyone focusing in the boat and making each stroke count. So I felt guilty.

True, I was doing the best I could, pulling water as much as it was possible. However, my mind wasn't entirely in the boat. I was thinking about Chelsea and how I was going to tell her my feelings and where I could tell her. These thoughts weren't constant, but rather a flash of contemplation between strokes, like a strobe light flash of consideration.

Reach, maybe the fountain of the stone dolphins, paddle in the water, or there is that coffee shop a block down from the hotel, pull back, or maybe a lounge somewhere. Paddle out, but which lounge, rotate, maybe dinner or, watch the timing, even a walk first.

There is one thing about trying to think of two different things at the same time; it sure makes the race go by fast and you don't have a moment to consider how utterly out of breath you are. Thus, before I knew it I was startled to hear the drummer and the steers person scream "Finish it! Finish it now!"

I poured myself into working the paddle as hard as I could, barely think about Chelsea's lovely legs.

"Hold the boat!"

I placed my paddle straight into the water and held tight. Seconds later a new command told us to relax.

"Let it ride."

I suddenly realized how utterly exhausted I was. I leaned forward, trying to pull air into my starving lungs. My stomach muscles felt like someone had kicked them. Then I felt a slap on my back from Greg.

"Great paddling, Harry. You were stroking like a man possessed. Absolutely perfect."

I tried to say thanks but nothing came out of my mouth but a croak.

Chelsea rubbed my back. "Hey, are you alright?"

I nodded. A few seconds later I managed to puff out, "Bit…out…of…breath."

She grinned at me. "You did great."

A minute later, we did the slow paddle back to the docks. I felt great that I managed to paddle so well, but I'm not sure if I could duplicate that ever again. I dropped off the paddle and the PFD and headed to join the others for the review of our last race.

Danielle read off the results. "Our official time is two minutes, twenty-eight and twelve ones hundreds of a second. We finished in third place, beating the Burning Dragons by twenty-two hundreds of a second. That means we go on to compete for the medal round of the Diamond division."

There were great cheers and chants of "Rodents, rodents."

I turned to Chelsea. "We did it, we're in medal competition."

"You should be proud of yourself. That extra effort you put in, leaving nothing in the tank, probably propelled us to third place."

I thought about it. We won by a fifth of a second over forth place and elimination. If I had put forth any less effort, that well could have dropped out of third. Of course, that was true for everyone on our boat, but I was probably the only one not focusing entirely in the boat during that frantic race. "Can we go and have a coffee someplace? I have a confession to make."

She grinned, "What, you snuck a dragon back with you to help us in the race?"

"No, it's too difficult to get a collar and leash on them."

I let her away from the crowd to a coffee shop well away from the dragon boat races. I kept the conversation light, explaining how I thought I was dreaming our whole adventure when my round rock disappeared from my room.

"So Sheldon is guarding it now," I finished.

"Well I was pretty sure I wasn't dreaming when I returned to the hotel room with half my clothes left on the other world."

I carried the coffee to the table where she sat by the window.

"Okay, so what's this confession all about?"

"You know how everyone is supposed to focus in the boat during a race?"

She nodded.

"I didn't. I was thinking about something else."

She looked puzzled. "What was that?"

"How I was going to tell you and where I was going to tell you something."

"I'm here now. What do you want to tell me?"

"That I love you."

She put down her coffee and covered her mouth with her fingers, looking down at the table. Then she looked back at me, her hand dropping away. "I love you, too."

I looked at her wet eyes and smiled, relieved my love was reciprocated.

Time went by pretty fast, and after our coffee went cold we walked around Kelowna. The final race for us was scheduled to start in less than an hour so we arrived at the tent site to begin the pre-race preparation. We snacked on food and drank juice or water. Then the stretching exercises. I hate stretching exercises. They're boring and I feel I'm ready to pull something out of place, like my back or elbow. But far be it for me to complain, at least aloud. I reached and pulled with the rest of them and then we ran around in a circle. Again, boring but at least there wasn't the danger of hurting something.

Then the wait began as we stood in line by the docks. We shuffled our feet and spoke in quiet voices, except for Sheldon who always moved huge volumes of air. I was worried that I wouldn't be able to perform as well as I did in the last race. My mind was still on other things, mainly Chelsea who stood next to me. I was in love and I was content to have a dumb smile on my face.

We were eventually allowed to enter the compound, and we made our way to the dock. I found a wet PFD that did fit and a paddle that was a bit on the short side but new looking. I rejoined our team in the line up and waited until we were allowed to go to the boats. I was nervous and happy, conflicting emotions depending whether I was thinking about the race or Chelsea. I sat in the boat wondering if I had the energy to duplicate the effort I had in the last race.

"Nervous?" Chelsea asked.

"Yeah. I hope I can do what I did in the last race. I was thinking during the last race how I would tell you how I felt, but I've done that now."

She smiled. "You need another distraction."

"I suppose so."

She leaned towards me and whispered in my ear, "If we get a medal, you can have me tonight."

I promptly dropped my paddle in the boat. A little too much distraction I suppose.

She giggled. "I didn't mean to make you anxious."

"Anxious? Let's get the damn race started. I have a mission to accomplish."

The horn finally sounded, signifying the start of the race. I dug in my paddle and pulled water. Not just pulled water; that would be an understatement. I moved water that was the equivalent of Niagara Falls. There were holes in the lake where my paddle swept through. I felt sorry for the steersperson, who probably was fighting to keep the boat from going around in circles.

I paddled with everything I had, in fact more than what I normally could. These weren't normal circumstances. Chelsea offered herself to me if we won. I wished the other paddlers in our boat would paddle harder. They looked like they thought it was evening practice.

Despite the lack of effort by the nineteen other paddlers, we managed to have a pretty good race. We crossed the finish line and then coasted when the command "Let it ride" was given.

I lifted my paddle out of the water, noting the shaft was bent. Then I slowly keeled over in the boat. I tried to brace myself with my arms but they refused to move, and just hung loosely by my sides as I did a face plant.

Chelsea grabbed me by my shoulders and tried to pull me back in the sitting position.

"Harry, Harry! Are you alright?"

My jaws opened and closed but I couldn't make any sound.

Greg helped me get back into a sitting position by pulling at my PFD. "You were paddling like a man possessed again. Where did you get that energy from?"

Chelsea gave me a kiss on the cheek. "You did great. Now just take it easy until we get back to the docks."

I didn't need any more encouragement. I sat quietly in the boat, barely holding my bent paddle.

After disembarking from the boat, we made our way to where the race results were posted. Sheldon pushed his way to the front and checked the results as they were added to the board. Then he made his way back to our group.

"We didn't make third place," he announced quietly. Then his face broke into a grin. "Second! We got Silver!" He laughed and half the women paddlers rushed forward to hug him.

One woman hugged me and I closed my eyes with a smile on my face. Maybe you thought we should have won the gold medal. That I, with my herculean effort, could propel us to first. One has to be realistic about such things. We won a silver medal under tough competition. The team that won gold, well they're probably thinking they should be at the next level. There is always another level a team can attain to. But we were a happy group and there would be a celebration tonight, along with the resulting hangovers the next day.

An hour later, we were sitting around in the beer gardens and toasting each other. Other teams came over and congratulated us on our medal. I shelled out a few dollars for a couple of pitchers of beer and a couple of hotdogs for Chelsea and myself.

Sheldon, being the social guy he is, moved around the table. He talked a lot, drank even more, and as far as I knew never laid down a dollar. He made it to where we sat and placed himself next to Chelsea. He put his big arm around her and gave her a squeeze.

"You two did a great job paddling today. Greg told me he had never seen anyone paddle with such determination as you, Harry, a guy who thought we canoed only weeks ago." He laughed his big laugh.

I smiled. "I felt inspired."

Chelsea gave me a mischievous look. "Harry really wanted the team to win a medal."

Sheldon nodded. "That's the team spirit, Harry. Very unselfish of you." He gave me a wink.

I wondered if he knew what Chelsea whispered to me. The man knows things he has no right to know. "Thanks, but it was the team that won. We all did our part."

He nodded. "By the way I still have your rock. I'll return it to you when we get back home so you don't have to worry about getting it on the plane." He finished his beer and poured himself another.

"Yeah, that was quite an adventure the three of us had. I'm amazed that such a place existed and that we made it back here. Good thing you left those marks inside the cave so we had a trail to follow on our way back."

"Oh, those marks weren't for our return here. The return path was fairly straight forward. No, the marks are for a return visit to the Givernich people."

I raised my eyebrows. "You're going back there?"

"Of course." Sheldon refilled his glass. "I was hoping you would accompany me. There are some mysteries I'd like to explore."

Chelsea took a drink of her own beer. "He better not be exploring the mystery of Ohwanwana. By the way, you never did tell us when or if you had been there before."

Sheldon looked to his left and right in case anyone was within hearing range and then gave us a Sheldon whisper. "I once was exploring that cave for a different reason and got lost. I finally emerged into the Givernich world. Details aren't important but remember their time line is not the same as ours. I was there over a hundred years ago their time.

Those marks are critical. If you go into that cave at different times, you will not see them. The cave will lead to a dead end or to a different world entirely."

Chelsea shook her head. "You live in a different universe than I do."

Sheldon laughed. "I do at that. But I have a gift for you two."

Chelsea gave a puzzled smile. "A gift?"

Sheldon held out a plastic card. "This is our last night here and I thought I'd switch rooms with Harry."

I could hardly believe my ears. Sheldon's room for mine. There had to be a catch.

"I just figured you and Chelsea would appreciate some alone time. Just make sure you cover your room bill tomorrow. My room cost, as you may know, was taken care of by the hotel manager."

Chelsea gave Sheldon a kiss on his cheeks. "Thanks Sheldon, you're always so thoughtful."

I smiled and exchanged the room keys with him, though I knew "thoughtful" Sheldon always seemed to stick me with a bill somehow.

After the beer drinking, it was time for the team to get our medals. The award ceremonies always involve a few speeches where the organizers are thanked for one task or another. Cheers are made that (once again) it was the best festival ever and that everyone was already looking forward to next year.

Then the different medals were handed out, starting with the bronze division and then moved up to the other levels. We received our medals and then joined the other teams as more medals were awarded and speeches delivered. I suppose it wasn't that long, but I was thinking about that hotel room and Chelsea. When the all the awards were dispersed, we said goodbye to some of the team members who were going to head back home right away. Some were driving but others had booked an early flight.

It was now late afternoon and the remaining team members decided to have dinner together. I took advantage of the few minutes to move my belongings to Sheldon's room. Chelsea did the same and together we went down the elevator to meet with the others. The meal seemed to take forever. Chelsea suggested that we pay for Sheldon's meal since he was giving up his hotel room for us. I cringed at the thought of buying him another meal, but knew she was right.

Finally, finally, finally I was alone with Chelsea in the hotel room. I took her in my arms and kissed her long and deeply. When we finally broke apart I began to undress her, kissed her some more and then...

Oh, come on. You don't think I'm going blab about the details here, do you? Remember, gentlemen don't tell. I'm sure Chelsea talked to all her female friends but I'm not going to say another word.

In the morning, we made it down to the lobby. I recognized a few paddlers from the River Rodents and other teams. We said hello and agreed to meet in the hotel restaurant for a final breakfast.

Several of the women paddlers smiled at us and one of them asked us if we slept well. Apparently, the news of our night together had spread quickly and was already common knowledge.

I nodded and said, "It was a very nice room," ignoring what they were really asking. "By the way, where is Sheldon?"

"Oh, he got up at five in the morning and left already. He's just amazing how he carries on."

Another female paddler added, "And he's always so thoughtful."

I immediately suffered a coughing spell.

I went to the front desk to pay up my portion of the hotel room. My roommate had already paid for his half and had even covered the internet fee. That was nice of him and I was happy to save a few dollars. Sheldon's adventure had cost me more than I budgeted for after I ended up paying for the supplies and gas.

I also handed in Sheldon's key. The clerk checked the information and then looked at me. "How do you wish to pay for this, sir? The same credit card?"

"I thought the room was already paid for."

"It is, sir, but not the incidentals. There is the bar service, room service, the movie charges, the massage, and the breakfast charge to the room."

"How much?"

"Two hundred and twenty six dollars, sir, plus tax."

That was more than my share of my original room. I handed over my charge card. "Does the hotel have a gun for hire among its services?"

The clerk looked troubled as he handed back my card.

Breakfast was good, mostly because I shared the table with Chelsea and some of the other River Rodent paddlers. It was typical hotel food, passable but overpriced. I paid cash for Chelsea and me, not being sure if my credit card was over its limit.

Our arrival back home was normal. Bored air hostesses, crackers to eat as an in flight meal with flat pop to drink, and finally the missing luggage. I walked a full hour to get to my conveniently parked car and then drove it back to airport to pick up Chelsea and our luggage.

Despite all that happened on the Air Cannotdo Airlines, I was in a good mood. I had Chelsea with me and a silver medal from our festival. My anger at Sheldon had not subsided and I was going to tell him off at our next practice. That tightwad was going to learn a lesson this time.

I told Chelsea what he had done as we walked to our first practice since the festival. "In a voice just as loud as he usually uses I'm going to announce how he stiffed me for his expenses at the hotel."

"Don't get yourself upset. Sheldon is just being Sheldon. I'm sure he just forgot and will make it up to you."

"He's pure evil."

She laughed. "You don't mean that."

I snarled, "I'm going to scream if I hear one more person say how thoughtful he is. His only thought is to stick me with a bill."

I saw him standing among the other paddlers, talking away as he gestured with not one, but two black paddles. The show off was probably going to use both paddles on our practice.

"Sheldon," I called out in a loud voice. I began to smile, thinking how I was going to make him feel small and cheap.

"Harry," he called back, "Just the man we were waiting for."

The other paddlers formed a semicircle around him. "On behalf of the River Rodents I want to say how much we appreciated your great contribution to gaining us a silver medal at the Kelowna Festival."

The rest of the team applauded as I looked on in surprise at their grinning faces.

"We want you to stay on as a River Rodent and as a token of our appreciation and what you mean to our club, I want to present you with this paddle."

He extended the black, carbon fibre paddle to me.

Danielle spoke up. "We all feel the same way about you, but it was Sheldon who insisted on buying it for you."

I took the paddle slowly from him, my eyes suddenly damp.

"Thank you, Sheldon. That was very thoughtful of you." As soon as I said those words, I felt like screaming. I had actually called Sheldon thoughtful.

The End

At The Edge Of Darkness
by
J H Wear

Prelude
Boston, New England
March 2, 1841

Rose-Marie brushed back the limp, damp hair clinging to his forehead, then gently stroked his cheek as he lay on the small bed.

"Don't worry, it won't be long now. Just try to relax, I'll be here to take good care of you."

He turned his head towards her, his eyes barely open. His vision seemed unfocused and incomplete. It didn't really matter. His memory of her was good enough. Dark red hair that framed her lovely face, golden eyes that seemed to radiate with their own light, and the pale skin that followed the delightful curves of her body. He remembered all of her and hated every part.

"Leave me! I would rather die than to be cursed with you or your life!" His voice came out in a whisper, rather than the shout he intended.

She blinked for a moment, and then smiled knowingly. "You say that now. But you're not in the right frame of mind. Soon you'll understand, when we're together. You once told me that you loved me. I believed you then and I still think you love me even if you deny it. You're fortunate that I'm willing to take the time to teach you, and to care for you." With her fingertips she traced a path from his face down his bare chest, resting them a moment on his stomach before repeating the action. She reached down and circled her fingers around his cock, smiling at her dominance over him.

His arms felt too heavy to slap her hands away, and again he cursed his weakness. He tried to speak, but found his mouth too dry, and now the heavy blanket of sleep started to cover him. His eyes shut one last time, and his life ended as he struggled against the darkness.

* * * *

"Water."

This time she heard him and moved quickly to obtain a cup. She supported his back as he gulped it down.

"More."

The second cup seemed to quench his thirst, and he fell back on his bed. He felt her hands pulling up the blanket to his shoulders, then quickly dropped back to something resembling sleep.

The next time he stayed awake longer and was able to eat a bit of stew. He still raged at her, calling her names and throwing out threats when she was there to listen. But she tolerated his behavior as something expected, and calmly went about her business of making him stronger.

"Would you like more bread?"

He grabbed the slice from her hand. "Don't you know I will kill you when I get strong enough?"

She sighed. "It will be a very long time before that happens. And it's not just the body, but also the mind that has strength." And then for a moment she bore at him with golden eyes that suspended him in a timeless trap and just as quickly released him. "I know how you feel, because once I felt that way towards my mentor."

She sat next to him on the small bed and ran her fingertips from his neck down his chest, coming to rest on his knee, pushing the thin cover down as she did so. Though she had released him from her direct mental control, he could still feel the remnants of its power, and couldn't do anything to stop her from touching him. He was more aware than ever of being naked on the small bed, unable to muster the strength to walk out of the room.

The woman seemed to understand his plight, and moved her hand to his upper leg, massaging his inner thigh gently. She slid her fingers up to his leg and dragged them over his groin before stopping to play with his pubic hair. She sported the look of a modest victory, such as one would use to gloat after winning a chess game. Despite his feelings towards her and his fear of what he was becoming, his own body started to betray him as his loins reacted to her touch. She pulled her hand away and stood up just as he was beginning to exert control on his arms again. Rose-Marie looked down at him, surveying his body, before pulling the blanket over him again.

"I could make you love me again, but I would rather it happens again on its own accord. And it will, you won't be able to stop yourself."

He said nothing more, fearing she was right. Who else but she could he have? Who else would care for him? He finished eating the bread. His stomach was full, but the hunger had not subsided. Rose-Marie had asked him if he wanted to feed, and he refused to admit he had the urge to do so. She merely smiled and went out that night to satisfy her own needs.

* * * *

"You must feed soon, or you'll get very sick, and then finally die."

"I would rather die than become the devil's instrument!"

She laughed, covering her mouth as she did so. "The devil's instrument? Where did you come up with that one? You are a predator, nothing more or less. Unless you think that lions are devil's instruments too? How about bears, or wolves, or hawks? You're still human, only of a superior form. You have the right to live, and the power to do it. So stop feeling sorry for yourself."

He glared at her, not knowing how to respond. She walked over to him, kissed him on his forehead and left the room. He was alone again with thoughts that swirled in his mind. He was a prisoner to his contemplation as well as to the room. Rose-Marie had done something to his mind that wouldn't allow him to leave the room, proof about her earlier convection that her mind's strength ranged far above his. But that didn't stop him from planning.

* * * *

The sound of footsteps down the hall stirred him from his half slumber. He turned away from the door as it opened, not wanting to give her any reason to think he needed her company.

"Look dear, what I have brought you."

He slowly turned to see what she had, and was startled by her gift.

"Isn't she lovely? Come here and hold her." The petite and pretty young woman had a glazed look in her eyes.

"No, let her go!" But even as he said the words he found himself standing up, and he could feel his upper gums starting to throb from pain.

"But she wants you. She needs you." Rose- Marie led the unresisting girl to him. "You shouldn't resist. It is the right thing to do. She wants you to do it."

Now he felt and tasted the trickle of his own blood as his gums split open to accommodate the new teeth. His hunger increased as the girl came closer, and he could only manage a slow shake of his head when she stood in front of him. He could feel the warmth of her body,

131

and the scent of her causing his new teeth to tingle, like an electric current ran through them.

Rose-Marie seemed to enjoy his torment, and laughed at his weakened resolve. "You must give in now. Look at her." With a hard pull she ripped open the girl's blouse, revealing two small breasts. She grabbed his hand and placed it on the exposed flesh, the nipples hard to his touch.

He was surprised to hear the girl softly moan with pleasure at his touch. He moved closer, his hands running over her bare chest as her cries grew louder. He felt dizzy, and as the room disappeared he could only focus on the helpless woman. He felt almost out of control as he started to kiss her lips, and then he suddenly plunged down to her neck. His blood boiled as he opened his jaw and...

It was the most glorious feeling. A bolt of electricity started at his mouth and perpetrated every part of his being. The rest of the room disappeared in his excitement as the explosion of physical and mental pleasure flooded him. His mind became linked to hers as he rode a constant wave of ecstasy. He could not get enough as he clung to his victim until she cried out, then went limp, and gradually fell to the floor.

"I think you've had enough. That was a rather long feeding for someone who would rather die."

"I don't know why I did that. I didn't mean to lose control." He slumped on the bed. "Is she going to be all right? Did I...?" He stopped speaking, knowing the answer.

"Just lie down and take it easy. The first feedings are like this." She lifted the body up and carried her to the door. "You will learn to temper your thirst. I'll take care of her."

* * * *

During the next few feedings he learned to use control. He still resented her but had held back his comments as he looked for a way to strike his revenge. She released her hold on him, knowing that he had no other place to turn. And she continued to teach him on how to survive.

"Only feed on the same victim twice. Three if you absolutely must, but after that there is a great risk of turning them into a vampire."

"Why do you care if they become vampires as well?"

"Because, dear Rodney, we do not need more competition for our feedings. More vampires will mean a greater chance of us being exposed, and the superstitious peasants will start hanging garlic bulbs at their doors." She shook her head in disgust. "But there's another good reason why you should not return to the same woman too many times."

"What is that?"

She leaned forward, her hand resting on his thigh. "I'm the jealous type. And I would kill her without a second thought to keep what is mine."

Her eyes showed no betrayal in what she said. And he sat horrified at the full implications of her words; he remained her prisoner for as long as he lived. Or as long as she did.

That night he came back late to the old house. She waited up for him, wearing a nightgown by the fireplace. He only nodded in reply to her greeting and slumped in a chair by the fire, feeling chilled to the bone.

"Any luck?"

"No. Not this time." In reality he didn't look for a victim at all, but spent the time walking up and down the streets thinking.

"You must be careful about staying out so late. Don't get caught in the morning sun, it would be unfortunate to lose you."

"I miss the sun, the daytime."

"I used to. But after a while you will forget about it, and learn to live after dusk."

"There must be something better to living at night, than only to feed and hide."

"There is." She opened her nightgown and dropped it to the floor. "Come to me, let us share the rest of the night together."

She was still beautiful to his eyes, but not his mind. Still, he felt his teeth sliding out of their concealment, ready to do his feeding.

"No, Rodney. You must never bite another vampire. A vampire's blood is poison to another. Like venom, it's very deadly even in small doses." She wrapped her arms around him. "So we will make love the old-fashioned way, and with no biting."

He took off his own clothes and they tumbled together by the fireplace. His thoughts only on her. Or, more accurately, on what she had told him. The sex was still good, though it paled in comparison to feeding. Part of the problem, he thought, was that it was hard to make love to someone you hated. Still he didn't have a problem obtaining an erection as he kissed her lips, neck and breasts. He sucked on her nipples as his fingers touched her clit and then slid inside. As soon as she was wet he inserted his cock inside her, wanting to finish as soon as he could, not caring that she also reached her climax.

* * * *

Rodney followed her when he had the chance and quickly figured out the type of men she preferred. Much like himself, which wasn't really a surprise. He also noticed how she would set up a future feeding by stalking the victim a few nights early, leaving them with a hypnotic suggestion that would make the rest of the seduction easier when the time came.

And now she had set up the next offering, the young man seemed quite taken by her beauty.

After she left, Rodney approached him. "Nice-looking woman."

The young man seemed nervous about talking to a stranger this late at night. Most strangers wanted some spare coin. And were prepared to roll you for it. Still, the young man couldn't ignore the comment, made in the relative security of the tavern.

"Yes, she is at that." "Tell me, are you going to meet her again?"

"Yes, I am."

"When and where?" Rodney stared at him, willing the information from him.

"Two nights from now, at Garland Bridge on the west side. At midnight."

"Now, listen very carefully. You will not meet her at the bridge. There has been a change of plans. Is that clear?"

"Yes."

But Rodney could tell it wasn't clear to his mind. Two contradicting orders. To meet or not to. "Good. Now, give me your hat and coat and go home. And do not go to the Garland Bridge two nights from now."

* * * *

Two nights later saw a troubled man trying to decide whether he should be at the bridge or not. He kept walking away and then returning. Then on his final return visit he saw the stranger, wearing his coat and hat, standing by the wooden posts that supported the bridge. The woman, the one with red hair, approached him from behind. The man kept his collar up and his head down as she spoke to him, only slowly turning sideways as she pulled at his arm. He could only hear her voice as she tried to maneuver him out of sight, the man declining to speak. Suddenly her mouth pounced at his neck; the man did not resist the attack, merely lifting his head. Then a moment later she began to shriek at him.

"You bastard! You have poisoned me! Why? Why? I loved you. Why did you do this?!" She fell to her knees, her hands pulling at his coat.

The stranger didn't reply at first, merely stepping backward in an attempt to distance himself from her.

"You damn bastard! I curse you!" She fell to the ground on her side, curling up from pain, her voice getting weaker.

"Sorry, but you left me no other choice."

Whether she heard him or not was difficult to say, for she became silent and lay still.

"I hope God forgives both of us. And I promise I will never do what you have done to me."

And that promise he kept. At least for another one hundred and fifty years.

Chapter One

"A vampire! Sheldon, are you serious?"

"Of course, Harry. Have I ever made up a story before?" The big guy finished off his beer in a quick gulp. "You don't think that I make them up do you?" He suddenly looked alarmed at the possibility that someone didn't believe everything he said.

Careful, we don't want to get him upset. As far as believing his stories, well, that was hard to say. Some of his stories were pretty fantastic, but he did tell them so well that...let us just say they sounded like the truth. "Of course not. They're a little different from my own experiences, but they are quite plausible." I hoped that would mollify him.

My name is Harry Webster. Most people know of me as a columnist for the local paper, writing about events in the city and special interest stories, like the sixty-eight year old grandmother taking up skiing for the first time. But I also write stories secretly under the name Edwin Drood, named after a character in the unfinished murder mystery of Charles Dickens. I use the cover of Harry Webster to hunt down those stories that can make it feel like a piece of ice has just touched your spine.

I met Sheldon at one of those forgettable grand openings and something about him made me wonder about him. According to his acquaintances he likes to tell tall tales; tales he insists are true. Second, it seems he dabbles in the arts, and I'm not talking about paintings. One young man confided in me he believes he's a warlock, prosperous perhaps, but I've seen stranger things, like vampires. Laugh at it as urban myth, but I've seen bits of evidence of their existence and apparently Sheldon knows one personally. Now if I can get him to talk about it without arousing his suspicions I might find out where this vampire is hiding.

"Good, because I only repeat what I know is the truth. But I must be going, I'm an old man and I need my sleep." He looked towards the bar and got Nancy's attention with a wave.

This was ridiculous. Sheldon may be old, how old is hard to say, but I doubt he goes to bed early. He keeps himself in shape, maybe by lifting weights or by swimming, and in truth has the body of a thirty year old. Only his white hair gives a hint of being a senior citizen. And man, can he attract the ladies. But the trouble now was to convince

Sheldon to stay and tell his tale of the vampire. His stories are always interesting, and though one may doubt their authenticity, they always make you wonder.

"How much do I owe you this time, my dear?"

"Only a couple of dollars. Do you really have to leave so soon?" Nancy placed the bill on the table, and rested a hand on his shoulder. "Gee, you smell nice. Is that a new aftershave?"

"I'm afraid so. An old man like myself needs his sleep. And, yes, that is a new aftershave. A lady acquaintance gave it to me as a gift." He picked up the bill. "Say, you bought me a drink. That was very kind of you."

Nancy beamed at him for noticing the drink. Like all women, she seemed to find him fascinating. Damn him. As for Nancy, she had dark features, a lovely smile and eyes that always had a sparkle to them. And tonight she wore her mini-skirt, a nice change from her usual jeans.

"Here's a ten spot. Keep the change and put it towards your college fund."

Incredible, he gives her a big tip, but to his buddies he's known as being a tight wad with his money. I have lost count of the number of lunches and drinks he has coerced out of us.

"Why, thank you Sheldon. You have a nice evening."

"Wait." I couldn't let Sheldon off the hook from his vampire story. "Nancy, why don't you bring us two more beers, and put it on my tab?"

Nancy looked at Sheldon for his reaction and he hesitated, and then very reluctantly nodded. "Well, I suppose one more won't hurt, if you insist, Harry." Nancy turned back towards the bar. "Oh, and Nancy, could you also bring me a steak sandwich? Medium rare."

Now she looked at me for the OK. A beer is one thing; food is another. I pondered my answer for a moment, and glanced at her legs. Rather nice legs. That was a good enough sign. "Sure, put the sandwich on my tab, too. Sheldon, I thought you ate supper."

"Oh, that was hours ago. And I shouldn't drink on an empty stomach. Us old men have to be careful, you know."

What does he mean 'us old men'?

* * * *

"Aha! So Rodney is also a vampire."

Sheldon looked mildly annoyed. "Of course he is. Did I give any indication that he wasn't?"

"No, but..."

"Well then stop making such obvious statements. Now where was I?"

"Drinking beer." On my tab I might add.

"Here's your steak sandwich, Sheldon." Nancy placed the plate before him, smiling away. "Do you want sour cream on your potato?"

"Yes, please. Make it two scoops and add some of those bacon bits as well."

I couldn't believe that he lived as long as he did eating food like that. Perhaps there is hope for me after all.

"Sheldon, this vampire you are talking about, doesn't seem much like, well, Dracula." Nancy placed one knee on an empty chair and leaned on our table towards Sheldon. "Like he's small, rather unimposing, wears glasses, and sleeps under an electric blanket. And he eats macaroni and cheese."

"That may be so, but since vampires were people of all walks of life before they became victims, shouldn't they represent all types of people as well? As for his diet he needs to feed off others, that is true. But that would not be his is only source of nourishment."

The trouble with Sheldon is that he could make preposterous situations seem quite reasonable. But there was something missing in his story. "What about a coffin. Don't vampires sleep in coffins?"

"Well, at one time they did. And there were several reasons for that. One, it provided protection against sunlight. Two, it offered refuge from intruders. When a vampire sleeps, which is not sleep so much as hibernation, they are rather defenceless. People are rather superstitious about opening coffins so they became good hiding places. And lastly the coffin provided some warmth for the vampire. They have trouble maintaining body heat and during periods of inactivity such as sleep they lose body heat easily. Incidentally, the reason vampires are pictured with a cape and high collar is also for warmth. The collar protects the neck from the chill air and the cape acts like a second coat."

"What about the glasses? And why were the eyes golden?" I notice the beer mugs were empty. "Nancy, why don't you bring a jug? This may take awhile."

"He was near-sighted, that's why he wore glasses. Though they didn't fit too well. But their eyes shone golden simply because of pigmentation. They're very good in seeing in the dark and like most creatures that can see well at night, their eyes would reflect what available light there was and that gave the appearance that they glowed."

Nancy stood up. "So he had good night vision. That would be handy in some of the bars around here. But it's hard to picture a vampire needing an electric blanket."

"Well, as matter of fact there was another reason he didn't sleep in a coffin."

"What was that?"

"The poor guy suffers from claustrophobia."

Chapter Two

The streetlights reflected back by the wet streets of Saint John. Though it had stopped raining hours ago the saturated air refused to accept any more moisture and the puddles of water remained behind. A lonely figure walked quickly through one of them towards home. With a turned up jacket collar, he had thrust his hands inside the pockets and had hunched up his shoulders. Still, perhaps in part of his small frame, he could not keep warm, and the occasional shiver ran through him. As he walked he would sometimes dart out a hand to push up his black-framed glasses as they slid down his nose.

The evening proved uneventful and he was anxious to make himself something to eat when he returned to his apartment. The chill air, with the weak smell of the ocean, had caused his hunger to mount. He was reviewing what was in his cupboards when he heard the laughter. At least two men by the sound of it. He rounded the final corner of his journey and the voices became much louder. He looked up and saw two young men approaching him. As they angled down the sidewalk, obviously suffering the effects of alcohol, they boomed out hearty laughs after each comment they made.

Unfortunately for him the type of people who lived in his neighborhood were not always the best of character. He started to hug the brick wall as they approached to allow them to pass. Now they noticed him, sized him up for a moment, and relinquished part of the sidewalk as they passed, lowering their voices marginally as well.

Relieved that they were not troublemakers, he hurried on his way to his third-floor walkup. When you stand only about five foot six it was not easy to avoid confrontations. He was certain he could have handled the men without too many difficulties but the fewer incidents, the better.

In his apartment he first secured the door and then turned on the stove. A few minutes later he had prepared macaroni and cheese along with a hot dog wiener. He sat down at the kitchen table, the only table in the apartment in fact, and wolfed down his supper. A few minutes later the plate sat in the sink as he undressed for bed. He secured the bedroom door, climbed into bed, and set the electric blanket on low. Sleep came easily to him, as usual.

Day break came to the good people of Saint John, and many of them were waking up or were already on their way to work. But in a small apartment bedroom a figure would sleep throughout the day. Actually you would have to look very carefully indeed to detect any breathing at all. Only the slow and shallow rise and fall of his chest indicated that Rodney was still alive.

* * * *

An hour after sunset, there was a stirring in the apartment's bedroom. The window effectively blocked sunlight from entering the room by a combination of aluminium foil and plywood, therefore Rodney depended on his biological clock as well as a clock radio, to inform him it was time to rise. He yawned, stretched, and gradually found his way to the door, and unlocked it.

Tea and toast. He had his usual breakfast as he listened to radio. Nothing much, except an appeal by the Red Cross for blood donations. He would pass on that.

"What is your blood type, sir?"

"Whatever type is available."

He took a quick shower, dressed, and headed out the door.

The sky shone clear, making it a nice change from the last three days of light rain. Still, the air felt cool, and he felt the need to hurry to work to avoid being outside longer than necessary. His path took him towards downtown and as he entered within the areas of restricted parking and heavier traffic he encountered a few others travelling down the sidewalks. He shied away from a group of young men standing outside a pizza joint. Probably too young to gain admittance to a bar, they would hang out in places they could get in if they had enough money. Individually they were not much of a bother. But in a group they had a tendency to exert their influence, usually on someone small such as himself. So he found himself skirting the outside of the sidewalk. He heard a comment made about him, superior hearing allowing him to overhear conversations, and he quickened his steps. Fortunately there was not a follow-up action to the remark, the wisecrack not made seriously. Still Rodney was always on guard, trying to avoid confrontations whenever possible. When it wasn't feasible, he was more than capable of defending himself. Vampires had a few advantages over others. They had higher degrees of smell and hearing, better night vision, faster reflexes and strength out of proportion to their size. Which was great in most circumstances, but might not suffice against a group. Especially if one of them had a weapon. And the last thing a vampire needs is situations where police might be involved. A daytime visit might be required to a police station or a courthouse.

So he mentally breathed a sigh of relief and headed down the block, turned a corner and almost tripped over a dog that was leaving a territorial mark. The canine looked at him, sensed something strange about him and hurried away. Many dogs acted that way to him. Some attacked while others thought of him as one of their own and would tag along with him throughout the night. Cats were better. They usually just ran away.

Halfway down the block two women were approaching him. He straightened up and slowed his pace a bit, not from the vampire aspect but from the nature of a man drawing close to attractive women. They were talking in low voices, sharing a joke as they giggled at a comment. Both were good-looking in different ways and were dressed for an evening of socializing. Their coats hid most of their clothes but the brunet was wearing tight jeans, while the lady with lighter hair wore a short skirt. The taller brunet was slim but was well endowed at top; her companion had a more hourglass figure and it was her that triggered a sudden change in his breathing.

Rodney looked at the legs, enjoying the sight and then looked up at her face. She was looking at him and he felt a moment of awkwardness, but only a moment. She had a lovely face that froze his eyes to her. As they passed she smiled, he smiled back, and he found his heart racing. He turned to watch her as they walked away and a feeling almost alien to him washed over him, a feeling a predator normally doesn't feel towards prey. His teeth started their outward journey but when he focused his thoughts on going to work they slid back to their hiding place.

Twenty minutes later he entered the side door of a three-story building with a key marked 'Do Not Copy' and went to a small door by the elevators. Inside the room was an assortment of mops, pails and cleaning supplies. Hauling them out, he proceeded to his circuit of wiping, cleaning, emptying and otherwise restoring the offices to their former state. A few hours later he finished, and now he replaced the items back in the closet. He opened his bag lunch, ate his sandwiches and then left the building. It was time for a vampire to do what he had to do to live and this time he didn't worry if his fangs started to expose themselves a bit.

* * * *

Sheldon refilled the beer glasses, picked his up, drank most of it in one long swallow and then refilled his glass. It was amazing what he could consume; he not only had a second supper with the steak sandwich but also out-drank me two to one. All the while telling his story. His jaws must be working overtime.

"This vampire had a job as a caretaker? Not quite the image I had of them."

"There's nothing wrong with being a caretaker!" One thing with Sheldon was that he was a bit unpredictable in reaction to offhand comments. Sheldon's raised voice caused a couple at a nearby table to glance in our direction. "I'll have you know that I know a number of people who are caretakers, and they are fine, educated people. Furthermore..."

"That's not what I meant." I waved my hands at him as he slowly increased the volume. "I was just surprised he worked at all. I thought that he might be independently wealthy."

"And that he lived in a castle?" Sheldon's outburst disappeared as rapidly as it appeared. His face was already losing its red color, and his body relaxed back into his chair. In a quieter, mater-of-fact voice Sheldon continued. "Really, you must realize that just about everyone needs some income. There aren't too many rich people who don't have to work and few of them are vampires."

Which implied that there were some vampires who were rich but I decided to let that go. "So why did he choose to be a caretaker?"

"Well, Rodney, he had to have an income somehow and very few jobs require only night work. Dayshifts are obviously not a consideration. The second problem is that he does not have proper identification. Simple things like a driver's license, credit cards, and bank accounts all require social insurance numbers. And the government does not easily hand out such numbers to people 187 years old."

"And being a caretaker gets around this problem?"

"Yes, first it is a night job. Second, he works under a contract, eliminating much of the normal identification information required by employers. He set up a bank account using false ID. He is a bit nervous about the income tax people asking questions but so far they haven't been too demanding. Just a few letters requesting more information."

Nancy came by in time to hear the last bit of the conversation. After refilling Sheldon's glass she joined into the question period. "What about other things like credit cards?"

"None of that. He really doesn't exist to any consumer credit companies. The government wouldn't know anything about him except for paying some taxes. When and if they start getting too close he will simply disappear, like he has a dozen times before by moving to another city."

"Doesn't he get kinda lonely?"

"Of course. No friends, though he does make a few acquaintances. The dilemma vampires face is that a solitary existence is the safest one for them. But how long can people live without company?"

"Can't he live with other vampires?" I drained the rest of my beer, and picked up the pitcher to refill it.

Sheldon held out his glass for a refill. Where does he put it? "No, vampires are too territorial to tolerate other vampires. Sometimes a couple will live together for a while but the relationship would be tedious. The nature of the vampire to feed on members of the opposite sex would cause jealousy. Vampires are predators and like most predators, they do not like competition."

"You said vampires prefer members of the opposite sex. Why would that be? Blood is blood, isn't it?"

"Well, not to Rodney. Let me explain by an example."

Chapter Three

Rodney moved quietly down the streets. The hunt was on, and his metabolism started to switch to a higher mode. His breathing became deeper, the senses keener. Soon he found himself in familiar territory, just outside the downtown area. He waited a short distance from a convenience store, and observed the people entering and leaving. He ignored the young men that entered left as a group. A couple came and left quickly, probably to pick up cigarettes. He waited for a lone person this time, not wanting to expend too much effort for this feeding by having to overpower two people. A single woman drove up and jumped out of her car. He moved across the street and waited by the outside of the building. The young blonde paid at the counter and headed out the door.

She saw him. He looked into her eyes. She hesitated a moment, the golden eyes holding her...then Rodney disappeared, watched her looked confused, and get into her car. . Rodney watched the car turn the corner and then continued to watch the store. She would have been fine, but as she came closer he could smell alcohol on her breath. He didn't like to feed on blood that wasn't healthy. Now a new car drove up. A woman in her thirties stepped out of her Honda and hurried into the store. The clerk looked at her as she came in and offered her a greeting as she approached him.

"Hi, could you tell me where you keep something for upset stomachs?"

"Just over there." He pointed with his arm. "At the far end aisle." Like most of the customers in the store she could locate milk, pop, magazines and cigarettes, but little else.

"Thanks. My daughter ate too much candy or cake at her friend's birthday party." She walked quickly to the area indicated to her, made a selection of pink fluid, and after a moment of hesitation, also picked a bottle of ginger ale. Two minutes later she paid for the items and left the store.

He was standing by her car, and she slowed her walk as she came closer. He was small in stature and did not pose a serious threat. Still, she felt a bit apprehensive as he approached. Until she looked at his eyes, golden eyes that held her gaze. Suddenly she understood, and opened the passenger door for him. She stepped into the driver's seat and drove out of the parking lot.

He guided her down unfamiliar streets, leaving the heavier travelled roads to a quiet one that wound its way past some residential areas before coming to open fields. The rural area had the look of unsuccessful farming; the pasture did not seem to be able to support either animals or crop. A bit farther down the road he directed her to park by a small grove of trees.

"It's getting really warm in here."

"Take off your jacket. It will be cooler."

She slipped off her jacket, still feeling the warmth that came from within her. Her breathing increased as he started to move his hands up and down her thighs and then began to kiss her neck. She closed her eyes, enjoying his touches. In the back of her mind she wanted him to stop, knew that it was wrong, but the thought was suppressed. Her skin started to tingle as hands started to move under her shirt and her mind could only focus on how good it felt. She shifted her position and after he helped pull off her shirt leaned forward so that he could remove her bra.

His lips moved down from her neck, kissing as he went downward. She moaned as he moved both his hands and lips over her body, feeling a flush of new heat; she felt more sensuous that she had ever felt before, not wanting him to stop. She started to cry out, urging him on as she undid her jeans and pushed them down. She thought she was having the most erotic dream she ever had and wasn't responsible for what happened. Rodney kissed her breasts and gently pinched her nipples with his fingers as he lowered his head. He licked at her pussy, encountering a problem with the steering wheel that banged on the back of his head when she reacted to his tongue. He swore, wishing he had moved her to the backseat first as she struggled to spread her legs, her jeans and panties bunched around her ankles.

Rodney touched her mind and determined that the moment was near. As her body started to tense up he moved back to her neck, then opened his mouth to expose his teeth to her soft skin. He pushed at her mind a bit more, giving her the final release the instant he bit down. She cried out loudly as he continued to feed, both of them wrapped up in their own passion. He was careful not to overfeed, and a minute later brought her back to a near normal state.

She was still in a bit of a daze as he helped her get dressed, and he carefully wiped away the blood from her neck. As they drove back to the convenience store he talked to her, reinforcing the story of what had happened.

As she headed home she hoped the medicine would help her daughter's stomach. And she was glad she could help the young couple who was lost, showing them the way to the highway. She didn't remember the woman very well, but the man was unusual. Something about his eyes.

* * * *

"So why did this vampire pick her?" Nancy was becoming more interested in the story as time progressed. Also she was becoming more interesting to look at, perhaps something to do with the beer.

"As I pointed out earlier, vampires prefer people with healthy blood. Rodney claims he can taste a definite difference between healthy blood and that of those who are under the weather."

"So that was why he refused the woman who had been drinking. Why did he take his victim out to the country to feed and what was the purpose of necking with her first?"

"Again it has to do with the taste of blood. Rodney claims, and I have no way of validating this, that blood fed from an aroused victim is much better. He said that trace chemicals make the feeding last longer, that he doesn't have to feed as often if he chooses a healthy female that is excited. I suppose males would provide the same benefit but he prefers to feed only on women. The reason for driving out to the deserted area was for privacy, it wouldn't be good to get caught feeding from someone's neck. The time to drive also allows for him to condition her mind both before and after. The victim believed only that she helped out a couple in trouble." Sheldon finished off his glass of beer and picked up the food menu again. "What are your chicken wings like?"

Chapter Four

Rodney opened the apartment door, did his usual quick glance to see if any intruders had entered during his absence, and then secured the door behind him. He went to the bathroom to brush his teeth, his breath after feeding could be most unpleasant, and then took a quick shower. He turned on his radio and then picked up the book he was currently reading. The book had his attention for a while but after an hour his thoughts drifted back to the events of the day. His feeding had gone rather well, he had received enough nourishment to last him for some time, perhaps a good week or week and a half. His victim had not suffered much, other than a loss of time, and there was little chance of his identity being disclosed.

All that was well and good. But his mind drifted to the lady walking on the sidewalk who had given him a smile. That made him feel good and it brought forth the realization that he was very lonely. His life was devoid of friends, and relationships of any kind did not seem possible. He remembered his own experience of being turned into a vampire. Perhaps he didn't have to force someone to be a vampire; they could still have an intimate relationship. The idea lingered for only a moment before he shoved it away and shook his head at the crazy thought. It wasn't feasible. His world opened the doors to a long life and a body that was physically better than other humans. However that meant other doors closed. He had to learn to accept what he could have and what he could not have.

He went to bed wishing for things a vampire shouldn't wish for.

* * * *

"So are we supposed to feel sorry for this vampire? Of course he's friendless. Who could be friends with someone who wanted to feed on their neck?" I didn't believe that Rodney should expect any better fate than he had.

"Your point has been made by others before. But the problem still remains that people enjoy relationships with others and when that is taken away we have a difficult situation."

Nancy placed the chicken wings on the table and took part in the conversation. "So what did he do? Give in to his loneliness and go after some girl?"

"Well, you will have to listen to my story to find out. But you have to remember the time when he first became a vampire, he vowed he would never do the same to another."

"I gather from the story that these vampires can turn another person only by repeated feedings, right? Otherwise the town would be swarming with vampires." Nancy was asking questions that I would have asked if I had not drunk so much beer. Well I still would have asked them but perhaps at a slower interval.

"Right. Some people can resist the virus better than others. But usually it would take at least three or four feedings within a year for the change to take place."

"Virus?"

"Yes, a virus actually causes the transformation of a person into a vampire. I'll explain that later."

"So why does he have to bite? Couldn't he just not bite people he liked?"

"Possibly, but the urge to bite would be very strong. And when a vampire is aroused, either by hunger pains or by sexual excitement, his teeth move outward. He can't really control or stop his teeth from moving past his lips. And the sight of those fangs is likely to disturb his friends."

"But what if they knew he was a vampire and learned not to be worried by their sight?"

"Rodney wouldn't trust his secret to anyone. A slip of a tongue could be the end for him. A vampire doesn't live long if he isn't a bit paranoid. Besides, wouldn't you be nervous around him if his teeth started to show? Even if you were friends?"

"I suppose so. But it would be kinda neat to know a vampire. And the thought of a vampire biting a neck is a rather alluring."

"That's one of the strange things about the relationship between vampires and people. The victim finds the predator erotically appealing. Many women find the image of being bitten in the neck by a vampire rather seductive." Sheldon shook his head slowly, unable to comprehend that thought.

Nancy laughed as she headed to the next table. "It just shows how strange us women can be." I noticed she was touching her neck with her fingertips as she walked away.

* * * *

"So he would also go to bars to pick women? That would seem easier than waiting for the right victim by the Seven-Eleven store." I watched horrified as Sheldon finished the last of the beer and signaled Nancy to bring another pitcher. If I drank much more I was going to have trouble walking out of here. Three glasses ago I had decided that I was going home by cab. Sheldon didn't even slow down.

"Well it would be at first glance. But most people in a bar have too much alcohol in their systems for Rodney's liking. They also have to be unattached and be able to follow him out of the bar without too much fuss. The second problem is that he cannot frequent the bar too much. Some of the patrons may start to get suspicious when young ladies leave with him on consecutive nights, without remembering what happened afterwards. The young lady who went with him this last time would ask questions on where they went. She would not be able to remember hardly any detail. Perhaps not even what he looked like. And if too many incidents like that occurred you can bet he would be in a difficult situation. People would talk and soon he would be noticed. So his method was to try a place, then not return for a few weeks. This meant he was always looking out for a new place, and new victims."

"You mentioned something about a virus that caused people to turn into vampires."

"That's right. The virus lives in the hollow of the vampire's teeth. It may also survive in other parts of the mouth, but is transmitted from the teeth during feeding. Usually the body has the ability to kill the virus the first time it is exposed. Most victims after a vampire feeding feel like they had a touch of the flu, as well as fatigue from the loss of blood. However the virus is normally killed easily after the first attack. If a second attack and then a third, or even a fourth attack was to occur too soon, the body would be unable to resist the virus. If enough of the virus survives it attacks the host's genes, altering them in subtle ways. That is the reason a person turning into a vampire succumbs to deep sleep, the body requires a lot of energy to transform itself. This deep sleep, of course, resembles that of a dead person. The loss of blood causes a pale complexion and combined with a lower body temperature gives an impression of death. Then they awaken, giving rise to stories of the walking dead."

"So a vampire is the result of a virus? Is there not a cure for it?"

"Well obviously not much research is placed into this virus. There are other side effects as well. The vampire becomes sterile. Procreation, which is strong in all species, is possible only through the creation of another vampire. I mentioned superior strength and reflexes and also an increased sense of smell. The eyes change so they can see extremely well in the dark; unfortunately they become too sensitive to light and a vampire becomes blind in normal daylight."

"What about their inability to stand sunlight at all?"

"Oh, there is that problem as well. Also, unfortunately for the vampire, the blood loses some of its effectiveness and the vampire requires a supplemental blood supply to keep it alive. I'll give you more details on that a bit later."

Chapter Five

The bar scene was always a nervous place for Rodney. There was a chance of being involved in a fight. He could handle himself quite well but if he got hurt, well, most hospitals did not understand a vampire's special needs. A small-framed man like himself sometimes stood as an easy target for those out to prove how tough they were. So he now felt a bit more relaxed as he checked out the shopping mall. Most people shopped or walked about in pairs. Some in an entire group. He kept looking, munching on a bag of chips as he did so. He looked in a couple of stores but did not see any potential. Then in a women's clothing store he saw her.

The woman who had given him a smile that night. Her hair was shoulder length and she tossed it as she held up a dress to her girlfriend and laughed. She wasn't tall but wore high heels with her short skirt. His heart started to race. He dropped his bag of chips and felt his teeth sliding out of his gums. Frantically he walked away, completely unnerved by what he felt. A minute later his teeth were again hidden and he stopped to rest on a mall bench.

This was not good; he couldn't afford to have feelings like that. Besides his teeth his loins indicated his interest in her, and that hadn't happened for a long, long time. He told himself to stay focused on the problem. He came here to find a victim. He needed to feed, so he better find someone else. He got up and went down the other side of the mall.

Inside the shoe store he watched another young woman make her purchase. She walked out of the store alone. He approached her, gazing at her eyes as he came closer.

"Yes?" She stopped to stare back at him.

Damn! He held her eyes but forgot to send a strong message on what he wanted. He tried to center his thoughts on the task at hand. Good. She started to move her mind to where he could bend her will. She nodded to his quietly spoken suggestion and headed to the exit doors.

They stepped out into the night air. He would lead her a few blocks to a secluded spot behind an old garage he had used before.

"Patricia! Where are you going?" A man burst through the exit doors. "What are you doing with my daughter? Who are you?" He stepped at a rapid pace. His hands clenched into fists. There wasn't time to give Patricia a message she could use as an excuse. Rodney panicked, and ran. His speed would have attracted attention if there were any people who could have seen him. In a flash he had covered the parking lot. He looked back at the man shaking his fist at him, still standing at the mall doors.

Rodney went back to his apartment. That woman had distracted him. None had ever done that to him before; at least to the extent it broke his concentration. And it had very nearly caused him a major problem. He should have verified that his target was alone. He mustn't let thoughts of that woman distract him again.

He wondered what her name was.

* * * *

After a restless sleep, for a vampire, Rodney strolled down the streets inhaling deeply the night air. He wasn't trying to pick up a scent though he had done so on occasion in the past. This time he just enjoyed the flavors that the night brought forth and a vampire's keen sense of smell could pick out many subtle nuances. He really needed to feed tonight but didn't feel the urgency yet. If he did fail there was always some food at the apartment that could hold him for a couple more days. When that couldn't sustain his needs any longer, he could always resort to the old standby of raw liver.

That had kept him going for up to a week in the past. But it couldn't give him the proper nourishment that human blood could. Especially the blood of young ladies. The thought sent his teeth out past his gums and he had to suppress his thoughts to cause them to retreat once more. No, his hunger felt more mental than physical this time. He sometimes only fed when he began to feel physically ill. But not tonight. He was going to enjoy this feeding. Rodney didn't consider why he felt this way. A vampire's needs are as complex as any person's. But in the back of his mind lingered the image of the woman. The one with the smile.

He walked down one street after another. Usually he had a plan, a destination. But not tonight. He let his legs carry him where they wanted. Pedestrian traffic was light since he was moving outside the downtown area. Near a small park he came across a single woman. She appeared to be alone, and moved quickly through the park so that he came up from behind her. He was ready to make his move when he heard the movement to his right. Twenty feet away walked a dog. He looked back at the woman and could now see a folded leash in her hand. Damn! That was close. He didn't want to tangle with a dog. He turned away and headed back up the street.

Old wives' tales tell of using garlic or a cross to ward off vampires. Some claimed a vampire didn't have a reflection. All of this was nonsense. But vampires did not go near dogs. The animals usually didn't like vampires, and were known to attack with little warning. And they were downright nasty when you were trying to feed on their master. Rodney could have handled the dog and then taken the woman. But it would have been more trouble than it was worth.

A block later he came upon a young lady carrying some groceries from her car.

"Hello."

"Uh, hi. Do I know you?"

Rodney quickly spoke a standard line that he used when a mind was ready to accept suggestions. He used the old friend proposal to bring down the subconscious guard a bit more. "Do you live by yourself?"

"Yes. I live alone." She stopped at her apartment door. "Would you like to come in?"

The apartment, a small one-bedroom crowded with furniture and pictures, gave Rodney a feeling of claustrophobia. He lost his composure for a moment but regained it in time to lead her to the bedroom. She stood at the doorway waiting for him to give directions, her face without a hint of expression. The bedroom was not filled with furniture like the rest of the apartment and the large window gave it a more open appearance. Rodney was able to relax a bit more, and watching her standing at the entrance made his needs come forward once more.

"It's time for you to get ready for bed." He waited for her to move towards the bed, and slowly begun to push new thoughts into her head. She responded as he expected, her breathing changing slightly, becoming deeper and more relaxed. She pulled off her shirt and jeans, discarding them on the floor. Rodney was pleased things were going smoothly for a change. He was working the thoughts into her mind with little effort, the young woman not resisting his suggestions at all. Now she removed her bra, allowing it to drop to the floor. She hooked her thumbs at the waistband of her panties, pushed them down, when he had an unexpected reaction.

He sneezed. And sneezed again. And again. With considerable effort he tried to keep focus on the job at hand. He found her thought patterns scramble, she was losing the dreamlike state where he could control her actions. He started to reshape the thoughts into the coherent pattern he needed. Good. She was back under his direction again.

But what caused this sudden attack of sneezes? A cat? Not likely, he would have felt its presence and the damn thing would have probably attacked him. Cats didn't like him much better than dogs did. He looked around where he was standing when he sneezed the first time. By the head of the bed. He picked up the pillow. And sneezed twice. It was the stupid pillow, or more precisely, the feathers inside it. Allergies to dust and feathers were something he could really do without. He should have taken his antihistamines with him. Rodney tossed the pillow into the closet, wondering how many other vampires suffered from allergies like he did. It would certainly make hanging around old castles difficult. But back to the main concern, namely the young lady who was now lying down on her bed, albeit without the pillow.

Rodney started kissing her neck but she resisted his advances slightly. He could feel her reluctance as he navigated around her mind, pushing here and pulling down resistance as he moved along. Her hands pushed against his chest, a feeble effort to stop the inevitable. He didn't hide in his mental probes what he was, some women found the thought of a vampire seducing them sensual and it did not matter what she knew now.

He continued kissing at her neck and then began a downward journey. He traced his tongue on her chest, and then moved his lips over her breast. She continued to push at his shoulders with her hands but her efforts weakened. Then like a key turning a tumbler in a lock he broke through her mindset. He was free to move her thoughts where he wanted them, the code was cracked and he could do what he wanted without her resistance. As he placed his lips on a nipple she moaned, and her hands lifted from his shoulders and fell above her head, signifying the end to her objection.

Because he was not seducing her in a car or an abandoned building, he took his time. It was relaxing not having to listen or watch for possible intruders. Under his guidance he sent her to ecstasy, holding her at the edge as she cried out. Her body had sheen from the film of perspiration and her hips shifted up as he traced his tongue along the length of her body. Her arms moved about continuously, sometimes her hands grabbed at him; sometimes they touched her own body, and at other times flailed above her head.

It was long enough, his teeth had been tingling for her blood for several minutes. He debated in his mind the best place to strike. The neck was his favorite place; the blood seemed to leap out into his teeth. But he had also fed from the thighs where puncher marks did not show as much, and occasionally from the inside of the elbow. He lifted himself from her legs, trying to decide, when she put her arms around him and pulled his head towards her. She lifted her head to expose her neck. The decision was made for him.

Afterwards, he told her to forget he was here, that she had met a blonde-haired man from Germany. He dressed, and threw a blanket over her. She still smiled in the afterglow as he left the bedroom. He looked at the groceries sitting on the kitchen table, walked over to them and checked their contents. He put the ice-cream in the freezer, meat and vegetables in the fridge. Nothing else was in danger of spoiling so he quietly slipped out of the apartment.

He entered the night air feeling good. He pulled his glasses from his shirt pocket and slipped them into place. The blurs suddenly sharpened into sharp edges of buildings and lights. It was a great night to be alive, even for a lonely vampire. Humming a tune seventy-five years old Rodney crossed the street to make his way home.

Chapter Six

"So is that it about the vampire? I had a feeling you might have killed him during the story." The story was a bit disappointing, the ending lacked a conclusion.

"Who said I was finished?"

Nancy reappeared with beer for Sheldon and coffee for me. "The girl he keeps thinking about, has a major part in the story, doesn't she?"

"Well I don't wish to give away anything. But you are right that she does make Rodney's situation more interesting."

Well it was a good thing she had brought me a coffee. It was obvious the beer was affecting my concentration; I had completely forgotten about the girl. I decided to keep quiet for awhile, lest Sheldon starts lecturing on knowing one's limit.

"Sheldon, how do vampires control the victim's minds, does he read them? Or does he just hypnotize them?"

"Well Nancy, initially there is a hypnotic suggestion involved, but what Rodney does after that is to trigger certain emotions. He said that it is like trying to pick up a broken egg off the floor with your fingers. You have to be agile but also gentle. Once he understands the type of thought patterns his victim has, he can guide them into place. He can't actually read minds, he just controls part of the thought patterns and gets some feedback on their emotional state."

* * * *

Rodney preferred to be unnoticed, privacy was important to avoid detection and possible questions about his lifestyle. Therefore he would change the places he searched for new victims and also alter his route to work. But since the evening he had received a smile from the passing woman, he had heavily favored one particular street as a walkway to work.

He didn't think it would hurt to overuse this street but also could not think of a logical reason he would continue to use it. So what if he saw her again; what possible good could come out of that? Ask her out? Would you like to go out with me? I promise I'll have you home by dawn.

Or did he plan to feed on her, on the one woman in all of Saint John who smiled at him?

Rodney stopped a half block from the street as he considered the question. Puzzled by his own inquires into his motives, for the moment he was oblivious to his surroundings. His thoughts jolted back to reality by the air brakes of a transit bus. His heart jumped a beat by the noise and he quickly started to move his feet again. The bus doors opened as he passed by, depositing three passengers. The first two, a young couple, grabbed each other's hands and disappeared. The last one caused his heart to skip another beat; it was the same woman he had been daydreaming about.

He stared open-mouthed at her. She immediately noticed the small man almost coming to a complete stop while his golden eyes peered at her.

At first she felt nervous, and then he looked vaguely familiar—had she seen him at a nightclub perhaps?— And as she looked back at him he caught himself and turned away embarrassed. Now she remembered him; he was walking in this area a few weeks back. She had commented to Shelly about his eyes being golden, their apparent size increased by his glasses. He not only looked shy and nervous, but his small stature did not cause one to be apprehensive in any event. She looked back at him as he quickly looked away but after a moment turned back at her and their eyes locked.

He appeared uncertain what to do. She knew how he felt, to look away again would appear rude. And to continue to stare would require him to say something or else he would look foolish. She felt some sympathy for his plight and felt some awkwardness herself at staring back at him.

Normally she did not make the first overture to a man but one of them should say something, and it looked like he was going to have trouble doing so. Already she could see him starting to blush and decided to initiate the dialogue; it appeared he lacked some social skills when meeting people.

"Hello. I think I've seen you in this area before."

"Uh, hi." He could feel blood rising to his face. Damn time to start blushing. The thought caused him to blush more. "Yeah, I walk this way to work. Sometimes." Why did I add sometimes? Great conversationalist.

"Oh, where do you work?" They fell in step with each other as the bus pulled away.

"I do work at the Crafton Building. Uh, do you work in this area?" Stop saying uh, she'll think you're an idiot.

"No, my girlfriend lives close by, we're going out for a bit to the bar. Isn't it kind of late to be going to work?" She noticed that though he had a small frame, he had an athlete's body. He moved fluidly and if he were to get rid of those glasses, or at least buy a better pair, he wouldn't be bad-looking at all. She still couldn't get over his eyes though.

"I do night work." Obviously, stupid! "I'm the caretaker for the building, so I do all the cleaning after hours." He looked at her eyes, and his heart raced a little. He was surprised that she showed interest in what he was saying. "Which bar are you going to?"

"Nighthawks, probably. Shelly, that's my girlfriend, and I will check it out. If it's too quiet, we'll try another spot."

"Well, if I finish up on time maybe I could head over there to see if you're still there. That is, if you don't mind."

"That would be great. What time would you be finishing up?" She stopped walking as they drew up to a walkup apartment.

"Around eleven."

"Okay, I'll be at Nighthawks some time between eleven and twelve. By the way, my name is Irene."

"Pleased to meet you Irene." You don't know how pleased. "My name is Rodney."

They parted and with his heart pounding he glanced back as she went up the apartment walkway. Though she wasn't tall her body had the right curves to it. Her skirt was on the short side and he hoped her legs wouldn't attract someone else before he got to the bar.

He thought about what had just happened; he had never once considered putting her under his spell and using mind control. That was really unusual. His teeth had started to slip out past his gums but then had stopped there. That did cause him to be careful how he pronounced words but he was grateful they did not show themselves. This woman was causing a strange reaction in him. A part of his mind warned of the danger up ahead. He didn't care. He was going to see this through and to hell with the consequences.

* * * *

"So Rodney, for the first time since becoming a vampire, has thrown caution to the wind. Vampires can live a very long time, several hundred years, but very few last even a normal person's lifespan."

The bar was now on the quiet side and as midnight approached a few more customers might wander in. But Nancy had everything under control. Tim, the bartender, was cleaning up at his own slow pace, which gave her time to sit down with us. The coffee hadn't had its desired effect yet as I was still under the influence of too much beer.

Which was why I had a quick look at her legs as she crossed them, the hem of her skirt rising higher. She should wear skirts more often.

Oh well, better be mindful to what Sheldon is saying before I get in trouble for not paying attention to his story. And a rather expensive story at that.

"So what will shorten a vampire's life, Sheldon?" I listened to myself speak, which is a sure sign that I have had too much to drink. "Besides a wooden steak through the heart."

"Really, that old story." He shook his head in amazement. "A wooden steak, an iron bar, a bullet, or even a knife. What does it matter? Anything that can stop your heart and kill you will also kill a vampire. They aren't supernatural beings after all. What kills them, more often than not, is disease. If you feed on the blood of other people you will catch whatever they have. True, a vampire has a more resilient immune system than most people, but there is only so much any body can take. AIDS killed many for instance. The problem many vampires had was that many of their victims were those not high on society's list. For example it is easier to go after victims in the less privileged neighborhoods than in the suburbs."

"What about sunlight? Doesn't that kill them as well?"

"Good point. Yes, sunlight is a risk to them, and will kill them if they are caught in daylight. The morning sun isn't too bad, they can survive that for almost an hour. The rest of the day would claim them much faster. Incidentally, even at night there is a danger from the so-called full spectrum lamps, which while not as powerful as natural sunlight, can cause extreme pain to a vampire."

"So why does sunlight affect them so much?" Nancy took a drink from her coffee laced with GM. She shifted position in her chair so that she faced Sheldon. Her interest in the story, or the storyteller was strong. That was okay because it gave me a better look at her legs.

"The virus, when it changed the genetic structure of the human cell, also causes porphyrias. In this case, erythropoietic porphyria. The cells can no longer make heme, which is an essential part of hemoglobin, and this is one of the reasons a vampire must obtain the blood of others. Second, the vampire cannot break down toxic precursors of heme. These are called porphyrins, and when the skin is exposed to sunlight, the proteins react. The skin blisters rapidly, and soon the vampire's skin looks like it is on fire. It isn't long before the vampire dies painfully from the ruptured skin."

160

Good grief. If I knew Latin or had a medical dictionary I might have followed his explanations or at least challenged his reasoning. As I mentioned before he always has an explanation behind his outrageous stories. "How come we never hear of anyone dying that way?"

"Simple. If a vampire is caught in the sunlight, rather than die painfully, they will jump off a building or throw themselves into a lake. Some even carry a gun or poison in the event they are caught out in the sun. And, of course, once they are dead no further skin reactions are possible. And that is the reason we do not hear of sunlight killing vampires." With that he took a large drink of his beer and placed the mug heavily on the table to reinforce that the matter was dealt with. A good storyteller, Sheldon does not allow questions to sidetrack him too long.

"Sheldon, does he meet up with that girl later on?" Nancy leaned forward, she sensed that the story was about to get interesting.

I sensed something as well and excused myself to go the washroom.

* * * *

Rodney hurried down the streets, walking as fast as he could. He would have run but that would have attracted too much attention. It was a long time since any woman took any sort of interest in him. Mind you, a lot of that was his own doing, making sure no one noticed him as much as possible. Women tend to ignore men hiding in shadows. But he felt he was ready now to meet someone.

He craved a chance to talk to someone not hypnotized, someone who would like him as he was. He was under no illusions about how far such a relationship could go. She could not find out he was a vampire. And he promised himself that he would never use her for feeding. It was time for a human-to-human relationship.

The bar was not crowded, and he was able to spot her right away, sitting at a large table with her friend and three other men. Rodney felt nervous approaching the group and they were laughing at a joke when Shelly turned and saw him. She touched her friend on the arm and spoke into her ear. Irene turned towards him, smiled, and then waved at him to come over.

"Rodney, this is my friend Shelly and this is Dean, Mark, Shairos." She pointed to each one in turn. Shelly said hello and waved her hand at him. She looked directly into his eyes, probably out of curiosity. Another part of him knew that his predator part always seemed to hold the eyes of possible victims.

Dean, on the short side himself but heavily built with muscle, stood and extended his hand. He was still taller than Rodney and the two locked eyes for a moment. Rodney could feel the strength in his handshake; Dean was putting a bit of extra effort in his hand grip. A warning that the lady was his? Showing off his strength? Or just didn't know how silly that was? Regardless, Rodney answered back with a grip of his own and he could see the surprise in the Dean's eyes.

Mark was casual in handshake, barely standing up as he did so. Tall and good looking, Mark looked at ease sitting between the two ladies. Shairos stood up completely, bowed his head slightly, and extended a weak handshake.

"Pull up a chair Rodney." Mark pointed out the empty chairs at the next table. Dean leaned back and pulled one across the floor from the next table. Rodney reluctantly walked over to sit between Shairos and Dean.

"Wait, Rodney, sit next to me. I want to ask you something." Irene motioned him to sit between Dean and herself. Dean gave him a dirty look but stood up from his chair, picked up his glass and moved to the new chair. Relieved, Rodney sat down.

Irene chatted with him immediately, the conversation centered on small talk, certainly nothing that required him to sit next to her. He felt grateful for the opportunity to sit next to her, whether it was because she liked him, or to push Dean farther away. This changed the chemistry of the table as well. Mark no longer was trying to woo both women, he sat up a bit straighter and began to talk more earnestly to Shelly. For her part Shelly seemed a bit miffed that Mark was making the moves on Irene earlier and only now turned attentions on her.

An hour later the two women went to the washroom, leaving the four men to eye each other. Rodney could perceive that Dean was hot under the collar. Mark was too drunk to care, and Shairos was unreadable, though he appeared pleased that he could join in the conversation for a bit.

"So, how long have you known Irene?" Dean leaned forward on the table and glared at Rodney.

Damn, this could be difficult. If I tell him I just met her he might not like that at all. He's looking for an excuse to fight me. "I met her a long time ago and was fortunate enough to run into her again." Rodney looked away from Dean and spoke to Shairos. "How did you meet Shelly and Irene?"

"We just met them this evening. We invited them to our table, which they accepted. We are hoping they will be able join us for a party afterwards."

"Shut up, Shairos, can't you see he's just trying to change the subject? We spent a few bucks on their drinks, and now he wants to take off with them." Dean face reddened and his voice amplified.

"Take it easy, Dean, we had a good time trying. You win some, you lose some. Rodney seems to have the inside track this time. Well, cheers to you Rodney. Hope you get some tonight. She sure looks hot." Mark was sitting relaxed in his chair, the body language belied the seriousness in his eyes.

"Well, to fuck with that nonsense. If he wants her, he better be ready to fight for her." Dean stood up, his fists clenched. The chair scraped loudly as he stood up, threatening to topple as it slid backwards. The noise caught the attention of the bartender and he put down the glass he held and began to slowly walk around the bar.

Mark stood up as well. "For Christ's sake Dean, you're twice his weight. If you win the fight you'll just be a bigger asshole than you already are. Sit down and drink your beer." Mark pointed his finger at him as he spoke.

Rodney was surprised by Mark's defense. Mark was unsteady on his feet but stood a foot taller than Dean, with a heavy build as well. The bartender now stood only a few feet away, ready to intervene. Rodney didn't know if he should stand up or not. Standing up could be seen as a provocation, sitting there made him feel foolish. He could feel perspiration at his back; he felt nervous and agitated. Is this what he deserved for trying to start a social life? He might be able to control Dean by hypnotizing him but that would require looking into his eyes. That might not work and Dean would see that as an invitation to a duel.

"Why are you sticking up for this creep?"

"I'm not. I'm just trying to stop you from making a fool of yourself and maybe getting arrested for manslaughter. But don't kid yourself, the way to him is through me."

The two men eyeballed each other for another few long seconds, then Dean sat down, looking straight ahead at no one. Mark sat down as well, and looked over to Rodney. Shairos had sat quietly through out the whole affair, turning his empty glass around and around. Rodney found himself slowly exhaling, sweat now trickling down from his armpits.

"Uh, thanks Mark."

"No problem kid. Dean is a helluva nice guy most of the time. Give you the shirt off his back. Except when he drinks. Goes nuts." Rodney was under the distinct impression that Dean and Mark had experienced this problem before. Mark may have been the stronger of the two but it was more his role as a big brother that kept Dean from acting out his threat.

The silenced endured for several seconds, and then the two ladies made it back, much to the relief of everyone. If they had heard the commotion they made no sign of it. A few minutes later they finished their drinks and indicated they had to leave.

"I have an early day tomorrow. It was nice meeting you guys. Thanks for the drinks." Shelly gave a sincere smile as she stood up.

Rodney felt nervous. How can I get Irene's phone number without reawakening Dean's outrage? "Irene, would you like some company back to the apartment?"

"That would be nice. Are you ready to go?"

"Yeah." He stood up. "Well, it was good meeting everyone." Mark gave him a thumbs up and a wink. Shairos merely nodded. But Dean stood up, causing Rodney to inhale sharply.

"Sorry about what I said. No hard feelings?" Dean stood up, his hands held limply at his sides. He didn't look directly at Rodney, but down towards the table.

"None at all." Rodney wasn't sure why the threat of violence always caused him to feel uptight. There was no doubt in his mind he could handle Dean easily, yet he remained frightened of him. It must be built in the programming I was born with, or something I learned when I was still a normal human being. But after a hundred and fifty years you would think..."

"What are thinking about?" Irene looked at him as they exited the bar.

"Nothing. Except that I am happy to have met you."

"Well I am happy to have met you too."

Encouraged, Rodney reached for her hand and was pleased she entwined her fingers into his. That made him feel good. Unfortunately he also felt his teeth slide outward. He tried to focus his thoughts elsewhere but his teeth would not return to their hiding place. He hoped he didn't have to try to talk until he could get control of his fangs. Irene drew her body closer to his as they walked. The teeth started to tingle. Out of desperation he used his free hand to pinch himself in the ribs, increasing the pressure until the pain was high enough that his teeth slid back.

The rest of the walk back was better; his teeth did not venture out again and he was able to have a conversation with Irene and Shelly as he walked between them.

After they reached Shelly's apartment they stood outside making more small talk. He was about to ask Irene for her phone number when Shelly invited him up to the apartment for a nightcap.

Rodney sat on the couch with Irene, while Shelly went into the kitchen for the drinks. Irene kicked off her shoes, which lowered her height a bit, and sat on the couch with Rodney. Irene started to talk to him and then swung one of her legs under her. He wasn't sure if she did that to increase her sitting height, or to face him better, but it did result in considerable more leg being exposed beneath the already short skirt. He tried not to stare, as that action might cause more teeth problems.

Shelly returned with three beers and Rodney was grateful for the interruption. His thoughts were going to get him into trouble. The beer tasted good though and Rodney couldn't remember the last time he drank so much.

"I want to see what you look like without glasses." Irene reached up and gently removed his glasses. She leaned back. "Hmm. Not bad at all. You should wear contacts. What do you think Shelly?"

"I think so. Either that or lighter framed glasses. Those..." She pointed at the glasses in Irene's hand, "... are too heavy a frame." Shelly looked into his eyes and felt it again. That sudden loss of where she was, the fall into infinity. The urge to obey commands lingered at the edge. And then it came, just before he turned away, the rush of warmth that started within her and moved outward. Almost sensual in nature. When he looked away the feeling disappeared. She wondered if she imagined it, perhaps from too much drink.

Rodney caught himself in time. When he first looked over to Shelly his vision became blurred without his glasses. He tried to focus his eyes on her but that effort had the effect of turning on his hypnotic powers and the normal suggestions associated with them. When he felt himself touching Shelly's mind he released her and looked away.

"Well, that's settled Rodney, you're going to have to get new glasses." Irene put on his glasses. "How do they look on me?"

"Terrible. But if you help me pick out a new pair, they're yours."

"I like these. It makes everyone look smaller than me."

"That's why I wear them too. When you're short, you have to give yourself a confidence boost." The drinks they had made almost every comment sound funny.

After a lull in the merriment, he asked them where they worked.

"We both work at Cox Industries. Shelly is the good-looking receptionist you see when you enter the door, and I," Irene cleared her throat. "am the training manager. I'm also the only person in the training department, but nevertheless, the training manager."

"So in what subject do you train?"

Irene ran her hands down Rodney's chest. "Sex education." This resulted in more laughter, a sure sign the alcohol was still working.

Rodney couldn't remember when he had had such a good time, in fact he couldn't ever remember having a good time in many years. But as all good times must come to an end this one did too,

"Excuse me, I have to go to the bathroom." Shelly got up and disappeared down the hall.

Irene still sat on her leg but now she leaned in towards Rodney. He didn't know too much about romance but even he knew she was being amorous. He placed a hand on her knee and slowly moved it upwards in massaging strokes. He looked at her and couldn't believe how lovely she looked. He felt his heart racing and could feel himself growing hard. Fortunately his teeth were not extending themselves past his lips. This was either due to his mental prowess, which ordered his teeth to stay home, or the effects of too much drink. She rose herself to her knees on the couch and looked down at him with soft eyes.

His heart nearly stopped as he stared at her, he felt frozen in time. Please don't let this end. His hand was still on her thigh and he moved it upward.

"I won't bite, you know." She moved her lips towards him, her eyes closing.

"I'll try not to." He whispered. His hand slid under skirt, resting on her buttocks.

The kiss lasted not long enough, and too long. He was scared his teeth would jump out at that moment. He darted his tongue into her mouth, fearful of the consequences of doing so but powerless to resist.

A moment later Shelly returned to the living room wearing a nightshirt with a Disney character on it. "Hey you two, don't set my couch on fire."

Rodney looked at her, while Irene was content to lean into him for a moment longer and then sat back, this time with both legs under her.

She gently pushed his hand off her backside as she did so. Shelly's nightshirt did little to hide her figure, the cotton clung to her enough to show her off and was short enough to display rather long legs.

"Sorry, I got carried away." He glanced back at Irene whose skirt was still up near her hips. The sight was hard for him to ignore but he turned his eyes back to Shelly. She was just sitting down and had to cross her legs for modesty. The sight of two women barely dressed caused him a serious problem, the bulge in his pants was evidence to that. As a man he was unsure of how to ease this type of frustration; a vampire would simply bite the neck of the closest woman. But he couldn't do that here. Or could he? Absolutely not. For once I have a chance to make friends, and I will act properly. He looked at his watch. Four o'clock in the morning! "I guess I better get going. I didn't realize the time."

"That's okay, we invited you in. And we don't have to get up until noon anyway." Shelly stifled a yawn. Rodney remembered that they had told the other men at the bar that they had to get up early, but understood that statement as a polite way of dumping them. Now he wanted to make sure that these ladies, in particular Irene, would see him again. "Do you suppose that I could have your phone number? I would like to see you again." He voiced his question to Irene who had readjusted her position so she now sat forward.

"Sure. Here, write down yours too."

The exchange of phone numbers done, he stood up to leave. Rodney had trouble remembering his number, not many requests were made for it. Shelly stood up as well and headed into the kitchen, giving Irene and Rodney their last bit of privacy but called out as she left, "Nice meeting you Rodney. Careful you don't bump into anything on your way out."

Rodney looked down and felt embarrassed by the protrusion in his pants. But he was grateful that his teeth had not ventured out again. Why he didn't know but he was thankful all the same.

Irene put her arms around his neck, kissing and pressing her body against his. If she cared about his erection she didn't let on. But he felt like he was ready to explode. "Sorry about kicking you out. Gotta save some for next time."

"That's okay. When can I call you next? Tomorrow?"

"No, Shelly and I are going out of town. Call me next week." Her arms fell to her side, indicating the good-byes were over.

"I will. Have a nice trip." With that he turned away, trying to look composed about it.

"Bye. Did you want me to call you a cab?"

"No, it's not far to walk. And I need the air." With that he turned and walked away, trying to look cool.

"Bye. Make sure you call."

* * * *

Irene closed the door and called to the kitchen. "Shelly, what do think?"

Shelly came out of the kitchen munching on an apple. "I think it was a good thing you were not alone with him tonight. Good grief girl, you were going hot and heavy on the couch with a man you just met."

"I know, I know. But it's been so long since...well its been a long time. But what do you think of him?"

"He's on the small side, so he's not what I'd call macho. But when he takes off his glasses, he's good enough looking. He's got to dress better, though. Those clothes do not make a fashion statement."

"He's pretty muscular, you know."

Shelly raised her eyebrows.

"Not big muscles because he is kind of skinny, but when I ran my hands over his shirt I could feel lots of muscle. He's really strong. But do you think he's nice enough, not like the creeps I usually end up with?"

Shelly thought for a moment. There was something about him she couldn't put her finger on. "Yeah, he's pretty nice. Seems a bit naive about things." She decided to hold back what happened when she looked into his eyes. "I'm not sure about something, though, so hold off going full board with him right away, okay?"

Irene thought for a moment. "I'll try. I'm getting tired of being burnt."

Shelly climbed into bed, sighed, and closed her eyes. She was a bit concerned about Irene. They had been friends a long time and had gone through different crisis together, mostly involving men. The last jerk messed her up good for a while and she was not keen to see her jump to another unknown so fast. And this one was a bit strange, but why exactly she could not pinpoint. She drifted off to sleep, her last thoughts were of golden eyes that hung by themselves in open space.

Irene hadn't expected to be spending the night at Shelly's. It wasn't a big deal, she had done that before. She took off her own clothes, and put on the T-shirt Shelly had lent her. She slipped under the covers on the couch. She laid awake thinking about him and found that she felt hot, aroused; the shirt was digging into her boobs. "What the hell, it's not as if Shelly would care." She murmured to herself, and took off the T-shirt. Sleeping in just her thong panties seemed the best option tonight.

* * * *

Nancy looked interested; the chance of romance in the story intrigued her. "Sheldon, was he really falling in love? And why was he so nervous with this woman? Hasn't he had lots of women before, even if only to feed on their blood?"

"Slow down on your questions, Nancy." He patted her arm. "Was he really falling in love? Well to answer that question, did you fall in love with your first boyfriend? Or maybe you just thought you did. But how can you tell the difference between love and infatuation? What you have to know is that feeding on young women that you have complete mental control over and trying to socialize with them when they are free to think as they please are two totally different things. He had avoided social interaction for so long he had to relearn social skills. And the social skills he knows are one hundred and fifty years old. As for knowing women, well let us say he knows how to please them in bed. That is a talent a vampire has to have if he wants a good feed. But before he gets to that point with Irene he has to learn how to treat her as a girlfriend. And he has just now started on that learning curve."

I had a question as well. "Sheldon, why did his teeth retract or at least not expose themselves?"

"Well, the alcohol had some effect on that. It does have a tendency to cause the muscles in that area to relax. But teeth come out when he's getting ready to feed, that is when he has a hunger for blood. When vampires are sexually aroused it is usually time for nourishment, the two normally go hand in hand. But the reason they come out is because the vampire is a predator, and the teeth appear much like a cat's claws come out when it is ready to attack. But Rodney in that instance gave a strong signal to his body, despite being very strongly aroused, that he was not in a predator mode. In other words he wanted something entirely different from these ladies. He had never distinguished the difference between feeding and sex so it took a while for his body to retract the teeth."

Chapter Seven

Rodney completed the first floor cleaning, and then dialed her number. He had it memorized the first time he had phoned, but kept the paper with her number on it in his wallet all the same. It rang once, twice and he was getting nervous. He had tried yesterday without any luck, and now for the second time today there didn't appear to be any response. Notions that she had given him the wrong number, that she was avoiding him plunged into his thoughts.

"Hello?"

"Hello, Irene? This is Rodney."

"Hi, Rodney, this is me."

He wasn't very good at small talk but managed to ask the appropriate questions on how work was, how her trip went, and generally tried to get her to do most of the talking. That part of the conversation went pretty well but when he tried arrange a time for them to get together, he was stymied. By the time he finished his shift it would be too late to go out.

"I guess we'll have to wait until the weekend to see each other Rodney."

"Yeah, I guess so."

"Well, you don't have much chance of finishing work early, do you?"

"No, well, sometimes I do. But it's more like finishing at ten thirty instead of eleven. That doesn't help much."

"No, it doesn't. But could you finish faster if I came down to help?"

"Sure, the work I do is easy enough to learn. Which evening could you come down?" His voice brightened.

"How about Thursday?"

The arrangements were made and after the call Rodney went happily back to work.

* * * *

Shelly got a call from Irene shortly after she had talked to Rodney and filled her in on the details of the dialogue. Irene seemed quite happy about the call and looked forward to Thursday evening's rendezvous.

But Shelly had some misgivings, partly because of Irene's tendency of falling too quickly for the wrong guys, and partly because of the spooky dream she had that night with the golden eyes. No, there was something more than a little different about this guy, she could sense it. "Look Irene, I know he seems like a nice guy but try to slow down a little. What are you doing Wednesday night?"

"Nothing much as far as I know. What did you have in mind?"

"Humor me a little. I know this tea reader. She's really good. I'll treat you, okay?"

"You want me to have my tea leaves read?"

"Please, I know it sounds silly, but I ..." How do you explain a bad dream? "Well, will you go?"

"Sure. I think they're kinda fun."

* * * *

The woman wasn't that old, perhaps around forty. But she dressed and acted like someone much older. Irene wasn't sure if her dress was part of the act but it didn't really matter. The reader studied the leaves of both women, and read Shelly's first.

"You are a kind person. You're trying to save someone, help someone? No matter, you always think of others. But you are troubled - by dreams." She looked up at Shelly who nodded. "Heed them, but be careful on how you interpret them. A mystery lurks within them. Other than that your life cycle is stable. You will meet a gentleman soon, a couple of months, who may be very satisfying to you." A few other comments were made, mostly of the nondescript nature that made them hard to discern.

She then looked into Irene's cup. "Very strange. I see that you have met someone. Be very careful, very careful." The reader looked up at her for emphasis.

"Why, what does it say about him?"

"Not too much. These are your leaves, not his. But..." She looked at the cup once more. "...He will have a great influence on you if you decide to be with him. Be cautious. He may hurt you without intention, but you will suffer just the same."

"Can you tell me anything more about him?" Irene looked anxious.

"Perhaps. But you would have to bring me something of his. Something personal. Then I could try."

"Is there anything else?"

The tea cup reader gave more indeterminate details, but both women were impressed by her ability to bring out some known facts. They walked off afterwards, talking over the experience.

"I'm glad for you that he called but don't go head over heels yet." Shelly could tell by the excitement in Irene's voice that she was getting her hopes up again. "Remember what the tea cup reader said."

"I know, I know. But we're just dating. And the tea cup reader didn't really say anything bad about him."

"That's because she was reading your leaves, not his. Tell you what, if you can get something personal from him and we take it back to the tea cup reader and she says good things about him, then I will lay off. Okay?"

"Oh, all right. I guess that can't hurt."

"Good, so you will get something personal from him?"

"I will. But it sounds like I don't trust him this way."

"What is there to trust? You just met him. You have been hurt too many times before. This time play it safe until you know."

"Okay. I'll see what I can do."

* * * *

Thursday evening arrived, and the Toyota navigated through the downtown streets. Irene finally parked and then let out a big sigh. She wasn't sure if she felt nervous or excited, or both. But her heart raced as she grabbed the gym bag from the front seat and walked to the building's rear door. She wore old clothes like he had suggested and took a change of clothes along to wear later.

Of course, just because they were old clothes didn't mean she couldn't look good wearing them. The jeans were tight-fitting and worn; there were holes at both knees as well as one on the seat. The white T-shirt had a faded print , some design that symbolized a forgotten rock group. The shirt had shrunk and thinned from repeated washings and when she tied the bottom in a knot, it helped to emphasize her figure. Not that it needed much help to be noticed anyway. Rodney opened the door to admit her, he was wearing his usual baggy pants of a non-descript brown. His flannel shirt was open and untucked over a plain T-shirt.

The usual greetings were offered, plus a kiss that indicated more was to follow. But for now work was to be done. He showed her how to go through the office areas, while he went to washrooms to clean up . They went to work and around eight thirty stopped for a break. They sat in the empty coffee room, where she drank a Diet Coke from the vending machine and he poured coffee from his thermos. As they continued with small talk Irene got up to look at the bulletin board and then various vending machine offerings.

"Are you hungry? Some of the stuff isn't too bad."

"No, just curious."

"Those are interesting jeans you have on. They look good on you."

"Thanks. I've had them a long time, they're really comfortable, but I can't wear them in public much." She slipped her fingers in the tear in the seat as an explanation.

The demonstration revealed a bit more of her cheek and he wondered if she wore any panties at all. That contemplation and the visual image of her backside consumed his thoughts when he became aware that she had asked him a question.

She had turned her head and was smiling at him, her fingers no longer pulling open the tear. "I asked how much longer until we are finished?"

"Sorry. About an hour should do it."

* * * *

They worked in the last office together at the end. Out of the corner of her eye she caught him looking at her several times, which was okay. That was what this outfit was supposed to do, attract his attention. But he seemed to react to it more than she expected.

"Rodney, can I ask a personal question?"

"Sure." He hoped it had nothing to do with him being a vampire.

"How old are you? I can't guess your age." Which was true, she and Shelly were stymied when trying to guess. His skin, being pale and smooth, gave no hint to his age. And his mannerisms reflected maturity while his inexperience showed in social skills.

He thought fast. It never occurred to him to think of an appropriate age to tell her. How old was she? He guessed about thirty and then added a few years for himself. "Thirty six."

"Oh. Well, you don't look it."

"Thanks. How old are you, or is that a secret?"

"No, I'm thirty-three. I guess we're about finished here. Are we still going out?"

"Sure, if you want to."

"I'll change then. My bag is downstairs. I'll meet you there."

He stood by the door waiting. He had finished cleaning up, put the cleaning equipment away, washed up and changed into street clothes, and still she wasn't ready. Then he heard the washroom door close, then the sound of high heels on a hard floor. She walked slowly and appeared around the corner.

"Sorry if I kept you waiting. It takes us ladies longer to get ready sometimes."

"That's okay, the wait is worth it." Which was true. She had reapplied makeup, altered her hair slightly and put on a semi-transparent top. The tight skirt almost reached her knees and had a slit at the front.

They went to her car. "Where to?"

"Go up to the light, turn left and go straight for a mile or so." As she swung out on the street, he noticed her perfume. It reminded him of someone from long ago. It wasn't the same fragrance, just the fact she wore it. "You smell nice. What's the name of your perfume?"

"Tresor. A friend gave it to me." She stopped at a set of lights. "Excuse me, it's a little hard to operate these pedals." She lifted up herself up, and pulled up on her skirt.

Rodney did his best not to gawk, keeping his eyes up as much as possible. But he did notice her bare legs, the slit in her skirt exposing them almost up to her crotch.

* * * *

Irene wasn't certain if she just happened to dress right, or if Rodney had picked a location that was appropriate to how she dressed. But the nightclub was perfect and had the right food menu for her appetite. They shared a bottle of wine together and talked. Talked about many things and found they enjoyed each other's company immensely. She suspected he was coming off a bad relationship, judging how eager he seemed for her company. She found she could learn little about his past, questions brought forth vague replies and a change of subject. Sometime before the dessert, and during the second bottle of wine, he kissed her deeply. After that time meant nothing to them. She looked into his golden eyes, normal size now that he had removed his glasses, and found that she trusted him.

As the waiter was bringing back the change, she leaned into him, relaxed. Irene felt his hand move up her thigh again, to rest as high as the slit would allow. His light fingers aroused her aroused her and she reminded herself that it would still be too soon to go to bed with him. She hoped he wouldn't persist too strongly; her resistance was getting weaker. But when she let him off at his own apartment he didn't ask twice about spending the night with her. Once he indicated that desire but after hearing some reluctance in her answer, he didn't repeat the invitation. She guessed that he was a bit nervous about the implications of that step and perhaps thought that it might be best that they waited a bit .

"Probably his last affair has made him reluctant for a bit with women." She mused.

She phoned him when she got home, as promised. It made her feel good that he worried about her safety.

* * * *

"He didn't try to sleep with you?"

"Well, yes, but he didn't push it. Which I was grateful for. After all that wine, well, I was on the weak side."

"Yes, we know all about you and wine, don't we?"

She laughed. "I can't help that. Anyway, I'm going to see him on Saturday."

"You didn't get an item from him, did you?"

"No, I didn't even think of that. And there really were no personal items I could get anyway. If I have a chance to, and if I remember, I will."

"Well, I am impressed he didn't try harder to bed you. But be careful, please."

"Don't worry. I think he really is special, unlike any other guy I've met before."

* * * *

Saturday evening found a nervous vampire phoning his girlfriend. He kept expecting the phone to ring without answer but on the second ring it was picked up. He wondered to himself what made her go out with him, he always thought of himself peculiar looking with his pale skin. But he decided that wasn't for him to figure out, and to be thankful she dated him.

They decided to meet at a small bar that served good food then plot the evening from there. He wore his usual baggy jeans and long-sleeved shirt. She came in a few minutes late, which didn't surprise him, wearing black stretch pants and a short yellow top. As it turned out, the steak sandwiches were excellent though she did wonder how someone could eat a very rare steak.

"It's an acquired taste. More beer?" The dark beer went down quickly during the meal, and after that he bought shooters, to toast their relationship. By that time it was getting too late to start looking for another place to go.

"We could go back to my place, if you like. There's a James Bond picture I haven't seen on TV tonight."

Lacking a better alternative they headed to her house, a small home that she had rented at a good price. On the way they stopped for more beer and chips. The movie had been on for half an hour by the time they turned the set on but it didn't take long to get up to speed on the plot. More beer and chips were consumed by the time the show ended, and both were in a good mood as they channel surfed, coming to stop at an old western.

"Isn't it cruel what they do to those poor calves?" Irene watched the calf being lassoed and then branded.

"Naw. They don't mind too much."

"Oh sure, how would you like that happening to you?" She elbowed him in the ribs for good measure.

"Well that's different. But I could demonstrate on you that it isn't all bad."

She turned to face him. "What do you mean by that?"

"I'll give a five second head start, then I'm going to catch you, tie you up, and then brand you. Or its equivalent."

"You wouldn't..."

"One."

"...Dare."

"Two. Three." He took off his belt.

"That's not..."

"Four. Better run while you can."

She took off running down the hallway. "...Fair."

"Five. Here I come." He walked down the hall.

Irene considered locking herself in the bathroom, but that meant if he could find a way to unlock the door, she would be trapped. And if he couldn't open the door, the game would end, ending any fun. She wasn't really concerned what he would do when he caught her. So she ran to the bedroom, thinking she could make a dash for the door again by running across the bed.

He entered the room with her on the far side of the bed. He moved towards where she was standing and then, as expected, she made a dash over the bed and to the door. She reached the hallway when she felt his hand pull at her waist. She carried on, breaking the grip. But in the living room he caught her again, one hand on her waist and the other on her leg. She made a low level scream as he gently allowed her to tumble to the floor.

She ended up on her side and when she tried to push him off with her free hand, felt the belt loop around her wrist. She tried to tumble away but her efforts were hampered by the coffee table. He turned her on her back, grabbed her other hand and put that through the belt loop as well and then wrapped the rest of the belt around them. The knot felt rather loose and she felt she could have slipped out of them without too much problem. She decided to give just a modest struggle anyway, just so he knew she wasn't giving in too easily.

"Now what are you going to do?"

He held her arms above her head with one of his and sat on her, looking at her. He looked like he was trying to read her mind, on what to do next, and in truth he was trying to read her emotional level to find if he could continue.

"I think I will relieve you of some of your garments."

"Excuse me? Remove my clothes?" She wiggled a bit more under him, and then relaxed again.

The yellow top had already slipped up to her bra during their struggles and now he eased it up with his free hand. He slid the top up to her hands. She took in a deep breath and looked down at her bra, noting the sheer lace wasn't hiding much of her breasts and her erect nipples. He began to circle his hand underneath her, feeling along the bra strap.

"That may take you awhile. The hook is at the front." She didn't want to make it too easy for him but his hand felt uncomfortable underneath. She also knew that by telling him where the hook was she gave him tacit approval to continue.

With a bit of effort using only one hand he managed to open the front, and then he pulled the bra up her arms as well. Still holding her wrists he kissed her quickly on the lips and then lightly kissed each of her nipples as well. She knew he was strong but it still surprised her when he easily slid her to a new position on the carpet.

"What was that for?"

"I'm getting tired of holding your wrists, so..." He picked up the edge of the coffee table and lowered one of the legs between her wrists. "... I'm going to let the coffee table leg do it for me. "Now I can concentrate on other matters."

"Which would be?"

"Removing more of your clothes."

"Oh, sure take advantage of a helpless lady."

He undid the zipper of her pants and then slowly pulled them off, taking his time looking at her legs as they were revealed.

"Now what are you thinking about? You have me tied up and undressed." She looked up at him staring at her, his mind obviously working at something. "Is there anything else?"

"Well, you still have your panties on."

"Believe me, there's not much to them."

"I believe you. Don't go away."

"Hardly." She watched him go to where the phone was. He looked through a small basket holding pens, scissors and other small hardware. He found what he was looking for and returned.

"Turn on your side."

"Why?"

"Time for your branding."

"My what!?"

He held up a red felt marker. "Your branding."

"What are you going to put there? What if it shows?"

"I'll put it where it won't. Turn on your side, or better still, your stomach."

"And if I don't agree to this branding?"

"I'll leave you tied up all night long."

She rolled on to her stomach and he noticed her panties were the thong type, which took away his attention for a moment. He set to work at drawing a large heart, shading the inside with the pen. She twitched from the movement of the felt pen, disturbing a line. "Hold still."

"And if I don't?" She wiggled her hips a bit.

"Then this." He smacked her on her cheek lightly twice. "Now hold still."

"Yes, Mr. Cowboy."

He finished the heart, then on the outside of the figure he wrote their names.

"Done."

"Good. Are you going to let me go now?"

Without answering he turned her over and pulled off her panties. He started kissing her neck, and then moved down until he reached her knees. He lingered at her breasts, stomach, hips and thighs. Then he returned to the space between her legs, his tongue licking at her pussy. Her moans and crying out became more frequent. He reached into her mind, helping to release the correct pattern, but was careful that she did not feel his presence. "Do you want me to stop and untie you?"

"Whatever. Do whatever you want, but don't stop." She panted out her response. Her hips and chest lifted up and down as she spoke.

178

He lifted up the coffee table to release her wrists, but didn't remove the belt holding them together. He then removed his own clothes and prepared to have sex without his fangs for the first time in a long, long time. His fangs had surfaced a few times during the evening but had quickly withdrawn each time. And though he had tried normal intercourse a few times since becoming a vampire, out of curiosity to see if the plumbing still worked, this was the first time he had done this to anyone he cared about since Rose-Marie. He felt like a born-again virgin.

Rodney was a vampire, and one thing a vampire becomes very good at is the art of making love. It is both a learned technique and a skill that comes from being able to read other people's emotions. Irene never believed that sex could be like that and later that night she knew she was falling in love, if not for the sex alone.

"You're going to stay the night?"

"I want to. But I can't. The sun in the morning is too strong and I will get very sick if I stay." He went to explain that he had a skin condition that couldn't take sunlight very well. She accepted his explanation rather well he thought, probably something to do with the amount of drinks they had.

"Then how about if I stay tonight at your place?"

"Well, I suppose so. If you will do what I ask."

"Which is?"

He grinned. "You'll find out."

* * * *

Irene left his apartment in the morning, amazed that she didn't wake him when she left. She put a note on his door and then quietly exited. She also took something extra, his shirt to wear back home. When they had left her place he would only let her wear her bathrobe, which was meant to be more revealing than concealing. Last night with the liquor in her it had seemed to be a fun thing to do, even when he pulled the top down and exposed her breasts. It was a good thing there wasn't any traffic at four in the morning. She giggled at the memory of herself going up to his apartment.

He had checked first that there was no one around. Then he opened her car door and made her stand while he tied her hands behind her back with the belt from the bathrobe. She had to walk to his apartment with her robe fluttering open. And then the sex after that, well she couldn't believe all the pent up frustration she must have had to explode like that. That felt fun at the time, but now she rejoiced that the shirt was on the long side as she walked barefoot to her car.

* * * *

"That was a rather interesting way to have sex for the first time." Nancy addressed the question to Sheldon as a statement. But she clearly expected an answer as if it was a question.

"I believe you may be referring to when Rodney tied up his girlfriend."

Nancy considered her words before answering. "Well, we all like different things. And it's nothing I haven't heard of before." She blushed. "I didn't say I get tied up for sex."

"Well that certainly is none of our business anyway. But for Rodney, to be a vampire is to command the other person. He is the one who must be in control, complete domination is essential. This is easy most of the time as we have seen in the past. So we have a situation where Rodney now associates sex with this act of dominance. And when he had sex with Irene, whom he did not want to exert mental control over, he tried to dominate her in other ways."

"Does that mean that every time Rodney is going to have sex with her, he has to tie her up?"

"No, he will learn that sex isn't just about dominance, but about love. But give him time, he's new at this game."

I took a quick swallow of my coffee, found it cold, and tried to remember when Nancy had poured it last. Still too much beer in the system. I did have a question, though. "Tell me, Sheldon, why did she allowed herself to tied up?"

"Well, for one it was just a game to her. On the conscious level it didn't mean being dominated. But in her previous relationship she had to do all the work, both household duties and financial ones, as well as be the emotionally strong one. She felt she had to care for both herself and her boyfriend. As a matter of fact that wasn't the first relationship where she had to carry the emotional load of a freeloader." Sheldon shook his head in annoyance. "On the subconscious level she was glad someone else was taking charge. With her hands tied it meant she didn't have to initiate anything, in fact she could tell herself that she was helpless and that he would take care of everything and make all the decisions."

Chapter Eight

Rodney read the note. Basically it said she would call later, that she would be doing some shopping. He was still feeling on cloud nine as the evening went on and tried to phone her, but got no answer. But he wasn't concerned and listened to the radio.

Irene did phone later and the two met for coffee, both still suffering a bit from the previous night's alcohol.

They didn't talk much but did a lot of hand holding and slow kisses.

"I'll return your shirt next time. I hope you didn't mind I took it."

"Of course not. But I warn you, I like the thought of you naked, and may try to do something like that again."

She blushed. "Well, it was fun for me too."

He didn't hear a negative in her voice, perhaps a tentative yes. "Tell you what. I'll call you during the week to check up on you, but maybe we can get together also where I work. I won't ask you to do any work, but I do have the whole building to myself. And maybe we could have some fun together."

"Sure. What did you have in mind exactly?"

"I just thought of it. I'll tell you more later."

"Something about me losing my clothes, I betcha."

"Maybe. But I hope you won't object in any event."

"No, I trust you. But let's make it for Wednesday and give my body a chance to recuperate."

"It's a date then. I'll phone Wednesday to give you some instructions."

* * * *

"How are things with you, Shelly?"

"Good. How was your coffee date? I hope it was tamer than your Saturday night one. Some day you'll have to give me the details."

"Well, maybe someday. But it was wild."

"Did you manage to get something of his?"

"Yes, I did. But I don't feel comfortable doing this."

"Come on, how can it hurt him? Look, if it turns out there is nothing, I personally will return it with an apology."

"Okay, I'll give it a try."

"Good. I phoned the cup reader and she is out of town or busy, but can see us on Thursday. I made an appointment for seven p.m."

* * * *

"Hello Irene? Are you still on for our date?"

"Sure. What did you have in mind?"

"Well, do you mind coming to the office building where I work?"

"No, not at all. What time did you want me to show up?"

"About nine p.m."

"Okay." A pause, then, "What should I wear? Anything special?"

"Well, if I get to pick out what you are going to wear, how about a short skirt and a light blouse. And high heels."

"That can be arranged. What about underwear? Do you prefer stockings, pantyhose or bare legs with the skirt?"

A moment of silence passed as Rodney thought. He hadn't really planned to be the one picking out her outfit. And choosing what she wore added suspense even though it didn't factor in to what he had planned. It made him feel good though that she was giving him the choice. "Uh, well, how about bare legs?"

"Okay, bare legs then."

"Good. And could you make your blouse of very light material?"

"Okay, you're the boss." She laughed a bit. "I'll wear a camisole underneath. The one I have in mind would be quite transparent."

"Good, I'm looking forward to seeing you."

"Me too."

* * * *

Irene arrived at the darkened building just after nine. The rear door was left ajar. She opened the door fully and stepped inside, then firmly closed it behind her.

"Hello?" She looked around then spotted the chair with the note on it. "Rodney? Are you there?" She walked over and picked up the note.

Irene:

Sorry that I am not downstairs to greet you, but I am busy working on the plans for this evening. Please go to third floor, room 312. A bottle of wine waiting for you.

Rodney

Irene was surprised by the note but the mystery aspect appealed to her. She went to the elevator, wondering what other plans were in store for the evening.

Room 312 was an unoccupied office. She noticed one overhead fluorescent tubing set shone in the corner of the room. As she approached she could see the bottle of wine on an empty cardboard box. Underneath the bottle lay another note.

Irene:

I hope you don't mind this method of putting some fun into the evening. If you don't care for this, call out, and we can do something else. If you wish to continue, read on.

Have a few sips of the wine, a rather nice red I think. When I talked to you on the phone you mentioned that you were going to wear a camisole underneath your blouse. If so, could you please remove it as well as your bra? Enjoy some more wine and then go to room 223.

Rodney

Irene drank a bit more wine, reread the note, and then considered his request. Actually she did find this note business interesting though not the type of evening she expected. She managed to drink about a third of the bottle before deciding she would slow down on her drinking. Having made her decision she stood behind a support pillar to remove her blouse, camisole and bra, before finally slipping her blouse back on.

Room 223 was a mail and photocopier room. The lights were on in the room but not anywhere else, which made it easy to find in the darkened hallway. On the table lay another note and sitting next to that was a plastic cup.

Irene:

The plastic cup contains three liquors; treat it like a shooter. After you consume it, please go to room 202 (it is on the far side of the building). And please remove your panties.

Irene sniffed the shooter. It smelled good, if a bit potent. She noticed the note didn't contain the line that if she wanted to stop, all she had to do was to call out. Apparently Rodney had thought that once she had reached this stage she was willing to follow through. She looked at the drink once more and then downed it, feeling the warmth spread from her stomach. "Wow, not bad." She went to the next step, lifting up her skirt and reaching up to pull off her panties. She wasn't sure what to do with them but like her camisole, she left them behind as she left the room.

Room 202 was a storage room for old files. Irene found the room rather small for even that purpose, but it could not be used very much.

It did contain a glass she presumed of the red wine. Another note awaited her. She drank the wine as she read.

Irene:

Thanks for being such a good sport. The next room is 355, the coffee room. Before you go there, please remove your skirt. I have turned up the heat a bit so you won't feel chilled.

Rodney

She closed the door, just in case someone could see her. She removed her skirt, then checked to see how much the blouse covered. The blouse was just barely long enough to cover her cheeks. Irene found herself growing more excited as each note gave her a new request.

The lunchroom still had its assortment of table and chairs. A white cloth covered one table with two chairs. Rodney was sitting in one chair, drinking a glass of wine. She stood at the doorway. "Well, here I am." She saw him look her up and down, wearing only her shoes and the transparent top. She did a quick spin around, noting he seemed transfixed by her.

"Do come in. Would you like another glass of wine?" Without waiting for an answer he poured her a glass. "I hope you didn't mind the run around, I thought you might enjoy a bit of mystery."

She took the wine and sat down, watching him. "No, I didn't mind that. But what was this bit about me having to get undressed? That doesn't seem to ever happen to you."

"Well, I guess I just thought of it first. I'm starving. How about you?"

"Sure, what do we have for dinner?"

He got up and removed two plates from the microwave. The plates contained take out portions from her favorite Italian restaurant. Along with the wine it made an excellent dinner. Though she felt exposed by what she was wearing, it felt sensual to be eating dinner in the office lunchroom almost naked with Rodney.

After the meal he was quiet, and then almost shyly he reached into a cupboard and produced a small present.

"I have something for you." He seemed reluctant to produce the small box and nervously extended it to her. "I bought this for you. I hope you like it"

"You didn't have to." She unwrapped it slowly, revealing a gold wristband with an intricate pattern. "It's beautiful."

He was beaming. "I wanted to get you something, because you mean so much to me."

She left her chair and hugged him. The hugs turned to kisses. The kisses led to other things. She ended up on the table where they had dinner, the plastic plates and containers tumbling to the floor. He mounted her as she wrapped her legs and arms around him.

"Hurry, the table is killing my back!"

* * * *

Irene's excitement didn't abate when she got home. She sat in her car looking around, wishing the night didn't have to end. She felt the jewellery around her wrist and smiled, glad she had found someone she could trust.

* * * *

"So you can see Rodney is making progress towards romance." Sheldon paused to take another drink. "He's starting to do romantic things such as buying a small gift and preparing dinner."

I saw Sheldon's point, but it didn't seem quite right. "But is it right what he's doing to her? After all she is falling for what she assumes to he a relatively normal guy. He has given no indication to her that he might not be what he seems."

Before Sheldon could answer, Nancy had a comment of her own. "And why did he use those notes to get her to undress? Couldn't he seduce her the way most men would?"

"Good questions. Yes, he should be more honest with her, or at least not seduce her into falling for him so fast. But he is blind as to what he is doing. He is intoxicated with the thought of a relationship and doesn't see the danger in what he is doing yet. As far as the notes are concerned, well Irene didn't mind so perhaps no harm done. But more to your point Nancy, he still is trying to exert control as a vampire. Where before he would use mental powers to get the women to undress he now substitutes written words to send out his commands. As I mentioned before he is learning and it is hard for him to drop his old habits."

"Hmm, the power of the written word. At least she wasn't opposed to it."

Chapter Nine

The cafe was not crowded, but evenings usually found it on the quiet side. The tea cup reader helped bring in some additional business, though tonight she had just one reading to do and that did not involve tea leaves.

Irene passed over the shirt reluctantly, still feeling guilty about the lack of trust it implied. Shelly sat next to her, sipping her tea. This time they drank a normal variety.

The reader shuffled the shirt in her hands, as if searching for a hidden object within it. She sighed, closed her eyes and then opened them again, staring past the two women sitting across from her.

"This shirt...it belongs to a very old man. He..."

"No, that can't be. Rodney is 36." Irene realized that she had interrupted. "Sorry."

"That is okay. But my dear, this shirt is worn by an old, old man. This much I am positive. But let me continue." She closed her eyes again. "He lives in a world of darkness. Shadows are around him. Ahh. I sense also the color red. Yes, that is very strong too." She opened her eyes again at her last statement. She then placed the shirt closer to her face but quickly removed it, holding it near her chest. "This is peculiar. This shirt gives me a bad feeling if I hold it too close to my face. I don't know why. But I can tell you more anyway. This man is very powerful, yes, very powerful."

"Do you mean strong? He is not that big."

"Actually, Shelly, he has really strong muscles though you can't tell from those bulky clothes he wears."

"No, I refer to mental prowess. Not just his intelligence, but his mental control."

"Anything else? Is he good for Irene to have a relationship with?"

"Hmm. His heart. Well he is not a bad person, but he is hiding a terrible secret from you, a terrible secret, and he's trying to run away from a problem. Yes, I see it now. For most of his life he has followed a path. But he was unhappy with it, so now he tries a new path. This makes him happy, but this cannot be. He is trying to be something he cannot be."

"Are you saying he can't change his character?"

"No, it is more than that. He is trying to be, how can I say it? It is like trying to be taller by standing on your toes. You can only do that for a little while. Soon he will have to go back to his original path."

"What if he doesn't go back?"

"Not possible, I think. But if he tries to stay on this new path, it would bring disaster to him. Death, perhaps."

"And the old path?"

"It would be dangerous to be near him when he goes back to his old way of living. Very dangerous."

"Is there anything else?"

"Yes, well, to him sex is very important. Sex, I sense this strongly, gives him life. That is very strange, but this I am sure is right."

"One other thing, if you don't mind. Can you tell me where and when he was born?" This was from Shelly, who kept looking at Irene as each revelation was made.

"Difficult to say. New England, about... well, I feel ... well over one hundred years ago. I must tell you something else. He has lost something a long time ago and now he wants to have it back, even if it costs him his life. Beware if you continue a relationship with him. It almost certainly will result in a tragedy."

A few more questions were asked, but the resulting answers sounded vague. Irene was beginning to doubt most of what she said.

"I know it is hard to believe what I told you. But I tell you something else, too, to help you believe. He lives alone, and works alone. He has recently bought you a gift ...of gold. His name is Robert, Rodney? It starts with the letter R, in any case. Ask him about Rose-Marie, it is she who made him."

"Made him?"

"This is what he feels."

Shelly and Irene left the cafe, Irene nervously rubbing her bracelet.

"She didn't say he was bad or anything like that. And she didn't know his age. I don't know what to think."

"Irene, she told you to stop seeing him or something awful was going to happen. Look, I know you fell for this guy, but he's bad news. I'm not saying he would intentionally hurt you, but you would be hurt just the same. Tell him it's going too fast and say it would be best if you didn't see him as much."

"I suppose it would be best if we did slow it down. I'll talk to him tomorrow night."

"Where are you meeting him?"

"The 8th Street Pub."

"How about if I join you two? I'll give you some support."

"That would be nice. I'm meeting him around eleven."

* * * *

After dropping Irene off at her house, Shelly paced in her apartment. The answer lay in front of her, but still out of reach. She tried to concentrate, but kept seeing those golden eyes and experiencing the memory of falling to nowhere for that brief moment. She went to the bathroom and turned on the shower, stripped off her clothes and stood under the hot water. She relaxed slowly, her mind forgetting about problems.

The sound of the telephone jarred her. She clutched at a towel and ran to the phone.

"Hello?"

"Hi, Shelly. We didn't interrupt you did we?"

"No, not at all Kim."

Kim rambled on as Shelly tried to dry herself with one hand, eventually giving up and letting the towel drop to the floor. Goosebumps starting forming on her skin.

"So if you're free Sunday, come over about two."

"Sure, I think I can make it. Does the baby need anything?"

"Not much, she has lots of relatives. Maybe a blanket or clothes. Well, if you like to get clothes, get them for a child about six months old. I think she has a lot right now."

"Say, Kim, are you good at puzzles?"

"No, but Frank is. What type of puzzle?"

"One from a book I'm reading. I have to determine an identity from some clues."

"What are the clues?"

"Darkness, the color red, very old but looks young, and, let's see...strong mental powers, and has a terrible secret."

"Gee, I don't know. Just a minute." Shelly heard the phone being covered. "Frank! Shelly needs help on a puzzle." The same clues were listed off.

"Shelly? Frank said that if you assume red is the color for blood then the only thing he can think of is a vampire."

"A vampire!"

"Well, that's Frank's guess. He's usually pretty good at that sort of thing."

"Okay, thanks Kim. I'll see you Sunday."

Standing naked and wet by the phone was chilly enough, but now she felt a new wave of cold sweeping through her, her muscles tightening up to the point where they hurt. Remembering his golden eyes once more she knew Frank was right.

* * * *

Friday at the office went by slowly. She talked to Irene, who still seemed confused about what she should do. Shelly, without trying to sound desperate, pointed out the arguments used before.

"That lady hit on some of the facts pretty good, like his name, and the bracelet. Don't you believe she's right about this other stuff as well?"

Reluctantly she agreed. But Shelly had seen this type of reaction before, including in herself. The heart often won the tug of war over logic.

That evening Shelly stood in front of her closet. What to wear to meet a vampire? Perhaps something in a high collar? Well even if she wasn't sure she considered a different plan. She knew men, and Rodney certainly acted like a horny guy. And she knew what to wear that gave her the upper hand over men at least most of the time. Out came the 'Phantom of the Opera' dress for lack of a better name. Before she left the apartment, she went to her jewellery box and picked out a special necklace.

* * * *

Rodney finished up putting the supplies away and then changed into less worn clothes. He decided he should do some shopping and get clothes closer to this decade's fashion. Closing and locking the outside door behind him, he headed towards the street corner.

Hurrying down the sidewalk, he didn't pay attention to her until she called out his name.

He turned and looked. Standing next to a car was a woman wearing a tight red skirt with a matching wrap which opened to reveal a translucent, white camisole. The image took his breath away for a moment and he could feel his teeth sliding out.

"Rodney, it's me, Shelly. We have to talk." She hoped her voice did not show the nervousness she felt and sounded properly authoritarian.

"Oh, hi Shelly. Sure, if you want." He spoke carefully so that he wouldn't lisp the words too badly, the teeth sometimes caused pronunciation problems. The teeth started their retreat slowly when he

189

caught a whiff of her perfume and the teeth started their outward journey again.

"Get in the car, I'll drive us to the bar."

He got in slowly, wondering what this visit concerned. Her emotional level was high and he could perceive that her outward appearance belied her apprehension.

She sat down carefully but the skirt still rose up. He quickly glanced at her legs, the top of the stockings now showed and then looked back at her face, lest he was caught taking unfair advantage of her predicament of trying to remain dignified in a bucket seat. Of course he also saw a fair bit of her bust but that seemed to be more of the intention of the garment rather than the result of an awkward position in a car. So he didn't feel abashed if he was seen looking for a moment. Still the effect of the way she dressed caused him to feel apprehensive and keep his mind from thinking much beyond what she was revealing, which was what she planned.

"Rodney, are you from New England originally?"

He didn't expect such a question and wondered why she had asked it. Still he could be honest about that. "Yes, I grew up there. How did you know?"

"Irene said that you were thirty-six years old."

"Un, yeah, that's right." Again he wondered what she leading up to but was still occupied with how she was dressed. He stole another look at her legs.

"Are you sure that wouldn't be one hundred and thirty-six years old?" Her voice blazed at him, demanding an answer. She kept her eyes away from him, refusing eye contact.

"What? What are you talking...."

"What are your plans for Irene? Do you love her?"

"Plans? What do you mean by plans?"

"Do you love her?" The questions came loud and fast as Shelly drove down the road.

"Yes, I love her. But why..."

"Then why are planning to turn her into a vampire?"

"I'm not going to do that. Why would you think...?" Rodney stopped. Did he just admit to being a vampire? Alarms went up as he tried to replay the conversation in his head.

"You're a vampire!" It was spoken as a statement and not a question. "So why wouldn't you turn Irene into one? I thought you loved her."

She finally turned to look at him.

He had almost folded into himself, his hands wrapped around his head, the back bent so that his face touched his legs. She heard his muffled sobs grow louder, almost into a wail. She pulled to a stop at the curb.

"I love her. I would never do to her what was done to me. Never!" With relief Rodney confessed, the secret he carried for so long came tumbling out. " I only wanted some love. I was so alone. Alone for a hundred and fifty seven fucking years. Alone for a hundred and fifty seven God Damn years!! Do you know what that was like? Can you even guess?" He burst into sobs again. He felt her arms around him, pulling him towards her. He cried for a long time, felt her hands stroke his hair as he buried his head into her bosom. She could feel the dampness on her camisole spreading, wondering how long he was going to cry, the torrent didn't seem like it would end soon. She also wondered if she should be holding a vampire like this.

After awhile the sobbing stopped, she felt him take a deep breath and then sit up. He looked straight ahead and then took the Kleenex tissue she offered.

"Sorry about that. I just..."

"I know. You don't have to explain. Here." She handed him his glasses that had fallen off when he was crying against her chest. Now she looked at his eyes, gold mixed with red and remembered the feeling of falling the first time they had met. "Rodney, we have to tell Irene the truth."

"I know. I didn't want to deceive her but I didn't know how to say it."

* * * *

Shelly and Rodney walked into the bar, with Shelly's red outfit getting lots of second looks. They joined Irene already sitting at a table that used high bar chairs, causing Shelly to wish her skirt didn't expose her legs quite so much.

Rodney heard two men, after watching him escort Shelly to sit with Irene, comment, "Some guys get all the luck."

Irene could tell something had happened. Rodney looked like an emotional wreck. She looked at Shelly who only nodded yes at her. They sat in silence for a few minutes, the waiter taking their order.

Finally Shelly spoke. "Rodney, why don't you tell Irene about Rose-Marie?"

A tight smile creased his lips. "Rose-Marie. Yes, Irene, I should tell you about her."

Irene was grateful that he started talking. Judging by the expressions of Shelly and Rodney, even small talk was doomed to failure.

"I fell in love with her a long time ago. She was beautiful. I can still picture her easily. She fell in love with me as well, in a fashion. She was quite eye-catching with her red hair, but one thing that really caught my attention was her golden eyes." He looked at Irene with his own golden eyes for emphasis.

Irene realized she now knew an important clue in his tale, two people with golden eyes.

"Before I met her my eyes were brown."

"How did they change?"

"Well, it turns out Rose-Marie, despite her good looks was very lonely. She wanted a companion. Me. And so she transformed me."

"Transformed you?"

"Rose-Marie was a vampire."

Irene almost jumped off of her stool. She might have run out of the bar but Shelly held up a restraining hand.

"It's okay. He is only going to tell us the truth. He won't attack you."

"She made me a vampire too. But I swore I would never do to another what she did to me." Rodney continued, as if he hadn't noticed Irene's reaction. He spoke without emotion but they could hear his passion at being able to talk about a secret hidden so long. Irene sat down again and started to relax as continued.

The three drank, conversed, and eventually the whole story, from Rose-Marie to when he met Irene and Shelly was told. He informed them about his ability to control others, about his allergies, and just about everything they wanted to know. He even held the crucifix Shelly wore on her necklace between his fingers, telling her that the cross had no ill effects on him. In fact, sometimes he went to midnight mass.

"So tell me Rodney, why didn't you just make me forget when I found out that you were a vampire?" Shelly took a drink, swinging back and forth on chair, looking better and better to Rodney.

"Because that was what Rose-Marie would have done. And in the emotional state I was in I wasn't sure I could pull that off. I vowed I was going to try to act human with you two, no special powers this time. On the subconscious level I guess I wanted to tell someone, wanted to be found out. And I had decided that if I got caught, well, then I would try to deal with the consequences. If you were yelling to everyone that I was a vampire that would be a different matter. I would do something to save my life, but not just because you found out my secret."

Irene was wearing jeans and a blouse. She felt underdressed compared to Shelly. When Rodney went to the washroom, Shelly explained to her that she wore her 'Phantom of the Opera' to throw Rodney off guard, so named because she bought it specifically to go to that opera. "This suit has that effect on men. They stop thinking for the first few minutes, it must scramble their brains. But I feel very conspicuous when I'm wearing it."

"I can see why. I feel like an old sea cow next to you."

"Don't be silly. You should undo some of the buttons on your blouse. It's pulling at the shoulders with the top button done up."

"Oh, sure. And what if Rodney gets all excited again? He's still dangerous." But she undid the top two buttons anyway, making her feel a bit better while sitting next to Shelly.

When Rodney returned they toasted to friendship and then left the bar, all under the influence. The bartender locked the door behind them.

"You know Irene, we shouldn't drive. Why don't we walk to my place and we can pick up the cars in the morning? Rodney, you can sleep on the couch if you like."

"Thanks, but I can't, the morning sun and all that. My apartment isn't far either and you two can stay there if you want."

"But would it be safe?"

"Honest, I won't bite." And the three burst into laughter at the almost joke.

* * * *

Irene woke up in the darkened room. She couldn't tell if her eyes were open at first, the blackness didn't change when she blinked. Then her eyes saw a dim glow from the nightlight in a wall plug. She got up carefully and stepped on a hand.

"Oops, sorry." she whispered. But there was no response. She went to the door, opened it slowly, and found something on the doorknob— her panties. She stepped out, closing the door carefully behind her.

She went to the bathroom, finished in there, and then went to the kitchen looking for coffee. After a few minutes she found the needed items, plugged in the coffeemaker and sat down. The only thing she wore was her panties; somewhere in the bedroom were the rest of her clothes. But how to find them in the dark was going to require coffee. Besides she knew from experience he wasn't going to wake up to discover her sitting without her clothes on. And that wouldn't be a big deal anyway.

The coffeemaker finished its task when the bedroom door opened again. Shelly stumbled out, went to the bathroom and stumbled out again. She was completely naked and didn't seem to care at that point.

"Is there any aspirin?" Shelly startled Irene. "What a hangover."

"Sure, I found some when I was looking for the coffee."

After coffee and pills both ladies were ready for the next problem. "I honestly don't remember taking off my clothes. Are they in the bedroom?" Shelley asked.

"Yes. And the reason you don't remember taking off your clothes is because you didn't. Rodney and I did. Actually you asked him to help you undress, something about not wanting to ruin your suit. Which reminds me, I want to borrow it sometime. He was more eager than me to undress you, so I let him do the work. He even carried you to the bed.

"So he took everything off?"

"Well, I guess so. We were all pretty drunk. It was nice of him to let us have the bed, though it was a bit small for two. He insisted sleeping on the floor. By the way he's naked too. So if you want to take a look at him, he'll never know."

"So you're the only one with anything left on from last night?"

"Uh, no. I found these clothes as I was getting up."

"Did he undress you too?"

"No. I went to lie down with my clothes on, but he stood at the foot of the bed, and ordered me to take off my clothes. Something about all of us should be naked or none of us."

"So you took off your clothes because he told you to?"

"Yes, well, he has a voice that sounds commanding, must be tied in with being a vampire. Anyway, I didn't mind, it's sometimes rather uncomfortable to have clothes on while you sleep."

"So we were sleeping nude last night, together in his bed and he was naked on the floor. Oh, my Lord. Was there any sex? Please say no."

"No sex. But you were sure kissing him last night. Good thing he has will power. And we weren't exactly sleeping together, more like passed out together."

"Oh my God. I was coming on to a vampire. You weren't mad, were you?"

"No, I was too drunk to care. Without saying much Rodney and I both understand that it's over as far as romance is concerned. But let's find our clothes, we can turn on the light and he won't wake up."

"And we can see what prince charming looks like too."

They returned to the bedroom and picked up their clothes. Shelly slipped on her skirt and jacket, and then stuffed the rest of her things in her purse. It was not a good morning to play around with garters and stockings.

"Do you think we should leave him on the floor like that?"

"Maybe not. Grab his feet and I'll grab his arms. We should be able to lift him onto the bed."

After they shuffled him on the bed Irene went into the kitchen and returned with a pen and paper. "Help me turn him on his stomach."

"Why?"

"I'll tell you about it later after a few drinks. But it is payback time right now." She drew a large heart on his cheek and inside it wrote 'Rodney, Irene and Shelly.' "There, help me turn him back. Vampires always sleep on their backs in the movies."

They covered him with the electric blanket, left him a note signed 'your friends' and exited the apartment to go home.

* * * *

"So that, my friends, is the story of a vampire. As you can see they are much like the rest of us looking for happiness."

"These women became his friends? Weren't they nervous with him?"

"No, Harry, they trusted him, as you trust Nancy not to overcharge you on our bill."

"This Rodney vampire person, he still searches for women for feeding? Does he ever feed on Irene or Shelly?" Nancy was reclining in her chair, her feet up on the opposite chair. As we were the only ones left in the bar she didn't have to look out for any other customers.

"No, he doesn't use those ladies for that. He would be scared that problems could arise. He would rather have them as friends. You see he finally realized he had to be what he was, a vampire. And being a vampire meant he had to give up on having a wife. But that didn't mean he couldn't have friends, it hadn't occurred to him before that he could. They have introduced him to others as well so his social life is quite good. Irene and Shelly are the only ones who know he's a vampire and keep that a secret. Now, to answer your first question, he still searches for new victims."

"Well, good thing for me he lives in Saint John. I would be worried if a vampire lurked around here. There are enough strange men without adding vampire to the equation."

"Oh, well to protect the identity of Rodney, and the ladies, I made up the fact he lives in New Brunswick. It wouldn't do to have someone search him out for some sensational news story, would it?"

Nancy's face fell. "You mean he might live here? He might attack me?" She felt her neck.

"Oh, don't worry. Chances are you'll never meet a vampire. Of course, if he did feed on you he would erase your memory of him anyway. So there's no point in concerning yourself about it."

"You mean to say he may have already fed on my blood? And I wouldn't know about it?"

"No, you wouldn't. Well, unless, you experience a loss of time. Have you ever wondered where the time went? That it went by inexplicably fast?"

"No. Wait, there was a time...Sheldon! Tell me the truth, does the vampire live here? Do you know if I have been attacked?"

"Oh, Nancy, really now. I assure you have not been attacked. Well, that is to my knowledge, I don't know everything."

I wish I had a pen and paper. I would have him sign a note stating that he did not know everything. First time I heard him admit that.

And so it ended, the three of us leaving the bar, with Nancy badgering Sheldon for more information. She locked the bar doors, imploring us to walk her to her car. She drove off in a hurry and I accepted Sheldon's offer for a ride home. He wasn't actually driving himself; he had a taxi waiting for him.

Fifteen minutes later he let me off. "Thanks Sheldon, for the ride. I hope Nancy isn't too scared to go to sleep." I leaned down and spoke to him through the open window.

"She shouldn't worry. I don't know of any men who are vampires in this area."

"That's good."

"Now, female vampires, that's a different story. Well, good night, Edwin. Sleep well."

"How do you know I use that name?"

"I may not know everything, but I do know a great many secrets..."

The taxi sped off before I could answer. Vampires, secrets…A tiny shudder ran over me. I thought about Sheldon's words—female vampires, that's a different story. Feeling nervous, I looked around. Did that shadow move?

The End

www.ingramcontent.com/pod-product-compliance
Lightning Source LLC
Chambersburg PA
CBHW030331180626
46810CB00003B/1313